BEGINNERS

Raymond Carver was born in Clatskanie, Oregon, in 1938. He grew up in Yakima, Washington; graduated from Humboldt State College in northern California; and attended the Iowa Writers' Workshop. He published his first short story in 1960, and his poetry and fiction appeared in periodicals and anthologies over the next two decades. Carver's stories reached a wider audience with the 1976 publication on *Will You Please Be Quiet, Please?* With the appearance of *What We Talk About When We Talk About Love* in 1981 his writing reached international recognition. Gordon Lish served as editor of both collections, but he surprised Carver by cutting the original manuscript of *What We Talk About* by more than half before its publication. Carver had dedicated the book to his fellow writer, companion, and future wife, Tess Gallagher, promising her that he would one day republish his stories at full length. *Beginners* restores the seventeen stories from *What We Talk About* to the forms in which he submitted them to his editor. All but four had previously appeared in literary magazines.

Carver went on to publish two more collections of stories, *Cathedral* and *Elephant*, each of which departed from the stringent 'minimalism' of *What We Talk About* and developed the nuanced empathy and expansiveness that was emerging in *Beginners*. His honours include one of the first Mildred and Harold Strauss Living Awards, nominations for the National Book Award and the Pulitzer Prize, and *Poetry* magazine's Levinson Prize. In 1988 he was inducted into the American Academy and Institute of Arts and Letters and was awarded an honorary Doctor of Letters degree by the University of Hartford. Raymond Carver died on August 2, 1988 at the age of fifty, shortly after completing a book of poems published posthumously as *A New Path to the Waterfall*. He was acclaimed 'America's Chekhov' in the *Sunday Times* after his death.

ALSO BY RAYMOND CARVER

Fiction

Furious Seasons

Will You Please Be Quiet, Please?

What We Talk About When We Talk About Love

Cathedral

Elephant

Where I'm Calling From: The Selected Stories
(with the author's foreword)

Short Cuts
(selected and with an introduction by Robert Altman)

Call If You Need Me: The Uncollected Fiction & Prose
(edited by William L. Stull with a foreword by Tess Gallagher)

Poetry

Near Klamath

Winter Insomnia

At Night the Salmon Move

Where Water Comes Together with Other Water

Ultramarine

In a Marine Light: Selected Poems

A New Path to the Waterfall
(with an introduction by Tess Gallagher)

All of Us: The Collected Poems
(edited by William L. Stull)

Essays, Poems, Stories

Fires

No Heroics, Please

RAYMOND CARVER

Beginners

The Original Version of *What We Talk About
When We Talk About Love*

TEXT ESTABLISHED BY

William L. Stull and Maureen P. Carroll

VINTAGE BOOKS
London

Published by Vintage 2010

6 8 10 9 7 5

Unpublished work by Raymond Carver
Copyright © Tess Gallagher 2009

Unpublished Editors' Preface and Notes
Copyright © William L. Stull and Maureen P. Caroll 2009

Raymond Carver has asserted his right under the Copyright, Designs
and Patents Act 1988 to be identified as the author of this work

First published in Great Britain in 2009 by
Jonathan Cape

Vintage
Random House, 20 Vauxhall Bridge Road,
London SW1V 2SA

www.vintage-books.co.uk

Addresses for companies within The Random House Group Limited
can be found at: www.randomhouse.co.uk/offices.htm

The Random House Group Limited Reg. No. 954009

A CIP catalogue record for this book
is available from the British Library

ISBN 9780099540328

The Random House Group Limited supports The Forest Stewardship
Council® (FSC®), the leading international forest-certification organisation.
Our books carrying the FSC label are printed on FSC®-certified paper.
FSC is the only forest-certification scheme supported by the leading
environmental organisations, including Greenpeace. Our
paper procurement policy can be found at
www.randomhouse.co.uk/environment

Printed and bound in Great Britain by Clays Ltd, St Ives PLC

Contents

Contents

Editors' Preface

> — but that is not the whole story.
>
> R.C., "Fat"

Beginners is the original version of seventeen short stories written by Raymond Carver and published, in editorially altered form, as *What We Talk About When We Talk About Love* by Alfred A. Knopf in April 1981.

The source of this edition—its base-text—is the manuscript that Carver delivered to Gordon Lish, then his editor at Knopf, in the spring of 1980. That manuscript, which Lish cut by more than fifty percent in two rounds of close line editing, is preserved in the Lilly Library of Indiana University. Carver's original stories have been recovered by transcribing his typewritten words that lie beneath Lish's handwritten alterations and deletions.

For ease of comparison, and because Carver provided no table of contents, the sequence of the stories in *Beginners* parallels their sequence in *What We Talk About When We Talk About Love*. In both books the penultimate story, albeit in markedly different forms, gives the collection its title. In Carver's manuscript, that story is called "Beginners" ("But it seems to me we're just rank beginners at love"). Having shortened "Beginners" by half, Lish adapted a line from elsewhere in Carver's text to yield the title "What We Talk About When We Talk About Love" for the story and the book.

Three months before taking his manuscript to New York City in May 1980, Carver wrote Lish that he had on hand three groups of stories. One group had previously appeared in little magazines or small-press books but had never been published by a major press. A second group either had appeared or were soon to appear in periodicals. A third group, by far the smallest, consisted of new stories still in typescript. These three groups of stories comprise *Beginners*.

In preparing the manuscript for Lish's editorial review, Carver made incidental changes to stories that had previously appeared in magazines or small-press books. These authorial revisions, including handwritten corrections, are preserved in *Beginners*. Obvious word omissions, misspellings, and inconsistencies in punctuation have been silently corrected. A brief publication history of each story is provided in the notes.

The restoration of *Beginners* has been the work of many years. We gratefully acknowledge the assistance of the staff of the Lilly Library of Indiana University in providing access to the papers of Gordon Lish and the archives of Noel Young's Capra Press. We warmly thank the staff of the Ohio State University Library, in particular Geoffrey D. Smith, head of Rare Books and Manuscripts, who has overseen the establishment of the Raymond Carver archive in the William Charvat Collection of American Fiction. For permission to reproduce Carver's writings, we thank the poet, essayist, and short story writer Tess Gallagher.

Raymond Carver dedicated *What We Talk About When We Talk About Love* to Tess Gallagher in 1981 with the promise that one day he would republish his stories at full length. His attempts to do so were cut short by his death, at age fifty, in 1988. Since then, we have pursued the restoration of *Beginners* with Ms. Gallagher's unwavering encouragement. It is to her that we dedicate the outcome of our efforts.

WILLIAM L. STULL
MAUREEN P. CARROLL

University of Hartford
West Hartford, Connecticut
18 May 2009

BEGINNERS

The Original Version of
What We Talk About When We Talk About Love

Why Don't You Dance?

IN the kitchen, he poured another drink and looked at the bedroom suite in his front yard. The mattress was stripped and the candy-striped sheets lay beside two pillows on the chiffonier. Except for that, things looked much the way they had in the bedroom—nightstand and reading lamp on his side of the bed, a nightstand and reading lamp on her side. *His* side, *her* side. He considered this as he sipped the whiskey. The chiffonier stood a few feet from the foot of the bed. He had emptied the drawers into cartons that morning, and the cartons were in the living room. A portable heater was next to the chiffonier. A rattan chair with a decorator pillow stood at the foot of the bed. The buffed aluminum kitchen set occupied a part of the driveway. A yellow muslin cloth, much too large, a gift, covered the table and hung down over the sides. A potted fern was on the table, along with a box of silverware, also a gift. A big console-model television set rested on a coffee table, and a few feet away from this, a sofa and chair and a floor lamp. He had run an extension cord from the house and everything was connected, things worked. The desk was pushed against the garage door. A few utensils were on the desk, along with a wall clock and two framed prints. There was also in the driveway a carton with cups, glasses, and plates, each object wrapped in newspaper. That morning he had cleared out the closets and, except for the three cartons in the living room, everything was out of the house. Now and then a car slowed and people stared. But no one stopped. It occurred to him that he wouldn't either.

"It must be a yard sale, for God's sake," the girl said to the boy.

This girl and boy were furnishing a little apartment.

"Let's see what they want for the bed," the girl said.

"I wonder what they want for the TV," the boy said.

He pulled into the driveway and stopped in front of the kitchen table.

They got out of the car and began to examine things. The girl touched the muslin cloth. The boy plugged in the blender and turned the dial to MINCE. She picked up a chafing dish. He turned on the television set and made careful adjustments. He sat down on the sofa to watch. He lit a cigarette, looked around, and flipped the match into the grass. The girl sat on the bed. She pushed off her shoes and lay back. She could see the evening star.

"Come here, Jack. Try this bed. Bring one of those pillows," she said.

"How is it?" he said.

"Try it," she said.

He looked around. The house was dark.

"I feel funny," he said. "Better see if anybody's home."

She bounced on the bed.

"Try it first," she said.

He lay down on the bed and put the pillow under his head.

"How does it feel?" the girl said.

"Feels firm," he said.

She turned on her side and put her arm around his neck.

"Kiss me," she said.

"Let's get up," he said.

"Kiss me. Kiss me, honey," she said.

She closed her eyes. She held him. He had to prize her fingers loose.

He said, "I'll see if anybody's home," but he just sat up.

The television set was still playing. Lights had gone on in houses up and down the street. He sat on the edge of the bed.

"Wouldn't it be funny if," the girl said and grinned and didn't finish.

He laughed. He switched on the reading lamp.

She brushed away a mosquito.

He stood up and tucked his shirt in.

"I'll see if anybody's home," he said. "I don't think anybody's home. But if they are, I'll see what things are going for."

"Whatever they ask, offer them ten dollars less," she said. "They must be desperate or something."

She sat on the bed and watched television.

"You might as well turn that up," the girl said and giggled.

"It's a pretty good TV," he said.

"Ask them how much," she said.

Max came down the sidewalk with a sack from the market. He had sandwiches, beer, and whiskey. He had continued to drink through the afternoon and had reached a place where now the drinking seemed to begin to sober him. But there were gaps. He had stopped at the bar next to the market, had listened to a song on the jukebox, and somehow it had gotten dark before he recalled the things in his yard.

He saw the car in the driveway and the girl on the bed. The television set was playing. Then he saw the boy on the porch. He started across the yard.

"Hello," he said to the girl. "You found the bed. That's good."

"Hello," the girl said, and got up. "I was just trying it out." She patted the bed. "It's a pretty good bed."

"It's a good bed," Max said. "What do I say next?"

He knew he should say something next. He put down the sack and took out the beer and whiskey.

"We thought nobody was here," the boy said. "We're interested in the bed and maybe the TV. Maybe the desk. How much do you want for the bed?"

"I was thinking fifty dollars for the bed," Max said.

"Would you take forty?" the girl asked.

"Okay, I'll take forty," Max said.

He took a glass out of the carton, took the newspaper off it, and broke the seal on the whiskey.

"How about the TV?" the boy said.

"Twenty-five."

"Would you take twenty?" the girl said.

"Twenty's okay. I could take twenty," Max said.

The girl looked at the boy.

"You kids, you want a drink?" Max said. "Glasses in that box. I'm going to sit down. I'm going to sit down on the sofa."

He sat on the sofa, leaned back, and stared at them.

The boy found two glasses and poured whiskey.

"How much of this do you want?" he said to the girl. They were only twenty years old, the boy and girl, a month or so apart.

"That's enough," she said. "I think I want water in mine."

She pulled out a chair and sat at the kitchen table.

"There's water in that faucet over there," Max said. "Turn on that faucet."

The boy added water to the whiskey, his and hers. He cleared his throat before he sat down at the kitchen table too. Then he grinned. Birds darted overhead for insects.

Max gazed at the television. He finished his drink. He reached to turn on the floor lamp and dropped his cigarette between the cushions. The girl got up to help him find it.

"You want anything else, honey?" the boy said.

He took out the checkbook. He poured more whiskey for himself and the girl.

"Oh, I want the desk," the girl said. "How much money is the desk?"

Max waved his hand at this preposterous question.

"Name a figure," he said.

He looked at them as they sat at the table. In the lamplight, there was something about the expression on their faces. For a minute this expression seemed conspiratorial, and then it became *tender*—there was no other word for it. The boy touched her hand.

"I'm going to turn off this TV and put on a record," Max announced. "This record player is going, too. Cheap. Name a figure."

He poured more whiskey and opened a beer.

"Everything goes."

The girl held out her glass and Max poured more whiskey.

"Thank you," she said.

"It goes right to your head," the boy said. "I'm getting a buzz on."

He finished his drink, waited, and poured another. He was writing a check when Max found the records.

"Pick something you like," Max said to the girl, and held the records before her.

The boy went on writing the check.

"Here," the girl said, pointing. She did not know the names on these records, but that was all right. This was an adventure. She got up from the table and sat down again. She didn't want to sit still.

"I'm making it out to cash," the boy said, still writing.

"Sure," Max said. He drank off the whiskey and followed it with some beer. He sat down again on the sofa and crossed one leg over the other.

They drank. They listened until the record ended. And then Max put on another.

"Why don't you kids dance?" Max said. "That's a good idea. Why don't you dance?"

"No, I don't think so," the boy said. "You want to dance, Carla?"

"Go ahead," Max said. "It's my driveway. You can dance."

Arms about each other, their bodies pressed together, the boy and girl moved up and down the driveway. They were dancing.

When the record ended, the girl asked Max to dance. She was still without her shoes.

"I'm drunk," he said.

"You're not drunk," the girl said.

"Well, I'm drunk," the boy said.

Max turned the record over and the girl came up to him. They began to dance.

The girl looked at the people gathered at the bay window across the street.

"Those people over there. Watching," she said. "Is it okay?"

"It's okay," Max said. "It's my driveway. We can dance. They thought they'd seen everything over here, but they haven't seen this," he said.

In a minute, he felt her warm breath on his neck, and he said: "I hope you like your bed."

"I will," the girl said.

"I hope the both of you do," Max said.

"Jack!" the girl said. "Wake up!"

Jack had his chin propped and was watching them sleepily.

"Jack," the girl said.

She closed and opened her eyes. She pushed her face into Max's shoulder. She pulled him closer.

"Jack," the girl murmured.

She looked at the bed and could not understand what it was doing in the yard. She looked over Max's shoulder at the sky. She held herself to Max. She was filled with an unbearable happiness.

—

The girl said later: "This guy was about middle-aged. All his belongings right out there in his yard. I'm not kidding. We got drunk and danced. In the driveway. Oh, my God. Don't laugh. He played records. Look at this phonograph. He gave it to us. These old records, too. Jack and I went to sleep in his bed. Jack was hungover and had to rent a trailer in the morning. To move all the guy's stuff. Once I woke up. He was covering us with a blanket, the guy was. This blanket. Feel it."

She kept talking. She told everyone. There was more, she knew that, but she couldn't get it into words. After a time, she quit talking about it.

Viewfinder

A MAN without hands came to the door to sell me a photograph of my house. Except for the chrome hooks, he was an ordinary-looking man of fifty or so.

"How did you lose your hands?" I asked, after he'd said what he wanted.

"That's another story," he said. "You want this picture of your house or not?"

"Come on in," I said. "I just made coffee."

I'd just made some Jell-O too, but I didn't tell him that.

"I might use your toilet," the man with no hands said.

I wanted to see how he would hold a cup of coffee using those hooks. I knew how he used the camera. It was an old Polaroid camera, big and black. It fastened to leather straps that looped over his shoulders and around his back, securing the camera to his chest. He would stand on the sidewalk in front of a house, locate the house in the viewfinder, depress the lever with one of his hooks, and out popped the picture in a minute or so. I'd been watching from the window.

"Where'd you say the toilet was?"

"Down there, turn right."

By this time, bending and hunching, he'd let himself out of the straps. He put the camera on the sofa and straightened his jacket. "You can look at this while I'm gone."

I took the photograph from him. There was a little rectangle of lawn, the driveway, carport, front steps, bay window, kitchen window. Why would I want a photograph of this tragedy? I looked closer and saw the outline of my head, *my head*, behind the kitchen window and a few steps back from the sink. I looked at the photograph for a time, and then I heard the toilet flush. He came down the hall, zipped and smiling, one hook holding his belt, the other tucking his shirt in.

"What do you think?" he said. "All right? Personally, I think it turned out fine, but then I know what I'm doing and, let's face it, it's not that hard shooting a house. Unless the weather's inclement, but when the weather's inclement I don't work

7

except inside. Special-assignment type work, you know." He plucked at his crotch.

"Here's coffee," I said.

"You're alone, right?" He looked at the living room. He shook his head. "Hard, hard." He sat next to the camera, leaned back with a sigh, and closed his eyes.

"Drink your coffee," I said. I sat in a chair across from him. A week before, three kids in baseball caps had come to the house. One of them had said, "Can we paint your address on the curb, sir? Everybody on the street's doing it. Just a dollar." Two boys waited on the sidewalk, one of them with a can of white paint at his feet, the other holding a brush. All three boys had their sleeves rolled.

"Three kids were by here awhile back wanting to paint my address on the curb. They wanted a dollar, too. You wouldn't know anything about that, would you?" It was a long shot. But I watched him just the same.

He leaned forward importantly, the cup balanced between his hooks. He carefully placed the cup on the little table. He looked at me. "That's crazy, you know. I work alone. Always have, always will. What are you saying?"

"I was trying to make a connection," I said. I had a headache. Coffee's no good for it, but sometimes Jell-O helps. I picked up the photograph. "I was in the kitchen," I said.

"I know. I saw you from the street."

"How often does that happen? Getting somebody in the picture along with the house? Usually I'm in the back."

"Happens all the time," he said. "It's a sure sell. Sometimes they see me shooting the house and they come out and ask me to make sure I get them in the picture. Maybe the lady of the house, she wants me to snap hubby washing his car. Or else there's junior working the lawnmower and she says, *get him, get him*, and I get him. Or the little family is gathered on the patio for a nice little lunch, and would I please." His right leg began to jiggle. "So they just up and left you, right? Packed up and left. It hurts. Kids I don't know about. Not anymore. I don't like kids. I don't even like my own kids. I work alone, as I said. The picture?"

"I'll take it," I said. I stood up for the cups. "You don't live around here. Where do you live?"

"Right now I have a room downtown. It's okay. I take a bus out, you know, and after I've worked all the neighborhoods, I go somewhere else. There's better ways to go, but I get by."

"What about your kids?" I waited with the cups and watched him struggle up from the sofa.

"Screw them. Their mother too! They're what gave me this." He brought the hooks up in front of my face. He turned and started pulling into his straps. "I'd like to forgive and forget, you know, but I can't. I still hurt. And that's the trouble. I can't forgive or forget."

I looked again at the hooks as they maneuvered the straps. It was wonderful to see what he could do with those hooks.

"Thanks for the coffee and the use of the toilet. You're going through the mill now. I sympathize." He raised and lowered his hooks. "What can I do?"

"Take more pictures," I said. "I want you to take pictures of me and the house both."

"It won't work," he said. "She won't come back."

"I don't want her back," I said.

He snorted. He looked at me. "I can give you a rate," he said. "Three for a dollar? If I went any lower I'd hardly come out."

We went outside. He adjusted the shutter. He told me where to stand, and we got down to it. We moved around the house. Very systematic, we were. Sometimes I'd look sideways. Other times I'd look straight into the camera. Just getting outside helped.

"Good," he'd say. "That's good. That one turned out real nice. Let's see," he said after we'd circled the house and were back in the driveway again. "That's twenty. You want any more?"

"Two or three more," I said. "On the roof. I'll go up and you can shoot me from down here."

"Jesus," he said. He looked up and down the street. "Well, sure, go ahead—but be careful."

"You were right," I said. "They did just up and move out. The whole kit and caboodle. You were right on target."

The man with no hands said: "You didn't need to say word one. I knew the instant you opened the door." He shook his hooks at me. "You feel like she cut the ground right out from

under you! Took your legs in the process. Look at this! This is
what they leave you with. Screw it," he said. "You want to get
up on that roof, or not? I've got to go," the man said.

I brought a chair out and put it under the edge of the carport. I still couldn't reach. He stood in the driveway and
watched me. I found a crate and put that on the chair. I
climbed onto the chair and then the crate. I raised up onto the
carport, walked to the roof, and made my way on hands and
knees across the shingles to a little flat place near the chimney.
I stood up and looked around. There was a breeze. I waved,
and he waved back with both hooks. Then I saw the rocks. It
was like a little rock nest there on the screen over the chimney
hole. Kids must have lobbed them up trying to land them in
the chimney.

I picked up one of the rocks. "Ready?" I called.

He had me located in his viewfinder.

"Okay," he answered.

I turned and threw back my arm. "Now!" I called. I hooked
that rock as far as I could, south.

"I don't know," I heard him say. "You moved," he said.
"We'll see in a minute," and in a minute he said, "By God, it's
okay." He looked at it. He held it up. "You know," he said,
"it's good."

"Once more," I called. I picked up another rock. I grinned.
I felt I could lift off. Fly.

"Now!" I called.

Where Is Everyone?

I'VE seen some things. I was going over to my mother's to stay a few nights, but just as I came to the top of the stairs I looked and she was on the sofa kissing a man. It was summer, the door was open, and the color TV was playing.

My mother is sixty-five and lonely. She belongs to a singles club. But even so, knowing all this, it was hard. I stood at the top of the stairs with my hand on the railing and watched as the man pulled her deeper into the kiss. She was kissing back, and the TV was going on the other side of the room. It was Sunday, about five in the afternoon. People from the apartment house were down below in the pool. I went back down the stairs and out to my car.

A lot has happened since that afternoon, and on the whole things are better now. But during those days, when my mother was putting out to men she'd just met, I was out of work, drinking, and crazy. My kids were crazy, and my wife was crazy and having a "thing" with an unemployed aerospace engineer she'd met at AA. He was crazy too. His name was Ross and he had five or six kids. He walked with a limp from a gunshot wound his first wife had given him. He didn't have a wife now; he wanted my wife. I don't know what we were all thinking of in those days. The second wife had come and gone, but it was his first wife who had shot him in the thigh some years back, giving him the limp, and who now had him in and out of court, or in jail, every six months or so for not meeting his support payments. I wish him well now. But it was different then. More than once in those days I mentioned weapons. I'd say to my wife, I'd shout it, "I'm going to kill him!" But nothing ever happened. Things lurched on. I never met the man, though we talked on the phone a few times. I did find a couple of pictures of him once when I was going through my wife's purse. He was a little guy, not too little, and he had a moustache and was wearing a striped jersey, waiting for a kid to come down the slide. In the other picture he was standing against a house—my house?—I couldn't tell—with his arms

crossed, dressed up, wearing a tie. Ross, you son of a bitch, I
hope you're okay now. I hope things are better for you too.

The last time he'd been jailed, a month before that Sunday,
I found out from my daughter that her mother had gone bail
for him. Daughter Kate, who was fifteen, didn't take to this
any better than I did. It wasn't that she had any loyalty to me
in this—she had no loyalties to me or her mother in anything
and was only too willing to sell either one of us down the river.
No, it was that there was a serious cash-flow problem in the
house and if money went to Ross, there'd be that much less for
what she needed. So Ross was on her list now. Also, she didn't
like his kids, she'd said, but she'd told me once before that in
general Ross was all right, even funny and interesting when he
wasn't drinking. He'd even told her fortune.

He spent his time repairing things, now that he could no
longer hold a job in the aerospace industry. But I'd seen his
house from the outside; and the place looked like a dumping
ground, with all kinds and makes of old appliances and equipment that would never wash or cook or play again—all of it
just standing in his open garage and in his drive and in the
front yard. He also kept some broken-down cars around that
he liked to tinker on. In the first stages of their affair my wife
had told me he "collected antique cars." Those were her
words. I'd seen some of his cars parked in front of his house
when I'd driven by there trying to see what I could see. Old
1950s and 1960s, dented cars with torn seat covers. They were
junkers, that's all. I knew. I had his number. We had things in
common, more than just driving old cars and trying to hold
on for dear life to the same woman. Still, handyman or not, he
couldn't manage to tune my wife's car properly or fix our TV
set when it broke down and we lost the picture. We had volume, but no picture. If we wanted to get the news, we'd have
to sit around the screen at night and listen to the set. I'd drink
and make some crack to my kids about Mr. Fixit. Even now I
don't know if my wife believed that stuff or not, about antique
cars and such. But she cared for him, she loved him even;
that's pretty clear now.

They'd met when Cynthia was trying to stay sober and was
going to meetings three or four times a week. I had been in
and out of AA for several months, though when Cynthia met

Ross I was out and drinking a fifth a day of anything I could get my hands on. But as I heard Cynthia say to someone over the phone about me, I'd had the exposure to AA and knew where to go when I really wanted help. Ross had been in AA and then had gone back to drinking again. Cynthia felt, I think, that maybe there was more hope for him than for me and tried to help him and so went to the meetings to keep herself sober, then went over to cook for him or clean his house. His kids were no help to him in this regard. Nobody lifted a hand around his house except Cynthia when she was there. But the less his kids pitched in, the more he loved them. It was strange. It was the opposite with me. I hated my kids during this time. I'd be on the sofa with a glass of vodka and grapefruit juice when one of them would come in from school and slam the door. One afternoon I screamed and got into a scuffle with my son. Cynthia had to break it up when I threatened to knock him to pieces. I said I would kill him. I said, "I gave you life and I can take it away."

Madness.

The kids, Katy and Mike, were only too happy to take advantage of this crumbling situation. They seemed to thrive on the threats and bullying they inflicted on each other and on us—the violence and dismay, the general bedlam. Right now, thinking about it even from this distance, it makes me set my heart against them. I remember years before, before I turned to drinking full time, reading an extraordinary scene in a novel by an Italian named Italo Svevo. The narrator's father was dying and the family had gathered around the bed, weeping and waiting for the old man to expire, when he opened his eyes to look at each of them for a last time. When his gaze fell on the narrator he suddenly stirred and something came into his eyes; and with his last burst of strength he raised up, flung himself across the bed, and slapped the face of his son as hard as he could. Then he fell back onto the bed and died. I often imagined my own deathbed scene in those days, and I saw myself doing the same thing, only I would hope to have the strength to slap each of my kids, and my last words for them would be what only a dying man would have the courage to utter.

But they saw craziness on every side, and it suited their purpose, I was convinced. They fattened on it. They liked being

able to call the shots, having the upper hand, while we bungled along letting them work on our guilt. They might have
been inconvenienced from time to time, but they ran things
their way. They weren't embarrassed or put out by any of the
activities that went on in our house either. To the contrary. It
gave them something to talk about with their friends. I've
heard them regaling their pals with the most frightful stories,
howling with laughter as they spilled out the lurid details of
what was happening to me and their mother. Except for being
financially dependent on Cynthia, who still somehow had a
teaching job and a monthly paycheck, they flat out ran the
show. And that's what it was too, a show.

Once Mike locked his mother out of the house after she'd
stayed overnight at Ross's house. . . . I don't know where I
was that night, probably at my mother's. I'd sleep over there
sometimes. I'd eat supper with her and she'd tell me how she
worried about all of us; then we'd watch TV and try to talk
about something else, try to hold a normal conversation about
something other than my family situation. She'd make a bed
for me on her sofa—the same sofa she used to make love on, I
supposed, but I'd sleep there anyway and be grateful. Cynthia
came home at seven o'clock one morning to get dressed for
school and found that Mike had locked all the doors and
windows and wouldn't let her in the house. She stood outside
his window and begged him to let her in—please, please, so
she could dress and go to school, for if she lost her job what
then? Where would he be? Where would any of us be then? He
said, "You don't live here anymore. Why should I let you in?"
That's what he said to her, standing behind his window, his
face all stopped up with rage. (She told me this later when she
was drunk and I was sober and holding her hands and letting
her talk.) "You don't live here," he said.

"Please, please, please, Mike," she pleaded. "Let me in."

He let her in and she swore at him. Like that, he punched
her hard on the shoulders several times—whop, whop, whop
—then hit her on top of the head and generally worked her
over. Finally she was able to change clothes, fix her face, and
rush off to school.

All this happened not too long ago, three years about. It was
something in those days.

I left my mother with the man on her sofa and drove around for a while, not wanting to go home and not wanting to sit in a bar that day either.

Sometimes Cynthia and I would talk about things—"reviewing the situation," we'd call it. But now and then on rare occasions we'd talk a little about things that bore no relation to the situation. One afternoon we were in the living room and she said, "When I was pregnant with Mike you carried me to the bathroom when I was so sick and pregnant I couldn't get out of bed. You carried me. No one else will ever do that, no one else could ever love me in that way, that much. We have that, no matter what. We've loved each other like nobody else could or ever will love the other again."

We looked at each other. Maybe we touched hands, I don't recall. Then I remembered the half-pint of whiskey or vodka or gin or scotch or tequila that I had hidden under the very sofa cushion we were sitting on (oh, happy days!) and I began to hope she might soon have to get up and move around—go to the kitchen, the bathroom, out to clean the garage.

"Maybe you could make us some coffee," I said. "A pot of coffee might be nice."

"Would you eat something? I can fix some soup."

"Maybe I could eat something, but I'll for sure drink a cup of coffee."

She went out to the kitchen. I waited until I heard her begin to run water. Then I reached under the cushion for the bottle, unscrewed the lid, and drank.

I never told these things at AA. I never said much at the meetings. I'd "pass," as they called it: when it came your turn to speak and you didn't say anything except "I'll pass tonight, thanks." But I would listen and shake my head and laugh in recognition at the awful stories I heard. Usually I was drunk when I went to those first meetings. You're scared and you need something more than cookies and instant coffee.

But those conversations touching on love or the past were rare. If we talked, we talked about business, survival, the bottom line of things. Money. Where is the money going to come from? The telephone was on the way out, the lights and gas threatened. What about Katy? She needs clothes. Her grades. That boyfriend of hers is a biker. Mike. What's going to happen to Mike? What's going to happen to us all? "My God," she'd say. But God wasn't having any of it. He'd washed his hands of us.

I wanted Mike to join the army, navy, or the coast guard. He was impossible. A dangerous character. Even Ross felt the army would be good for him, Cynthia had told me, and she hadn't liked him telling her that a bit. But I was pleased to hear this and to find out that Ross and I were in agreement on the matter. Ross went up a peg in my estimation. But it angered Cynthia because, miserable as Mike was to have around, despite his violent streak, she thought it was just a phase that would soon pass. She didn't want him in the army. But Ross told Cynthia that Mike belonged in the army where he'd learn respect and manners. He told her this after there'd been a pushing and shoving match out in his drive in the early morning hours and Mike had thrown him down on the pavement.

Ross loved Cynthia, but he also had a twenty-two-year-old girl named Beverly who was pregnant with his baby, though Ross assured Cynthia he loved her, not Beverly. They didn't even sleep together any longer, he told Cynthia, but Beverly was carrying his baby and he loved all his children, even the unborn, and he couldn't just give her the boot, could he? He wept when he told all this to Cynthia. He was drunk. (Someone was always drunk in those days.) I can imagine the scene.

Ross had graduated from California Polytechnic Institute and gone right to work at the NASA operation in Mountain View. He worked there for ten years, until it all fell in on him. I never met him, as I said, but we talked on the phone several times, about one thing and another. I called him once when I was drunk and Cynthia and I were debating some sad point or another. One of his children answered the phone and when Ross came on the line I asked him whether, if I pulled out (I had no intention of pulling out, of course; it was just harassment), he intended to support Cynthia and our kids. He said he was carving a roast, that's what he said, and they were just going to sit down and eat their dinner, he and his children. Could he call me back? I hung up. When he called, after an hour or so, I'd forgotten about the earlier call. Cynthia answered the phone and said "Yes" and then "Yes" again, and I knew it was Ross and that he was asking if I was drunk. I grabbed the phone. "Well, are you going to support them or not?" He said he was sorry for his part in all of this but, no, he guessed he couldn't support them. "So it's No, you can't support them," I said, and looked at Cynthia as if this should settle everything. He said, "Yes, it's no." But Cynthia didn't bat an eye. I figured later they'd already talked that situation over thoroughly, so it was no surprise. She already knew.

He was in his mid-thirties when he went under. I used to make fun of him when I had the chance. I called him "the weasel," after his photograph. "That's what your mother's boyfriend looks like," I'd say to my kids if they were around and we were talking, "like a weasel." We'd laugh. Or else "Mr. Fixit." That was my favorite name for him. God bless and keep you, Ross. I don't hold anything against you now. But in those days when I called him the weasel or Mr. Fixit and threatened his life, he was something of a fallen hero to my kids and to Cynthia too, I suppose, because he'd helped put men on the moon. He'd worked, I was told time and again, on the moon project shots, and he was close friends with Buzz Aldrin and Neil Armstrong. He'd told Cynthia, and Cynthia had told the kids, who'd told me, that when the astronauts came to town he was going to introduce them. But they never came to town, or if they did they forgot to contact Ross. Soon after the moon probes, fortune's wheel turned and Ross's drinking increased. He began missing work. Somewhere then the troubles with his first wife started. Toward the end he began taking the drink to work with him in a thermos. It's a modern operation out there, I've seen it—cafeteria lines, executive dining rooms, and the like, Mr. Coffees in every office. But he brought his own thermos to work, and after a while people began to know and to talk. He was laid off, or else he quit—nobody could ever give me a straight answer when I asked. He kept drinking, of course. You do that. Then he commenced working on ruined appliances and doing TV repair work and fixing cars. He was interested in astrology, auras, I Ching—that business. I don't doubt that he was bright enough and interesting and quirky, like most of our ex-friends. I told Cynthia I was sure she wouldn't care for him (I couldn't yet bring myself to use the word "love" then, about that relationship) if he wasn't, basically, a good man. "One of *us*," was how I put it, trying to be large about it. He wasn't a bad or an evil man, Ross. "No one's evil," I said once to Cynthia when we were discussing my own affair.

My dad died in his sleep, drunk, eight years ago. It was a Friday night and he was fifty-four years old. He came home from work at the sawmill, took some sausage out of the freezer for his breakfast the next morning, and sat down at the kitchen table, where he opened a quart of Four Roses. He was in good enough spirits in those days, glad to be back on a job after being out of work for three or four years with blood poisoning and then something that caused him to have shock treatments. (I was married and living in another town during that time. I had the kids and a job, enough troubles of my own, so I couldn't follow his too closely.) That night he moved into the living room with his bottle, a bowl of ice cubes and a glass, and drank and watched TV until my mother came in from work at the coffee shop.

They had a few words about the whiskey, as they always did. She didn't drink much herself. When I was grown, I only saw her drink at Thanksgiving, Christmas, and New Year's—eggnog or buttered rums, and then never too many. The one time she had had too much to drink, years before (I heard this from my dad, who laughed about it when he told it), they'd gone to a little place outside Eureka and she'd had a great many whiskey sours. Just as they got into the car to leave, she started to get sick and had to open the door. Somehow her false teeth came out, the car moved forward a little, and a tire passed over her dentures. After that she never drank except on holidays and then never to excess.

My dad kept on drinking that Friday night and tried to ignore my mother, who sat out in the kitchen and smoked and tried to write a letter to her sister in Little Rock. Finally he got up and went to bed. My mother went to bed not long after, when she was sure he was asleep. She said later she noticed nothing out of the ordinary except maybe his snoring seemed heavier and deeper and she couldn't get him to turn on his side. But she went to sleep. She woke up when my dad's sphincter muscles and bladder let go. It was just sunrise. Birds were singing. My dad was still on his back, eyes closed and mouth open. My mother looked at him and cried his name.

I kept driving around. It was dark by now. I drove by my house, every light ablaze, but Cynthia's car wasn't in the drive. I went to a bar where I sometimes drank and called home. Katy answered and said her mother wasn't there, and where was I? She needed five dollars. I shouted something and hung up. Then I called collect to a woman six hundred miles away whom I hadn't seen in months, a good woman who, the last time I'd seen her, had said she would pray for me.

She accepted the charges. She asked where I was calling from. She asked how I was. "Are you all right?" she said.

We talked. I asked about her husband. He'd been a friend of mine and was now living away from her and the children.

"He's still in Richland," she said. "How did all this happen to us?" she asked. "We started out good people." We talked a while longer, then she said she still loved me and that she would continue to pray for me.

"Pray for me," I said. "Yes." Then we said good-bye and hung up.

Later I called home again, but this time no one answered. I dialed my mother's number. She picked up the phone on the first ring, her voice cautious, as if expecting trouble.

"It's me," I said. "I'm sorry to be calling."

"No, no, honey, I was up," she said. "Where are you? Is anything the matter? I thought you were coming over today. I looked for you. Are you calling from home?"

"I'm not at home," I said. "I don't know where everyone is at home. I just called there."

"Old Ken was over here today," she went on, "that old bastard. He came over this afternoon. I haven't seen him in a month and he just shows up, the old thing. I don't like him. All he wants to do is talk about himself and brag on himself and how he lived on Guam and had three girlfriends at the same time and how he's traveled to this place and that place. He's just an old braggart, that's all he is. I met him at that dance I told you about, but I don't like him."

"Is it all right if I come over?" I said.

"Honey, why don't you? I'll fix us something to eat. I'm hungry myself. I haven't eaten anything since this afternoon. Old Ken brought some Colonel Sanders over this afternoon. Come over and I'll fix us some scrambled eggs. Do you want me to come get you? Honey, are you all right?"

I drove over. She kissed me when I came in the door. I turned my face. I hated for her to smell the vodka. The TV was on.

"Wash your hands," she said as she studied me. "It's ready."

Later she made a bed for me on the sofa. I went into the bathroom. She kept a pair of my dad's pajamas in there. I took them out of the drawer, looked at them, and began undressing. When I came out she was in the kitchen. I fixed the pillow and lay down. She finished with what she was doing, turned off the kitchen light, and sat down at the end of the sofa.

"Honey, I don't want to be the one to tell you this," she said. "It hurts me to tell you, but even the kids know it and they've told me. We've talked about it. But Cynthia is seeing another man."

"That's okay," I said. "I know that," I said and looked at the TV. "His name is Ross and he's an alcoholic. He's like me."

"Honey, you're going to have to do something for yourself," she said.

"I know it," I said. I kept looking at the TV.

She leaned over and hugged me. She held me a minute. Then she let go and wiped her eyes. "I'll get you up in the morning," she said.

"I don't have much to do tomorrow. I might sleep in awhile after you go." I thought: after you get up, after you've gone to the bathroom and gotten dressed, then I'll get into your bed and lie there and doze and listen to your radio out in the kitchen giving the news and weather.

"Honey, I'm so worried about you."

"Don't worry," I said. I shook my head.

"You get some rest now," she said. "You need to sleep."

"I'll sleep. I'm very sleepy."

"Watch television as long as you want," she said.

I nodded.

She bent and kissed me. Her lips seemed bruised and swollen. She drew the blanket over me. Then she went into her bedroom. She left the door open, and in a minute I could hear her snoring.

I lay there staring at the TV. There were images of uniformed men on the screen, a low murmur, then tanks and a man using a flamethrower. I couldn't hear it, but I didn't want to get up. I kept staring until I felt my eyes close. But I woke up with a start, the pajamas damp with sweat. A snowy light filled the room. There was a roaring coming at me. The room clamored. I lay there. I didn't move.

Gazebo

THAT morning she pours Teacher's scotch over my belly and licks it off. In the afternoon she tries to jump out the window. I can't stand this anymore, and I tell her so. I go, "Holly, this can't continue. This is crazy. This has got to stop."

We are sitting on the sofa in one of the upstairs suites. There were any number of vacancies to choose from, but we needed a suite, a place to move around in and be able to talk. So we'd locked up the motel office that morning and gone upstairs to a suite.

She goes, "Duane, this is killing."

We are drinking Teacher's with ice and water. We'd slept awhile between morning and afternoon. Then she was out of bed and threatening to climb out the window in her undergarments. I had to get her in a hold. We were only two floors up, but even so.

"I've had it," she goes. "I can't take it anymore." She puts the back of her hand to her cheek and closes her eyes. She turns her head back and forth and makes this humming noise. I could die seeing her like this.

"Take what?" I go, though of course I know. "Holly?"

"I don't have to spell it out for you again," she goes. "I've lost self-control. I've lost my pride. I used to be a proud woman."

She's an attractive woman just past thirty. She is tall and has long black hair and green eyes, the only green-eyed woman I've ever known. In the old days I used to comment on her green eyes, and she'd tell me she knew she was meant for something special. And didn't I know it. I feel so awful from one thing and the other.

Downstairs in the office I can hear the telephone ringing again. It has been ringing off and on all day. Even when I was dozing earlier I could hear it. I'd open my eyes and look at the ceiling and listen to it ring and wonder at what was happening to us.

"My heart is broken," she goes. "It's turned to a piece of stone. I'm no longer responsible. That's what's as bad as anything, that I'm not responsible anymore. I don't even want to get up mornings. Duane, it's taken a long time to come to this decision, but we have to go our separate ways. It's over, Duane. We may as well admit it."

"Holly," I go. I reach for her hand, but she draws it away.

When we'd first moved down here and taken over as motel managers we thought we were out of the woods. Free rent and utilities plus three hundred a month, you couldn't beat it. Holly took care of the books, she was good with figures, and she did most of the renting of the units. She liked people and people liked her back. I saw to the grounds, mowed the grass and cut weeds, kept the swimming pool clean, did minor repairs. Everything was fine for the first year. I was holding down another job nights, a swing shift, and we were getting ahead, rich in plans. Then one morning, I don't know, I'd just laid some bathroom tile in one of the units when this little Mexican maid comes in to clean. Holly had hired her. I can't really say I'd noticed her before, though we spoke when we saw each other. She called me Mister. Anyway, one thing and the other, we talked. She wasn't dumb, she was cute and had a nice way about her. She liked to smile, would listen with great intent when you said something, and looked you in the eyes when she talked. After that morning I started paying attention when I'd see her. She was a neat, compact little woman with fine white teeth. I used to watch her mouth when she laughed. She started calling me by my first name. One morning I was in another unit replacing a washer for one of the bathroom faucets. She didn't know I was there. She came in and turned on the TV as maids are in the habit of doing while they clean. I stopped what I was doing and stepped outside the bathroom. She was surprised to see me. She smiled and said my name. We looked at each other. I walked over and closed the door behind her. I put my arms around her. Then we lay down on the bed.

"Holly, you're still a proud woman," I go. "You're still number one. Come on, Holly."

She shakes her head. "Something's died in me," she goes. "It took a long time for it to die, but it's dead. You've killed something, just like you'd take an ax to it. Everything is dirt now." She finishes her drink. Then she begins to cry. I make to hug her, but she gets up and goes into the bathroom.

I freshen our drinks and look out the window. Two cars
with out-of-state plates are parked in front of the office. The
drivers, two men, are standing in front of the office, talking.
One of them finishes saying something to the other, looks
around at the units and pulls his chin. A woman has her face
up to the glass, hand shielding her eyes, peering inside. She
tries the door. The phone begins ringing in the office.

"Even when we were making love a while ago you were
thinking of her," Holly goes, as she returns from the bathroom. "Duane, this is so hurtful." She takes the drink I give
her.

"Holly," I go.

"No, it's true, Duane." She walks up and down the room in
her underpants and bra with the drink in her hand. "You've
gone outside the marriage. It's our trust you've broken.
Maybe that sounds old-fashioned to you. I don't care. Now I
just feel like, I don't know what, like dirt, that's what I feel
like. I'm confused. I don't have a purpose anymore. You were
my purpose."

This time she lets me take her hand. I get down on my knees
on the carpet and put her fingers against my temples. I love
her, Christ, yes, I love her. But at that very minute too I'm
thinking of Juanita, her fingers rubbing my neck that time.
This is awful. I don't know what's going to happen.

I go, "Holly, honey, I love you." But I don't know what else
to say or what else I can offer under the circumstances. She
runs her fingers back and forth across my forehead as if she is a
blind person being asked to describe my face.

In the lot someone leans on a horn, stops, starts again.
Holly takes her hand away, wipes her eyes. She goes, "Fix me a
drink. This one's too weak. Let them blow their horns, I don't
care. I think I'll move to Nevada."

"Don't talk crazy," I go.

"I'm not talking crazy," she goes. "I just said I think I'll
move to Nevada. Nothing's crazy about that. Maybe I can find
someone there who'll love me. You can stay here with your
Mexican maid. I think I'll move to Nevada. Either that or I'm
going to kill myself."

"Holly!"

"Holly nothing," she goes. She sits on the sofa and draws

her knees up under her chin. It's getting dark outside and inside. I pull the curtain and switch on the table lamp.

"I said fix me another drink, son of a bitch," she goes. "Fuck those horn-blowers. Let them go down the street to the Travelodge. Is that where your Mexican girlfriend works now? The Travelodge? I'll bet she helps that Sleepy Bear get into his pajamas every night. Well, fix me another drink and put some scotch in it this time." She sets her lips and gives me a fierce look.

Drinking's funny. When I look back on it, all of our important decisions have been taken when we were drinking. Even when we talked about having to cut back on our drinking, we'd be sitting at the kitchen table or out at a picnic table in the park with a six-pack or a bottle of whiskey in front of us. When we decided to move down here and take this motel job, leave our town, friends and relations, everything, we sat up all night drinking and talking, weighing the pros and cons, getting drunk over it. But we used to be able to handle it. And this morning when Holly suggests we need a serious talk about our lives, the first thing I do before we lock the office and go upstairs for our talk is run to the liquor store for the Teacher's.

I pour the last of it into our glasses and add another ice cube and a little water.

Holly gets off the sofa and stretches out across the bed. She goes, "Did you make love to her in this bed, too?"

"I did not."

"Well, it doesn't matter," she goes. "Not much matters anymore, anyway. I've got to recover myself though, that much is for sure."

I don't answer. I feel wiped out. I give her the glass and sit down in the big chair. I sip my drink and think, What now?

"Duane?" she goes.

"Holly?" My fingers curl around the glass. My heart has slowed. I wait. Holly was my true love.

The thing with Juanita had gone on five days a week between the hours of ten and eleven for six weeks. At first we contrived to meet in one unit or another as she was making her rounds. I'd just walk in where she was working and shut the door behind me. But after a time that seemed risky and she adjusted her routine so that we began meeting in 22, a unit at the end of the motel that faced east, toward the mountains, whose front door couldn't be seen from the office window. We were sweet with each other, but swift. We were swift and sweet at the same time. But it was fine. It was entirely new and unexpected, that much more pleasure. Then one fine morning, Bobbi, the other maid, she walks in on us. These women worked together, but they were not friends. Like that she went to the office and told Holly. Why she'd do such a thing I couldn't understand then and still can't. Juanita was scared and ashamed. She dressed and drove home. I saw Bobbi outside a while later and sent her home too. I wound up putting the units in order myself that day. Holly kept to the office, drinking, I suspect. I stayed clear. But when I came into the apartment before I went to work she was in the bedroom with the door closed. I listened. I heard her asking the employment service for another maid. I heard her hang up the telephone. Then she began that hum. I was undone. I went on to work, but I knew there'd be a reckoning.

I think Holly and I could maybe have weathered that. Even though she was wild drunk when I got in from work that night and threw a glass at me and said awful things we could never either of us forget. I slapped her for the first time ever that night and then begged her forgiveness for slapping her and for getting involved with someone. I begged her to forgive me. There was a lot of crying and soul-searching, and more drinking; we were up most of the night. Then we went to bed exhausted and made love. It simply was not mentioned again, the business with Juanita. There'd been the outburst, and then we proceeded to act as if the other hadn't happened. So maybe she was willing to forgive me, if not to forget it, and life could go on. What we hadn't counted on was that I would find myself missing Juanita and sometimes unable to sleep nights for thinking about her. I'd lie in bed after Holly was asleep and think about Juanita's white teeth, and then I'd think about her breasts. The nipples were dark and warm to the touch and there were little hairs growing just below the nipples. She had hair under her arms as well. I must have been crazy. After a couple of weeks of this I realized I had to see her again, God help me. I called one evening from work and we arranged that

I would stop by. I went to her house that night after work. She
was separated from her husband and lived in a little house with
two children. I got there just after midnight. I was uncomfortable, but Juanita knew it and put me at ease right away. We
drank a beer at the kitchen table. She got up and stood behind
my chair and rubbed my neck and told me to relax, relax and
let go. In her robe, she sat down at my feet and took my hand
and began to clean under my fingernails with a little file. Then
I kissed her and lifted her up, and we walked into the bedroom. In an hour or so I dressed, kissed her good-bye, and
went home to the motel.

Holly knew. Two people who have been so close, you can't
keep that kind of thing secret for long. Nor would you want
to. You know something like that can't go on and on, something has to give. Worse, you know you're in a constant state
of deception. It's no kind of life. I held on to the night job, a
monkey could do that work, but things were going downhill
fast at the motel. We just didn't have the heart for it any
longer. I stopped cleaning the swimming pool, and it began to
fill with algae so that guests couldn't use it. I didn't repair any
more faucets or lay any more tile or do any touch-up painting.
Even if we'd had the heart for it, there was just never enough
time with one thing and the other, the drinking especially.
That consumes a great deal of time and effort if you devote
yourself to it fully. Holly began some very serious drinking of
her own during this time. When I came in from work, whether
I'd been by Juanita's or not, Holly would either be asleep and
snoring, the bedroom smelling of whiskey, or else she'd be up
at the kitchen table smoking her filter tip, a glass of something
in front of her, eyes red and staring as I came in the door. She
was not registering guests either, charging too much or
else, most often, not collecting enough. Sometimes she'd as-
sign three people to a room with only one double bed, or else
she'd put a single party in one of the suites that had a king-size
bed and a sofa and charge the party for a single room only, that
sort of thing. Guests complained and sometimes there were
words. People would load up and go somewhere else after de-
manding their money back. There was a threatening letter
from the motel management people. Then another letter, cer-
tified. Telephone calls. Someone was coming down from the

city to look into matters. But we had stopped caring, and that's a fact. We knew things had to change, our days at the motel were numbered, a new wind was blowing—our lives fouled and ready for a shake-up. Holly's a smart woman, and I think she knew all this before I did, that the bottom had fallen out.

Then that Saturday morning we woke up with hangovers after an all-night rehashing of the situation that hadn't got us anywhere. We opened our eyes and turned in bed to look at each other. We both knew it at the same time, that we'd reached the end of something. We got up and dressed, had coffee as usual, and that's when she said we had to talk, talk now, without interruption, no phone calls, no guests. That's when I drove to the liquor store. When I came back we locked it up and went upstairs with ice, glasses, and the Teacher's. We propped up pillows and lay in bed and drank and didn't discuss anything at all. We watched color TV and frolicked and let the phone ring away downstairs. We drank scotch and ate cheese crisps from the machine down the hall. There was a funny sense of anything could happen now that we realized everything was lost. We knew without having to say it that something had ended, but what was about to begin and take its place, neither of us could think on yet. We dozed and sometime later in the day Holly raised herself off my arm. I opened my eyes at the movement. She sat up in bed. Then she screamed and rushed away from me toward the window.

"When we were just kids before we married?" Holly goes. "When we drove around every night and spent every possible minute together and talked and had big plans and hopes? Do you remember?" She was sitting in the center of the bed, holding her knees and her drink.

"I remember, Holly."

"You weren't my first boyfriend, my first boyfriend was named Wyatt and my folks didn't think much of him, but you were my first lover. You were my first lover then, and you've been my only lover since. Imagine. I didn't think I was missing that much. Now, who knows what I was missing all those years? But I was happy. Yes, I was. You were my everything, just like the song. But I don't know now what was wrong with

me all those years loving just you and only you. My God, I've
had the opportunities."

"I know you have," I go. "You're an attractive woman. I
know you've had the opportunities."

"But I didn't take them up on it, that's the point," she goes.
"I didn't. I couldn't go outside the marriage. It was beyond,
beyond comprehension."

"Holly, please," I go. "No more now, honey. Let's not tor-
ture ourselves. What is it that we should do now?"

"Listen," she goes. "Do you remember that time we drove out
to that old farm place outside of Yakima, out past Terrace
Heights? We were just driving around, it was a Saturday, like
today. We came to those orchards and then we were on a little dirt
road and it was so hot and dusty. We kept going and came to
that old farmhouse. We stopped and went up to the door and
knocked and asked if we could have a drink of cool water. Can
you imagine us doing something like that now, going up to a
strange house and asking for a drink of water?"

"We'd be shot."

"Those old people must be dead now," she goes, "side by
side out there in Terrace Heights cemetery. But that day the
old farmer and his wife, they not only gave us a glass of water,
they invited us in for cake. We talked and ate cake in the
kitchen, and later they asked if they could show us around.
They were so kind to us. I haven't forgotten. I appreciate
kindness like that. They showed us through the house. They
were so nice with each other. I still remember the inside of that
house. I've dreamed about it from time to time, the inside of
that house, those rooms, but I never told you those dreams. A
person has to have some secrets, right? But they showed us
around on the inside, those nice big rooms and their furnishings.
Then they took us out back. We walked around and they
pointed out that little—what did they call it? Gazebo. I'd
never seen one before. It was in a field under some trees. It
had a little peaked roof. But the paint was gone and weeds
were growing up over the steps. The woman said that years
before, before we were born even, musicians had come out
there to play on Sundays. She and her husband and their
friends and neighbors would sit around in their Sunday clothes

and listen to music and drink lemonade. I had a flash then, I don't know what else to call it. But I looked at that woman and her husband and I thought, someday we'll be old like that. Old but dignified, you know, like they were. Still loving each other more and more, taking care of one another, grandchildren coming to visit. All those things. I remember you were wearing cutoffs that day, and I remember standing there looking at the gazebo and thinking about those musicians when I happened to glance down at your bare legs. I thought to myself, I'll love those legs even when they're old and thin and the hair on them has turned white. I'll love them even then, I thought, they'll still be *my* legs. You know what I'm saying? Duane? Then they walked with us to the car and shook hands with us. They said we were nice young people. They invited us to come back, but of course we never did. They're dead now, they'd have to be dead. But here we are. I know something now I didn't know then. Don't I know it! It's such a good thing, isn't it, a person can't look into the future? But now here we are in this awful town, a couple of people who drink too much, running a motel with a dirty old swimming pool in front of it. And you in love with someone else. Duane, I've been closer to you than to anyone on earth. I feel crucified."

I can't say anything for a minute. Then I go, "Holly, these things, we'll look back on them someday when we're old, and we will be old together, you'll see, and we'll go, 'Remember that motel with the cruddy swimming pool?' and then we'll laugh at the things we did crazy. You'll see. It'll be all right. Holly?"

But Holly sits there on the bed with her empty glass and just looks at me. Then she shakes her head. She knows.

I move over to the window and look from behind the curtain. Someone says something below and rattles the door to the office. I wait. I tighten my fingers on the glass. I pray for a sign from Holly. I pray without closing my eyes. I hear a car start. Then another. The cars turn on their lights against the building and, one after the other, pull away and out into the traffic.

"Duane," Holly goes.

In this, as in most matters, she was right.

Want to See Something?

I WAS in bed when I heard the gate unlatch. I listened carefully. I didn't hear anything else. But I had heard that. I tried to wake Cliff, but he was passed out. So I got up and went to the window. A big moon hung over the mountains that surrounded the city. It was a white moon and covered with scars, easy enough to imagine a face there—eye sockets, nose, even the lips. There was enough light that I could see everything in the backyard, lawn chairs, the willow tree, clotheslines strung between the poles, my petunias, and the fence enclosing the yard, the gate standing open.

But nobody was moving around outside. There were no dark shadows. Everything lay in bright moonlight, and the smallest things came to my attention. The clothespins standing in orderly rows on the line, for instance. And the two empty lawn chairs. I put my hands on the cool glass, hiding the moon, and looked some more. I listened. Then I went back to bed. But I couldn't sleep. I kept turning over. I thought about the gate standing open like an invitation. Cliff's breathing was ragged. His mouth gaped and his arms hugged his pale, bare chest. He was taking up his side of the bed and most of mine. I pushed and pushed on him. But he just groaned. I stayed in bed awhile longer until finally I decided it was no use. I got up and found my slippers. I went to the kitchen where I made a cup of tea and sat with it at the kitchen table. I smoked one of Cliff's unfiltereds. It was late. I didn't want to look at the time. I had to get up for work in a few hours. Cliff had to get up too, but he'd gone to bed hours ago and would be okay when the alarm went off. Maybe he'd have a headache. But he'd put away lots of coffee and take his time in the bathroom. Four aspirin and he'd be all right. I drank the tea and smoked another cigarette. After a while I decided I'd go out and fasten the gate. So I found my robe. Then I went to the back door. I looked and could see stars, but it was the moon that drew my attention and lighted everything—houses and trees, utility poles and power lines, the entire neighborhood. I peered around the backyard before I stepped off the porch. A little breeze came along that made me close the robe. I started toward the open gate.

There was a noise at the fence that separated our house from Sam Lawton's. I looked quickly. Sam was leaning with his arms on the fence, gazing at me. He raised a fist to his mouth and gave a dry cough.

"Evening, Nancy," he said.

I said, "Sam, you scared me. What are you doing up, Sam? Did you hear something? I heard my gate unlatch."

"I've been out here awhile, but I haven't heard anything," he said. "Haven't seen anything either. It might have been the wind. That's it. Still, if it was latched it shouldn't have come open." He was chewing something. He looked at the open gate and then he looked at me again and shrugged. His hair was silvery in the moonlight and stood up on his head. It was so light out I could see his long nose, even the deep lines in his face.

I said, "What are you doing up, Sam?" and moved closer to the fence.

"Hunting," he said. "I'm hunting. Want to see something? Come over here, Nancy, and I'll show you something."

"I'll come around," I said, and started along the side of our house to the front gate. I let myself out and went down the sidewalk. I felt strange, walking around outside in my nightgown and robe. I thought to myself that I must remember this, walking around outside in my nightgown. I could see Sam standing near the side of his house in his robe, his pajamas stopping just at the tops of his white and tan oxfords. He was holding a big flashlight in one hand and a can of something in the other. He motioned me with his light. I opened the gate.

Sam and Cliff used to be friends. Then one night they were drinking. They had an argument. The next thing, Sam had built a fence between the houses. Then Cliff decided to build his own fence. That was not long after Sam had lost Millie, remarried, and become a father again. All in the space of little more than a year. Millie, Sam's first wife, was a good friend of mine up until she died. She was only forty-five when she had heart failure. Apparently it hit her just as she turned their car into the driveway. She slumped over the wheel, the car kept going and knocked through the back of the carport. When Sam ran out of the house, he found her dead. Sometimes at night we'd hear a howling sound from over there that he must have been making. We'd look at each other when we heard that and not be able to say anything. I'd shiver. Cliff would fix himself another drink.

Sam and Millie had a daughter who'd left home at sixteen and gone to San Francisco to become a flower child. From time to time over the years she'd sent cards. But she never came back home. Sam tried but he couldn't locate her when Millie died. He wept and said he lost the daughter first and then the mother. Millie was buried, Sam howled, and then after a little while he started going out with Laurie something-or-other, a younger woman, a schoolteacher who did income tax preparations on the side. It was a brief courtship. They were both lonely and in need. So they married, and then they had a baby. But here's the sad thing. The baby was albino. I saw it a few days after they brought it home from the hospital. It was an albino, no question of that, right down to its poor little fingertips. Its eyes were tinged with pink around the iris instead of being white, and the hair on its head was as white as an old person's. Its head seemed overlarge too. But I haven't been around that many babies, so that could have been imagination on my part. The first time I saw it, Laurie was standing on the other side of its crib, arms crossed, the skin on the backs of her hands broken out, anxiety making her lips twitch. I know she was afraid I'd peep into the crib and gasp or something. But I was prepared. Cliff had already filled me in. In any case, I'm usually good at covering up my real feelings. So I reached down touched each of its tiny white cheeks and tried to smile. I said its name. I said, "Sammy." But I thought I would cry when I said it. I was prepared, but still I couldn't meet Laurie's eyes for the longest while. She stood there waiting while I silently gave thanks that this was her baby. No, I wouldn't want a baby like that for anything. I counted my blessings that Cliff and I had long ago decided against children. But according to Cliff, who's no judge, Sam's personality changed after the baby was born. He became short-tempered and impatient, mad at the world, Cliff said. Then he and Cliff had the argument, and Sam built his fence. We hadn't talked in a long while, any of us.

"Look at this," Sam said, hitching his pajamas and squatting down with the robe fanned over his knees. He pointed his light at the ground.

I looked and saw some thick white slugs curled on a bare patch of dirt.

"I just gave them a dose of this," he said, raising a can of something that looked like Ajax. But it was a bigger and heavier can than Ajax and had a skull and crossbones on the label. "Slugs are taking over," he said, working something in his mouth. He turned his head to one side and spit what could have been tobacco. "I have to keep at this nearly every night to just come close to staying up with them." He turned his light onto a glass jar that was nearly filled with the things. "I put bait out for them at night, and then every chance I get come out here with this stuff and hunt them down. Bastards are all over. Your backyard has them too, I'll bet. If mine does, yours does. It's a crime what they can do to a yard. And your flowers. Look over here," he said. He got up. He took my arm and moved me over to some rosebushes. He showed me little holes in the leaves. "Slugs," he said. "Everywhere you look around here at night, slugs. I lay out bait and then I come out and try to pick off the ones who don't eat the little banquet I've fixed up for them," he said. "An awful invention, a slug. But I save them up in that jar there, and when the jar is full and they're nice and ripe, I sprinkle them under the roses. They make good fertilizer." He moved his light slowly over the rosebush. After a minute he said, "Some life, isn't it?" and shook his head.

A plane passed overhead. I raised my eyes and saw its blinking lights and behind the lights, clear as anything in the night sky, the long white stream of its exhaust. I imagined the people on the plane as they sat belted into their seats, some of them involved in reading, some of them just staring out their windows.

I turned back to Sam. I said, "How're Laurie and Sam junior?"

"They're fine. You know," he said and shrugged. He chewed on whatever it was he was chewing. "Laurie's a good woman. The best. She's a good woman," he said again. "I don't know what I'd do if I didn't have her. I think if it wasn't for her I'd want to be with Millie, where she is. Wherever that is. I guess that's nowhere, as far as I can tell. That's my idea on the matter. Nowhere," he said. "Death is nowhere, Nancy. You can quote me if you want." He spat again. "Sammy's sick.

You know he gets these colds. Hard for him to shake them. She's taking him to the doctor again tomorrow. How're you folks? How's Clifford?"

I said, "He's fine. Same as ever. Same old Cliff." I didn't know what else to say. I looked at the rosebush once more. "He's asleep now," I said.

"Sometimes when I'm out here after these damn slugs, I'll glance over the fence in your direction," he said. "Once—," he stopped and laughed quietly. "Excuse me, Nancy, but it strikes me kind of funny now. But once I looked over the fence and saw Cliff out there in your backyard, peeing onto those petunias. I started to say something, make a little joke of some kind. But I didn't. From the looks of things, I think he'd been drinking so I didn't know how he'd take it, if I'd said anything. He didn't see me. So I just kept quiet. I'm sorry Cliff and me had that falling out," he said.

I nodded slowly. "I think he is too, Sam." After a minute I said, "You and he were friends." But the picture of Cliff standing unzipped over the petunias stayed in my head. I closed my eyes and tried to get rid of it.

"That's true, we were good friends," Sam said. Then he went on. "I come out here nights after Laurie and the baby are asleep. Gives me something to do, is one thing. You folks are asleep. Everybody's asleep. I don't sleep good anymore. And what I'm doing is worth doing, I believe that. Look there now," he said and drew a sharp breath. "There's one there. See him? Right there where my light is." He had the beam directed onto the dirt under the rosebush. Then I saw the slug move. "You watch this," Sam said.

I closed my arms under my breasts and bent over where he was shining his light. The slug stopped and turned its blind head from side to side. Then Sam was over it with the can, sprinkling, sprinkling. "Goddamn these slimy things," he said. "God, I hate them." The slug began to writhe and twist this way and that. Then it curled and then it straightened out. It curled again and lay still. Sam picked up a toy shovel. He scooped the slug into that. He held the jar away from him, unscrewed the lid, and dropped the slug into the jar. He fastened the lid once more and set the jar on the ground.

"I quit drinking," Sam said. "I didn't exactly quit, I just cut way back. Had to. For a while it was getting so I didn't know up from down. We keep it around the house still, but I don't have much to do with it anymore."

I nodded. He looked at me and he kept looking. I had the feeling he was waiting for me to say something. But I didn't say anything. What was there to say? Nothing. "I'd better get back," I said.

"Sure," he said. "Well, I'll continue with what I'm doing awhile longer, and then I'll head in too."

I said, "Good night, Sam."

"Good night, Nancy," he said. "Listen." He stopped chewing, and with his tongue pushed whatever it was behind his lower lip. "Tell old Cliff I said hello."

I said, "I will. I'll tell him you said hello, Sam."

He nodded. He ran his hand through his silvery hair as if he were going to make it lay down for once. "'Night, Nancy."

I went back to the front of the house and down the sidewalk. I stopped for a minute with my hand on our gate and looked around the still neighborhood. I don't know why, but I suddenly felt a long way away from everybody I had known and loved when I was a girl. I missed people. For a minute I stood there and wished I could get back to that time. Then with my next thought I understood clearly I couldn't do that. No. But it came to me then that my life did not remotely resemble the life I thought I'd have when I had been young and looking ahead to things. I couldn't remember now what I'd wanted to do with my life in those years, but like everybody else I'd had plans. Cliff was somebody who had plans too, and that's how we'd met and why we'd stayed together.

I went in and turned off all the lights. In the bedroom I took off the robe, folded it, put it within reach so I could get to it after the alarm went off. Without looking at the time, I checked again to make sure the stem was out on the clock. Then I got into bed, pulled the covers up, and closed my eyes. Cliff started to snore. I poked him, but it didn't do any good. He kept on. I listened to his snores. Then I remembered I'd forgotten to latch the gate. Finally I opened my eyes and just lay there, letting my eyes move around over things in the room. After a time I turned on my side and put an arm over Cliff's waist. I gave him a little shake. He stopped snoring for a minute. Then he cleared his throat. He swallowed. Something caught and rattled in his chest. He sighed heavily, then started up again, snoring.

I said, "Cliff," and shook him, hard. "Cliff, listen to me." He moaned. A shudder went through him. For a minute he seemed to have stopped breathing, to be down at the bottom of something. Of their own accord, my fingers dug into the soft flesh over his hip. I held my own breath, waiting for his to start again. There was a space and then his breathing, deep and regular once more. I brought my hand up to his chest. It lay there, fingers spread, then beginning to tap, as if thinking what to do next. "Cliff?" I said again. "Cliff." I put my hand to his throat. I found the pulse. Then I cupped his stubbled chin and felt the warm breath on the back of my hand. I looked closely at his face and began to trace his features with the tips of my fingers. I touched his heavy closed eyelids. I stroked the lines in his forehead.

I said, "Cliff, listen to me, honey." I started out everything I was going to say to him by saying I loved him. I told him I had always loved him and always would love him. Those were things that needed saying before the other things. Then I began to talk. It didn't matter that he was someplace else and couldn't hear any of what I was saying. Besides, in mid-sentence it occurred to me he already knew everything I was saying, maybe better than I knew, and had for a long time. When I thought that, I stopped talking for a minute and looked at him with new regard. Nevertheless, I wanted to finish what I'd started. I went on telling him, without rancor or heat of any sort, everything that was on my mind. I wound up by saying it out, the worst and last of it, that I felt we were going nowhere fast, and it was time to admit it, even though there was maybe no help for it.

Just so many words, you might think. But I felt better for having said them. And so I wiped the tears off my cheeks and lay back down. Cliff's breathing seemed normal, though loud to the point I couldn't hear my own. I thought for a minute of the world outside my house, and then I didn't have any more thoughts except I thought maybe I could sleep.

The Fling

IT's October, a damp day outside. From my hotel room window I can look out and see much of this gray midwestern city; just now, lights are coming on here and there in some of the buildings, and smoke from the tall stacks at the edge of town is rising in a slow thick climb into the darkening sky. Except for a branch of the university campus located here—a poor relation, really—there isn't much to recommend the place.

I want to relate a story my father told me last year when I stopped over briefly in Sacramento. It concerns some sordid events that he was involved in nearly two years before that, before he and my mother were divorced. It could be asked that if it is important enough to warrant the telling—my time and energy, your time and energy—then why haven't I told it before this? I'd have no answer for that. In the first place, I don't know if it is that important—at least to anyone except my father and the others involved. Secondly, and perhaps more to the point, what business is it of mine? That question is more difficult to answer. I admit I feel that I acted badly that day with regard to my father, that I perhaps failed him at a time when I could have helped. Yet something else tells me that he was beyond help, beyond anything I could do for him, and that the only thing that transpired between us in those few hours was that he caused me—*forced* might be the better word —to peer into my own abyss; and nothing comes of nothing as Pearl Bailey says, and we all know from experience.

I'm a book salesman representing a well-known midwestern textbook firm. My home base is Chicago, my territory Illinois, parts of Iowa and Wisconsin. I had been attending the Western Book Publishers Association convention out in Los Angeles when it occurred to me, sheerly on the spur of the moment, to visit a few hours with my father on my way back to Chicago. I hesitated because, since his divorce, there was a very large part of me that didn't want to see him again, but before I could change my mind, I fished his address out of my wallet and proceeded to send him a telegram. The next morning I sent my things on to Chicago and boarded a plane for Sacramento.

The sky was slightly overcast; it was a cool, damp September morning.

It took me a minute to pick him out. He was standing a few steps behind the gate when I saw him, white hair, glasses, brown Sta-Prest cotton pants, a gray nylon jacket over a white shirt open at the throat. He was staring at me, and I realized he must have had me in view since I stepped off the plane.

"Dad, how are you?"

"Les."

We shook hands quickly and began to move toward the terminal.

"How's Mary and the kids?"

I looked at him closely before answering. Of course, he didn't know we'd been living apart for nearly six months. "Everyone's fine," I answered.

He opened a white confectionery sack. "I picked them up a little something, maybe you could take it back with you. Not much. Some Almond Roca for Mary, a Cootie game for Ed, and a Barbie doll. Jean'll like that, won't she?"

"Sure she will."

"Don't forget this when you leave."

I nodded. We moved out of the way as a group of nuns, flushed and talking excitedly, headed for the boarding area. He'd aged. "Well, shall we have a drink or a cup of coffee?"

"Anything you say. I don't have a car," he apologized. "Really don't need one around here. I had a cab bring me out."

"We don't have to go anyplace. Let's go to the bar and have a drink. It's early, but I could use a drink."

We located the lounge and I waved him into a booth while I went over to the bar. My mouth was dry and I asked for a glass of orange juice while I waited. I looked over at my father; his hands were clasped together on the table and he gazed out the tinted window that overlooked the field. A large plane was taking passengers and another was landing farther out. A woman in her late thirties, red hair, wearing a white knit suit, was sitting between two well-dressed younger men a few stools down. One of the men was close to her ear, telling her something.

"Here we are, Dad. Cheers." He nodded and we each took a long drink and then lighted cigarettes. "Well, how're you getting along?"

He shrugged and opened his hands. "So-so."

I leaned back in the seat and drew a long breath. He had an air of woe about him that I couldn't help but find a little irritating.

"I guess the Chicago airport would make three or four of this one," he said.

"More than that."

"Thought it was big."

"When did you start wearing glasses?"

"Not long ago. A few months."

After a minute or two I said, "I think it's time for another one." The bartender looked our way and I nodded. This time a slender pleasant girl in a red and black dress came to take our order. All the stools at the bar were taken now, and there were a few men in business suits sitting at the tables in the booths. A fishnet hung from the ceiling with a number of colored Japanese floats tossed inside. Petula Clark was singing "Downtown" from the jukebox. I remembered again that my father was living alone, working nights as a lathe operator in a machine shop, and it all seemed impossible. Suddenly the woman at the bar laughed loudly and leaned back on her stool, holding onto the sleeves of the men who sat on either side of her. The girl came back with the drinks, and this time my father and I clinked glasses.

"I liked to have died over it myself," he said slowly. His arms rested heavily on either side of his glass. "You're an educated man, Les. Maybe you can understand."

I nodded slightly, not meeting his eyes, and waited for him to go on. He began to talk in a low monotonous drone that annoyed me immediately. I turned the ashtray on its edge to read what was on the bottom: HARRAH'S CLUB RENO AND LAKE TAHOE. Good places to have fun.

"She was a Stanley products woman. A little woman, small feet and hands and coal black hair. She wasn't the most beautiful woman in the world, but she had nice ways about her. She was thirty years old and had kids but, but she was a decent woman, whatever happened.

"Your mother was always buying something from her, a broom or a mop, some kind of pie filling, you know your mother. It was a Saturday, and I was home alone and your mother was gone someplace. I don't know where she was. She wasn't working. I was in the front room reading the paper and drinking a cup of coffee, just taking it easy. There was a knock on the door and it was this little woman, Sally Wain. She said she had some things for my wife, Mrs. Palmer. 'I'm Mr. Palmer,' I said. 'Mrs. Palmer is not here right now.' I asked her just to step in, you know, and I'd pay her for the things. She didn't know whether she should or not, just stood there a minute holding this little paper sack and the receipt with it.

" 'Here, I'll take that,' I said. 'Why don't you come in and sit down a minute till I see if I can find some money.'

" 'That's all right,' she said. 'You can owe it. I can pick it up anytime. I have lots of people do that; it's all right.' She smiled to let me know it was all right.

" 'No, no,' I said. 'I've got it, I'd rather pay it now. Save you a trip back and save me owing another bill. Come in,' I said again, and held open the screen door. 'It isn't polite to have you standing out there.' It was around eleven or twelve o'clock in the morning."

He coughed and took one of my cigarettes from the pack on the table. The woman at the bar laughed again, and I looked over at her and then back at my father.

"She stepped in then and I said, 'Just a minute, please,' and went into the bedroom to look for my wallet. I looked around on the dresser but couldn't find it. I found some change and matches, and my comb, but I couldn't find my wallet. Your mother had gone through that morning cleaning up. I went back to the front room and said, 'Well, I'll turn up some money yet.'

" 'Please don't bother,' she said.

" 'No bother,' I answered. 'Have to find my wallet, anyway. Make yourself at home.'

" 'Look here,' I said, stopping by the kitchen door. 'You hear about that big holdup back east?' I pointed to the newspaper. 'I was just reading about it.'

" 'I saw it on television last night,' she said. 'They had pictures and interviewed the cops.'

" 'They got away clean,' I said.

" 'Pretty slick of them, wasn't it?' she said.

" 'I think everybody at some time or another dreams about pulling the perfect crime, don't they?'

" 'But not many people get away with it,' she said. She picked up the paper. There was a picture of an armored car on the front page and the headlines said something like million-dollar robbery, something like that. You remember that, Les? When those guys dressed up as policemen?

"I didn't know what else to say, we were just standing there looking at each other. I turned and went on out to the porch and looked for my pants in the hamper where I figured your mother had put them. I found the wallet in my back pocket and went back to the other room and asked how much I owed.

" 'We can do business now,' I said.

"It was three or four dollars, and I paid her. Then, I don't know why, I asked her what she'd do with it if she had it, all the money those guys got away with.

"She laughed out loud at that and showed her teeth.

"I don't know what came over me then, Les. Fifty-five years old. Grown kids. I knew better than that. This woman was barely half my age with little kids in school. She did this Stanley job just the hours they were in school, just to give her something to do. She got a little spending money from it, naturally, but mainly it was just to keep occupied. She didn't have to work. They had enough to get by on. Her husband, Larry, he, he was a driver for Consolidated Freight. Made good money. Teamster, you know. He made enough for them to live on without her having to work. It wasn't a have-to case."

He stopped and wiped his face. "I want to try and make you understand."

"You don't have to say any more," I said. "I'm not asking you anything. Anybody can make a mistake. I understand."

He shook his head. "I have to tell somebody this, Les. I haven't told this to anybody, but I want to tell you this and I want you to understand."

"She had two boys, Stan and Freddy. They were in school, about a year apart. I never met them, thank God, but later on she showed me some pictures of them. She laughed when I said that about the money, said she guessed she'd quit selling Stanley products, and they'd move to San Diego and buy a house there. She had relatives in San Diego, and if they had that much money, she said, they'd move down there and open a sporting goods store. That's what they'd always talked about doing, opening a sporting goods store, if they ever got enough ahead."

I lit another cigarette, glanced at my watch, and crossed and recrossed my legs under the table. The bartender looked over at us, and I raised my glass. He motioned to the girl who was taking an order at another table.

"She was sitting down on the couch now, more relaxed and just skimming the newspaper, when she looked up and asked if I had a cigarette. Said she'd left hers in her other purse, and she hadn't had a smoke since she left her house. Said she hated to buy from a machine when she had a carton at home. I gave her a cigarette and I held a match for her, but my fingers were shaking."

He stopped again and looked at the table for a minute. The woman at the bar had her arms locked through the arms of the man on each side of her, and the three of them were singing along with the music from the jukebox: *That summer wind, came blowin' in, a-cross the sea.* I ran my fingers up and down the glass and waited sadly for him to go on.

"It's kind of fuzzy after that. I remember I asked her if she wanted any coffee. Said I'd just made a fresh pot, but she said she had to be going, though maybe she had time for one cup. We never mentioned your mother the whole time, either of us, the fact she may just walk in any minute. I went out to the kitchen and waited for the coffee to heat, and by that time I had a case of the nerves so that the cups rattled when I brought them in . . . I'll tell you, Les, I'll swear before God, I never once stepped out on your mother the whole time we were married. Not once. Maybe there were times when I felt like it, or that I had the chance . . . You don't know your mother like I do. Sometimes she was, she could be—"

"That's enough of that," I said. "You don't have to say another word in that direction."

"I didn't mean anything by that. I loved your mother. You don't know. I just wanted you to try and understand . . . I brought in the coffee, and Sally'd taken off her coat by then. I sat down on the other end of the couch from her and we got to talking more personal. She said she had two kids in Roosevelt grade school, and Larry, he was a driver and was sometimes gone for a week or two at a time. Up to Seattle, or down to Los Angeles, or else to Phoenix, Arizona. Always someplace. Pretty soon we just began to feel good talking with one another, you know, and enjoying just sitting there talking. She said her mother and father were both dead and she'd been raised by an aunt there in Redding. She'd met Larry when they were both going to high school, and they'd gotten married, but she was proud of the fact she'd gone on to school till she finished. But pretty soon she gave a little laugh at something I'd said that could maybe be taken two ways, and she kept laughing, and then she asked if I'd heard the one about the traveling shoe salesman who called on the widow woman. We laughed quite a bit after she told that one, and then I told her one a little worse, and she giggled at that, and then smoked another cigarette. One thing was leading to another, and pretty soon I'd eased over beside her.

"I'm ashamed telling you this, my own flesh and blood, but I kissed her then. I guess I was clumsy and awkward, but I put her head back on the couch and kissed her, and I felt her tongue touch my lips. I don't, don't know quite how to say this, Les, but I raped her. I don't mean raped her against her will, nothing like that, but I raped her all the same, fumbling and pulling at her like a fifteen-year-old kid. She didn't encourage me, if you know what I mean, but she didn't do anything to stop me either . . . I don't know, a man can just go along, go along, obeying all the rules and then, then all of a sudden . . .

"But it was all over in a minute or two. She got up and straightened her clothes and looked embarrassed. I didn't really know what to do and I went out to the kitchen and got more coffee for us. When I came back in she had her coat on and was ready to leave. I put the coffee down and went over and squeezed her.

"She said, 'You must think I'm a whore or something.' Something like that, and looked down at her shoes. I squeezed her again and said, 'You know that isn't true.'

"Well, she left. We didn't say good-bye or see you later. She just turned and slipped out the door and I watched her get into her car down the block and drive off.

"I was all excited and mixed up. I straightened things around the couch and turned over the cushions, folded all the newspapers and even washed the two cups we'd used, and cleaned out the coffee pot. All the time I was thinking about how I was going to face your mother. I knew I had to get out for a while and have a chance to think. I went down to Kelly's and stayed there all afternoon drinking beer.

"That was the way it started. After that, nothing happened for two or three weeks. Your mother and I got along the same as always, and after the first two or three days I stopped thinking about the other. I mean, I remembered everything all right—how could I forget it?—I just stopped thinking about any of it. Then one Saturday I was out working on the lawn mower in the front yard when I saw her stop on the other side of the street. She got out of the car with a mop and a couple or three little paper bags in her hand, making a delivery. Now your mother was right in the house where she could see everything, if she just happened to look out the window, but I knew I had to have a chance to say something to Sally. I watched, and when she came out of the house across the street I sauntered over as ordinary-looking as I could, carrying a screwdriver and a pair of pliers in my hand like I might have some kind of legitimate business with her. When I walked up to the side of the car she was already inside and had to lean over and roll the window down. I said, 'Hello, Sally, how's everything?'

" 'All right,' she said.

" 'I'd like to see you again,' I said.

"She just looked at me. Not mad-like, or anything, just looked at me straight and even and kept her hands on the wheel.

" 'Like to see you,' I said again, and my mouth was thick. 'Sally.'

"She pulled her lip between her teeth and then let go and said, 'You want to come tonight? Larry's gone out of town to Salem, Oregon. We could have a beer.'

"I nodded and took a step back from the car. 'After nine o'clock,' she added. 'I'll leave the light on.'

"I nodded again, and she started up and pulled away, dragging the clutch. I walked back across the street, and my legs were weak."

Over near the bar a lean, dark man in a red shirt began to play the accordion. It was a Latin number and he played with feeling, rocking the big instrument back and forth in his arms, sometimes lifting his leg and rolling it over his thigh. The woman sat with her back to the bar and listened, holding a drink. She listened to him and watched him play and began to move back and forth on her stool in time with the music.

"Some live music," I said to distract my father, who merely glanced in that direction then finished his drink.

Suddenly the woman slid down off the stool, took a few steps toward the center of the floor, and commenced to dance. She tossed her head from side to side and snapped her fingers on both hands as her heels hit the floor. Everyone in the place watched her dance. The bartender stopped mixing drinks. People began to look in from outside and soon a little crowd had collected at the door to watch, and still she danced. I think people were at first fascinated, but a little horrified and embarrassed for her, too. I was, anyway. At one point her long red hair pulled loose and fell down her back, but she only cried out and stamped her heels faster and faster. She raised her arms above her head and began to snap her fingers and move about in a small circle in the middle of the floor. She was surrounded by men now, but above their heads I could see her hands and her white fingers, snapping. Then, with a last staccato stamping of her heels and a final yip, it was finished. The music stopped, the woman cast her head forward, hair flinging out over her face, and dropped to one knee. The accordion player led the applause, and the men nearest her backed away to give her room. She stayed there on the floor a minute, head bowed, taking long breaths, before she got to her feet. She seemed dazed. She licked the hair that clung to her lips and looked around at the faces. Men continued to applaud. She smiled and nodded slowly and formally, turning slowly until she had taken in everyone. Then she made her way back to the bar and picked up her drink.

"Did you see that?" I asked.

"I saw it."

He couldn't have appeared less interested. For a moment he seemed utterly contemptible to me, and I had to look away. I knew I was being silly, that I'd be gone in another hour, but it was all I could do to keep from telling him then what I thought of his dirty affair, and what it had done to my mother.

The jukebox started in the middle of a record. The woman sat at the bar still, only leaning on her elbow now, staring at herself in the mirror. There were three drinks in front of her, and one of the men, the one who had been talking to her earlier, had moved off, down toward the end of the bar. The other man had the flat of his hand against the lower part of her back. I drew a long breath, put a smile on my lips, and turned to my father.

"So that's the way it went for a while," he started in again. "Larry had a pretty regular schedule, and I'd find myself over there every night I had the chance. I'd tell your mother I was going to the Elks, or else I told her I had some work to finish up at the shop. Anything, anything to be gone a few hours.

"The first time, that same night, I parked the car three or four blocks away and walked up the street and then right on past her house. I walked with my hands in my coat and at a good pace and walked right on by her house, trying to get my nerve up. She had the porch light on all right, and all the shades pulled. I walked to the end of the block and then came back, slower, and walked up the sidewalk to her door. I know if I'd found Larry there to answer the door, that'd been the end of that. I'd have said I was looking for directions and gone on. And never come back. My heart was pounding in my ears. Just before I rang the bell, I worked the wedding ring off my finger and dropped it in my pocket. I guess, I guess right then, that minute on the porch before she opened the door, that was the only time I considered, I mean really considered, what I was doing to your mother. Just in that minute before Sally opened the door, I knew for a minute what I was doing, and that what I was doing was dead wrong.

"But I did it, and I must have been crazy! I must have been crazy all along, Les, and didn't know it, just laying in wait for me. Why? Why'd I do it? An old bastard like me with grown kids. Why'd she do it? That son-of-a-bitching slut!" He set his jaws and brooded for a minute. "No, I don't mean that. I was crazy about her, I admit it . . . I was even over there days when I had the chance. When I knew Larry'd be gone, I'd slip out of the shop in the afternoon and beat it over there. Her

kids were always in school. Thank God for that, I never
bumped into them. It'd be a lot harder now if I had . . . But
that first time, that was the hardest time of all.

"We were both pretty nervous. We sat up for a long time in
the kitchen drinking beer, and she began to tell me a lot about
herself, secret thoughts, she called them. I began to relax and
feel more at ease too, and I found myself telling her things.
About you, for instance; you working and saving your money
and going to school and then going back to Chicago to live.
She said she'd been to Chicago on a train when she was a little
girl. I told her about what I'd done with my life—not very
much until then, I said. And I told her some of the things I
still wanted to do, things that I still planned on doing. She
made me feel that way when I was around her, like I didn't
have it all behind me. I told her I wasn't too old to still have
plans. 'People need plans,' she said. 'You have to have plans.
When I get too old to make plans and look forward to something, that's when they can come and put me away.' That's
what she said, and more, and I began to think I loved her. We
sat there talking about everything under the sun for I don't
know how long, before I put my arms around her."

He took off his glasses and shut his eyes for a minute. "I
haven't talked about this to anybody. I know I'm probably
getting a little tight, and I don't want any more to drink, but
I've got to tell this to somebody. I can't keep it in any longer.
So, so if I'm bothering you with all this you'll just have to,
you'll just have to please oblige me by listening a little longer."

I didn't answer. I looked out at the field, then looked at my
watch.

"Listen!—What time does your plane leave? Can you take a
later one? Let me buy us another drink, Les. Order us two
more. I'll speed it up, I'll be through with this in a minute. You
don't know how much I need to get some of this off my chest.
Listen.

"She kept his picture in the bedroom right by the
bed . . . I want to tell it all, Les . . . First it bothered me,
seeing his picture there as we climbed into bed, the last thing I
saw before she turned out the light. But that was just the first
few times. After a while I got used to having it there. I mean, I
liked it, him smiling over at us, nice and quiet, as we got into

his bed. I almost got to looking forward to it, and would have missed it if it hadn't been there. Got to where I was even liking to do it best in the afternoons, because there was always plenty of light then, and I could look over and see him whenever I wanted."

He shook his head and it seemed to wobble a little. "Hard to believe, isn't it? Don't hardly recognize your father anymore, do you? . . . Well, it all came to a bad end. You know that. Your mother left me, as she had every right to do. You know all that. She said, said she couldn't bear to look at me anymore. But even that's not so important."

"What do you mean," I said, "that's not important?"

"I'll tell you, Les. I'll tell you what's the most important thing here involved. You see there are things, things far more important than that. More important than your mother's leaving me. That's, in the long run, that's nothing . . . We were in bed one night. It must have been around eleven o'clock because I always made it a point to be home before midnight. The kids were asleep. We were just laying there in bed talking, Sally and me, my arm around her waist. I was kind of dozing, I guess, listening to her talk. It was pleasant just dozing and kind of half listening. At the same time, I was awake and I remember thinking that pretty soon I'd have to get up and go on home, when a car pulled into the driveway and somebody got out and slammed the door.

"'My God,' she screams, 'it's Larry!' I jumped out of bed and was still in the hallway trying to get my clothes on when I heard him come onto the porch and open the door. I must have gone crazy. I seem to remember thinking that if I ran out the back door he'd pin me up against that big fence in the backyard and maybe kill me. Sally was making a funny kind of sound. Like she couldn't get her breath. She had her robe on but it was undone, and she stood in the kitchen shaking her head back and forth. All this was happening all at once. There I was, half naked with all my clothes in my hand, and Larry was opening the front door. I jumped. I jumped right into their big front-room window, right through the glass. I landed in some bushes, jumped up with the glass still falling off me, and started off running down the street."

You crazier than hell old son of a bitch, you. It was grotesque.

The whole story was insane. It would have been ludicrous, all of it, if it hadn't been for my mother. I looked at him steadily for a minute, but he didn't meet my eyes.

"You got away, though? He didn't come after you, or anything?"

He didn't answer, just stared at the empty glass in front of him, and I looked at my watch again. I stretched. I had a small insistent ache behind my eyes. "I guess I'd better be getting out there soon." I ran my hand over my chin and straightened my collar. "I guess that's all there is to it, huh? You and mother split up then, and you moved down here to Sacramento. She's still in Redding. Isn't that about it?"

"No, that's not exactly right. I mean, that's true, yes, yes, but—" He raised his voice. "You don't know anything, do you? You don't really know anything. You're thirty-two years old, but, but you don't know anything except how to sell books." He glared at me. Behind his glasses his eyes looked red and tiny and far away. I just sat there and didn't feel anything one way or the other. It was almost time to go. "No. No, that's not all . . . I'm sorry. I'll tell you what else happened. If, if he'd just beat her up or something, or else come after me, come looking for me at my home. Anything. I deserved it, whatever he had to dish out . . . But he didn't. He didn't do anything like that. I guess, guess he just broke up and went all to pieces. He just . . . went to pieces. He lay down on the couch and cried. She stayed out in the kitchen, and she cried too, got down on her knees and prayed to God out loud and said she was sorry, sorry, but after a while she heard the door close and came back out to the living room and he was gone. He didn't take the car, that was still there in the driveway. He walked. He walked downtown and rented a room there at the Jefferson, down on Third. He got hold of a paring knife at some all-night drugstore and went up to his room and began, began sticking it in his stomach, trying to kill himself . . . Somebody tried to get in there a couple of days later and he was still alive, and there were thirty or forty of those little knife wounds in him and blood all over the room, but he was still alive. He'd cut his guts all to pieces, the doctor said. He died up in the hospital a day or two later. The doctors said there was nothing they could do for him. He just died, never opened his mouth or asked for anybody. Just died and with his insides all cut to pieces.

"I feel like, Les, that I died up there. Part of me did. Your mother was right in leaving me. She should've left me. But they shouldn't have had to bury Larry Wain! I don't want to die, Les, it isn't that. I guess if you'd get right down to it, I'd rather it was him under the ground and not me. If there was a choice had to be made . . . I don't know what any of it's all about, life and death, those things. I believe you only have one life and that's that; but, but it's hard to walk around with that other on my conscience. It keeps coming back to me, I mean, and I can't get it out of my head that he should be dead for something I caused."

He started to say something else, but shook his head. Then he leaned forward slightly across the table, lips parted still, trying to find my eyes. He wanted something. He was trying to involve me in it someway, all right, but it was more than that, he wanted something else. An answer, maybe, when there were no answers. Maybe simply a gesture on my part, a touch on the arm, perhaps. Maybe that would have been enough.

I loosened my collar and wiped my forehead with my wrist. I cleared my throat, still unable to meet his eyes. I felt a shaky, irrational fear begin to work through me, and the pain behind my eyes grew stronger. He kept staring at me until I began to squirm, until we both realized I had nothing to give him, nothing to give to anyone for that matter. I was all smooth surface with nothing inside except emptiness. I was shocked. I blinked my eyes once or twice. My fingers trembled as I lighted a cigarette, but I took care not to let him notice.

"Maybe you think it isn't the right thing for me to say, but I think there must have been something wrong with the man to begin with. To do something like that just because his wife was chippying around. I mean, a man would have to be half crazy to begin with to do something like that . . . But you don't understand."

"I know it's terrible, having it on your conscience, but you can't go on blaming yourself forever."

"Forever." He looked around. "How long is that?"

We sat there for a few minutes longer without saying anything. We'd finished our drinks long ago, and the girl hadn't come back.

"You want another one?" I said. "I'm buying."

"You got time for another?" he asked, looking at me closely. Then: "No. No, I don't think we'd better. You've got a plane to catch."

We got up from the booth. I helped him into his coat and we started out, my hand guiding his elbow. The bartender looked at us and said, "Thanks, fellas." I waved. My arm felt stiff.

"Let's get a breath of air," I said. We walked down the stairs and outside and squinted in the bright afternoon glare. The sun had just gone behind some clouds and we stood outside the door and didn't say anything. People kept brushing past us. All of them seemed in a hurry except one man in jeans who carried a leather overnight kit and walked past us with a bloody nose. The handkerchief he held to his face appeared stiff with blood and he looked at us as he passed. A Negro cabbie asked if he could take us somewhere.

"I'll put you in a cab, Dad, and send you home. What's your address?"

"No, no," he said and took an unsteady step back from the curb. "I'll see you off."

"That's all right. I think it'd be better if we said good-bye here, out here in front. I don't like good-byes anyway. You know how that goes," I added.

We shook hands. "Don't worry about anything, that's the important thing right now. None of us, none of us is perfect. Just get back on your feet and don't worry."

I don't know if he heard me. He didn't answer anyway. The cabbie opened the rear door and then turned to me and said, "Where to?"

"He's okay. He can tell you."

The cabbie shrugged and shut the door and walked around to the front.

"Take it easy now and write, will you, Dad?" He nodded. "Take care of yourself," I finished. He looked back at me out of the window as the cab pulled away, and that was the last I've seen of him. Halfway to Chicago, I remembered I'd left his sack of gifts in the lounge.

He hasn't written, I haven't heard from him since then. I'd write to him and see how he's getting along, but I'm afraid I've lost his address. But, tell me, after all, what could he expect from someone like me?

A Small, Good Thing

SATURDAY afternoon she drove to the little bakery in the shopping center. After looking through a loose-leaf binder with photographs of cakes taped onto the pages, she ordered chocolate, his favorite. The cake she chose was decorated with a spaceship and launching pad under a sprinkling of white stars at one end of the cake, and a planet made of red frosting at the other end. His name, SCOTTY, would be in raised green letters beneath the planet. The baker, who was an older man with a thick neck, listened without saying anything when she told him Scotty would be eight years old next Monday. The baker wore a white apron that looked like a smock. Straps cut under his arms, went around in back and then back in front again where they were secured under his big waist. He wiped his hands on the front of the apron as he listened to her. He kept his eyes down on the photographs and let her talk. He let her take her time. He'd just come to work and he'd be there all night, baking, and he was in no real hurry.

She decided on the space cake, and then gave the baker her name, Ann Weiss, and her telephone number. The cake would be ready on Monday morning, just out of the oven, in plenty of time for Scotty's party that afternoon. The baker was not jolly. There were no pleasantries between them, just the minimum exchange of words, the necessary information. He made her feel uncomfortable, and she didn't like that. While he was bent over the counter with the pencil in his hand, she studied his coarse features and wondered if he'd ever done anything else with his life besides be a baker. She was a mother and thirty-three years old, and it seemed to her that everyone, especially someone the baker's age—a man old enough to be her father—must have children who'd gone through this special time of cakes and birthday parties. There must be that between them, she thought. But he was abrupt with her, not rude, just abrupt. She gave up trying to make friends with him. She looked into the back of the bakery and could see a long, heavy wooden table with aluminum pie pans stacked at one end, and beside the table a metal container filled with empty racks. There was an enormous oven. A radio was playing country-western music.

The baker finished printing the information on the special-order card and closed up the binder. He looked at her and said, "Monday morning." She thanked him and drove home.

On Monday afternoon, Scotty was walking home from school with a friend. They were passing a bag of potato chips back and forth and Scotty was trying to find out what his friend was giving him for his birthday that afternoon. Without looking, he stepped off the curb at an intersection and was immediately knocked down by a car. He fell on his side with his head in the gutter and his legs out in the road. His eyes were closed, but his legs began to move back and forth as if he were trying to climb over something. His friend dropped the potato chips and started to cry. The car had gone a hundred feet or so and stopped in the middle of the road. A man in the driver's seat looked back over his shoulder. He waited until the boy got unsteadily to his feet. They boy wobbled a little. He looked dazed, but okay. The driver put the car into gear and drove away.

Scotty didn't cry, but he didn't have anything to say about anything, either. He wouldn't answer when his friend asked him what it felt like to be hit by a car. He walked straight to his front door, where his friend left him and ran home. But after Scotty went inside and was telling his mother about it, she sitting beside him on the sofa, holding his hands in her lap and saying, "Scotty, honey, are you sure you feel all right, baby?" and thinking she would call the doctor anyway, he suddenly lay back on the sofa, closed his eyes, and went limp. When she couldn't wake him up, she hurried to the telephone and called her husband at work. Howard told her to remain calm, remain calm, and then he called an ambulance for Scotty and left for the hospital himself.

Of course, the birthday party was canceled. The boy was in the hospital with a mild concussion and suffering from shock. There'd been vomiting, and his lungs had taken in fluid which needed pumping out that afternoon. Now he simply seemed to be in a very deep sleep—but no coma, Dr. Francis had emphasized; no coma, when he saw the alarm in the parents' eyes.

At eleven o'clock that Monday night when the boy seemed to be resting comfortably enough after the many X-rays and the lab work, and it was now just a matter of his waking up and coming around, Howard left the hospital. He and Ann had been at the hospital with Scotty since that afternoon, and he was going home for a short while to bathe and to change clothes. "I'll be back in an hour," he said. She nodded. "It's fine," she said. "I'll be right here." He kissed her on the forehead, and they touched hands. She sat in a chair beside the bed, looking at Scotty. She kept waiting for him to wake up and be all right. Then she could begin to relax.

Howard drove home from the hospital. He took the wet, dark streets faster than he should have, then caught himself and slowed down. Until now, his life had gone smoothly and to his satisfaction—college, marriage, another year of college for the advanced degree in business, a junior partnership in an investment firm. Fatherhood. He was happy and, so far, lucky—he knew that. His parents were still living, his brothers and his sister were established, his friends from college had gone out to take their places in the world. So far he had kept away from any real harm, from those forces he knew existed and that could cripple or bring down a man, if the luck went bad, if things suddenly turned. He pulled into the driveway and parked. His left leg had begun to tremble. He sat in the car for a minute and tried to deal with the present situation in a rational manner. Scotty had been hit by a car and was in the hospital, but he was going to be all right. He closed his eyes and ran his hand over his face. In a minute, he got out of the car and went up to the front door. The dog, Slug, was barking inside the house. The telephone kept ringing while he unlocked the door and fumbled for the light switch. He shouldn't have left the hospital, he shouldn't have, he cursed himself. He picked up the receiver and said, "I just walked in the door! Hello!"

"There's a cake here that wasn't picked up," said the man's voice on the other end of the line.

"What? What are you saying?" Howard asked.

"A cake," the voice said. "A sixteen-dollar cake."

Howard held the receiver against his ear, trying to understand. "I don't know anything about a cake," he said. "Jesus, what are you talking about?"

"Don't give me that," the voice said.

Howard hung up the telephone. He went into the kitchen and poured himself some whiskey. He called the hospital, but Scotty's condition remained the same; he was still sleeping and nothing had changed there. While water poured into the tub, he lathered his face and shaved. He had stretched out in the tub and closed his eyes when the telephone began ringing again. He hauled himself out, grabbed a towel, and hurried through the house, saying, "Stupid, stupid," for having left the hospital. But when he picked up the receiver and shouted, "Hello!" there was no sound at the other end of the line. Then the caller hung up.

He arrived back at the hospital a little after midnight. Ann still sat in the chair beside the bed. She looked up at Howard and then she looked back at Scotty. The boy's eyes stayed closed, his head was still wrapped in the bandages. His breathing was quiet and regular. From an apparatus over the bed hung a bottle of glucose with a tube distending from the bottle to the boy's right arm.

"How is he?" Howard said. "What's all this?" waving at the glucose and the tube.

"Dr. Francis's orders," she said. "He needs nourishment. Dr. Francis said he needs to keep up his strength. Why doesn't he wake up, Howard?" she said. "I don't understand, if he's all right."

Howard put his hand at the back of her head and ran his fingers through the hair. "He's going to be all right, honey. He'll wake up in a little while. Dr. Francis knows what's what."

In a little while he said, "Maybe you should go home and get a little rest for yourself. I'll stay here. Just don't put up with this creep who keeps calling. Hang up right away."

"Who's calling?" she asked.

"I don't know who, just somebody with nothing better to do than call up people. You go ahead now."

She shook her head. "No," she said, "I'm fine."

"Really," he said. "Go home for a while, if you want, and then come back and spell me in the morning. It'll be all right. What did Dr. Francis say? He said Scotty's going to be all right. We don't have to worry. He's just sleeping now, that's all."

A nurse pushed the door open. She nodded at them as she

went to the bedside. She took the left arm out from under the covers and put her fingers on the wrist, found the pulse, and then consulted her watch. In a little while she put the arm back under the covers and moved to the foot of the bed, where she wrote something on a clipboard attached to the bed.

"How is he?" Ann said. Howard's hand was a weight on her shoulder. She was aware of pressure in his fingers.

"He's stable," the nurse said. Then she said, "Doctor will be in again shortly. Doctor's back in the hospital. He's making rounds right now."

"I was saying maybe she'd want to go home and get a little rest," Howard said. "After the doctor comes," he added.

"She could do that," the nurse said. "I think you should both feel free to do that, if you wish." The nurse was a big Scandinavian woman with blond hair, and heavy breasts that filled the front of her uniform. There was a trace of an accent in her speech.

"We'll see what the doctor says," Ann said. "I want to talk to him. I don't think he should keep sleeping like this. I don't think that's a good sign." She brought her hand up to her eyes and leaned her head forward a little. Howard's grip tightened on her shoulder, and then his hand moved to her neck where his fingers began to knead the muscles there.

"Dr. Francis will be here in a few minutes," the nurse said. Then she left the room.

Howard gazed at his son for a time, the small chest quietly rising and then falling under the covers. For the first time since the terrible minutes after Ann's telephone call at the office, he felt a genuine fear starting in his limbs. He began shaking his head, trying to keep it away. Scotty was fine, except instead of sleeping at home in his own bed, he was in a hospital bed with bandages around his head and a tube in his arm. But it was what he needed right now, this help.

Dr. Francis came in and shook hands with Howard, though they'd just seen each other a few hours before. Ann got up from the chair. "Doctor?"

"Ann," he said and nodded. "Let's just first see how he's doing," the doctor said. He moved to the side of the bed and took the boy's pulse. He peeled back one eyelid and then the other. Howard and Ann stood beside the doctor and watched.

Ann made a little noise as Scotty's eyelid rolled back and disclosed a white, pupilless space. Then the doctor turned back the covers and listened to the boy's heart and lungs with his stethoscope. He pressed his fingers here and there on the abdomen. When he was finished he went to the end of the bed and studied the chart. He noted the time on his watch, scribbled something on the chart, and then looked at Howard and Ann, who were waiting.

"Doctor, how is he?" Howard said. "What's the matter with him exactly?"

"Why doesn't he wake up?" Ann said.

The doctor was a handsome, big-shouldered man with a tan face. He wore a three-piece blue suit, a striped tie, and ivory cuff links. His gray hair was combed, and he looked as if he could have just come from a concert. "He's all right," the doctor said. "Nothing to shout about, he could be better, I think. But he's all right. Still, I wish he'd wake up. He should wake up pretty soon." The doctor looked at the boy again. "We'll know some more in a couple of hours, after the results of a few more tests are in. But he's all right, believe me, except for that hairline fracture of the skull. He does have that."

"Oh, no," Ann said.

"And a bit of a concussion, as I said before. Of course, you know he's in shock," the doctor said. "Sometimes you see this in shock cases."

"But he's out of any real danger?" Howard said. "You said before he's not in a coma. You wouldn't call this a coma then, would you, Doctor?" Howard waited and looked at the doctor.

"No, I don't want to call it a coma," the doctor said and glanced over at the boy once more. "He's just in a very deep sleep. It's a restorative, a measure the body is taking on its own. He's out of any real danger, I'd say that for certain, yes. But we'll know more when he wakes up and the other tests are in. Don't worry," the doctor said.

"It's a coma," Ann said. "Of sorts."

"It's not a coma yet, not exactly," the doctor said. "I wouldn't want to call it coma. Not yet, anyway. He's suffered shock. In shock cases this kind of reaction is common enough; it's a temporary reaction to bodily trauma. Coma—well, coma is a deep, prolonged unconsciousness that could go on for days, or weeks even. Scotty's not in that area, not as far as we can tell, anyway. I'm just certain his condition will show improvement by morning. I'm betting that it will, anyway. We'll know more when he wakes up, which shouldn't be long now. Of course, you may do as you like, stay here or go home for a while, but by all means feel free to leave for a while if you want. This is not easy, I know." The doctor gazed at the boy again, watching him, and then he turned to Ann and said, "You try not to worry, little mother. Believe me, we're doing all that can be done. It's just a question of a little more time now." He nodded at her, shook hands with Howard again, and left the room.

Ann put her hand on Scotty's forehead and kept it there for a while. "At least he doesn't have a fever," she said. Then she said, "My God, he feels so cold, though. Howard? Is he supposed to feel like this? Feel his head."

Howard put his hand on the boy's forehead. His own breathing slowed. "I think he's supposed to feel this way right now," he said. "He's in shock, remember? That's what the doctor said. The doctor was just in here. He would have said something if Scotty wasn't okay."

Ann stood there awhile longer, working her lip with her teeth. Then she moved over to her chair and sat down.

Howard sat in the chair beside her. They looked at each other. He wanted to say something else and reassure her, but he was afraid to. He took her hand and put it in his lap, and this made him feel better, her hand being there. He picked up her hand and squeezed it, then just held it. They sat like that for a while, watching the boy and not talking. From time to time he squeezed her hand. Finally, she took her hand away and rubbed her temples.

"I've been praying," she said.

He nodded.

She said, "I almost thought I'd forgotten how, but it came back to me. All I had to do was close my eyes and say, Please, God, help us—help Scotty; and then the rest was easy. The words were right there. Maybe if you prayed too," she said to him.

"I've already prayed," he said. "I prayed this afternoon—yesterday afternoon, after you called, while I was driving to the hospital. I've been praying," he said.

"That's good," she said. Almost for the first time, she felt they were together in it, this trouble. Then she realized it had only been happening to her and to Scotty. She hadn't let Howard into it, though he was there and needed all along. She could see he was tired. The way his head looked heavy and angled into his chest. She felt a good tenderness toward him. She felt glad to be his wife.

The same nurse came in later and took the boy's pulse again and checked the flow from the bottle hanging above the bed.

In an hour another doctor came in. He said his name was Parsons, from radiology. He had a bushy moustache. He was wearing loafers and a white smock over a western shirt and a pair of jeans.

"We're going to take him downstairs for more pictures," he told them. "We need to do some more pictures, and we want to do a scan."

"What's that?" Ann said. "A scan?" She stood between this new doctor and the bed. "I thought you'd already taken all your X-rays."

"I'm afraid we need some more," he said. "Nothing to be alarmed about. We just need some more pictures, and we want to do a brain scan on him."

"My God," Ann said.

"It's perfectly normal procedure in cases like this," the new doctor said. "We just need to find out for sure why he isn't back awake yet. It's normal medical procedure, and nothing to be alarmed about. We'll be taking him down in a few minutes," the doctor said.

In a little while two orderlies came into the room with a gurney. They were black-haired, dark-complexioned men in white uniforms, and they said a few words to each other in a foreign tongue as they unhooked the boy from the tube and moved him from his bed to the gurney. Then they wheeled him from the room. Howard and Ann got on the same elevator. Ann stood beside the gurney and gazed at the boy, who was lying so still. She closed her eyes as the elevator began its descent. The orderlies stood at either end of the gurney without saying anything, though once one of the men made a comment to the other in their own language, and the other man nodded slowly in response.

Later that morning, just as the sun was beginning to lighten the windows in the waiting room outside the X-ray department, they brought the boy out and moved him back up to his room. Howard and Ann rode up on the elevator with him once more, and once more they took up their places beside the bed.

They waited all day, but still the boy did not wake up. Occasionally one of them would leave the room to go downstairs to the cafeteria to drink coffee or fruit juice and then, as if suddenly remembering and feeling guilty, jump up from the table and hurry back to the room. Dr. Francis came again that afternoon and examined the boy once more and then left after telling them he was coming along and could wake up any minute now. Nurses, different nurses than the night before, came in from time to time. Then a young woman from the lab knocked and came into the room. She wore white slacks and a white blouse and carried a little tray of things which she put on the stand beside the bed. Without a word to them, she took blood from the boy's arm. Howard closed his eyes as the woman found the right place on the boy's arm and pushed the needle in.

"I don't understand this," Ann said to the woman.

"Doctor's orders," the young woman said. "I do what I'm told to do. They say draw that one, I draw. What's wrong with him, anyway?" she said. "He's a sweetie."

"He was hit by a car," Howard said. "A hit-and-run."

The young woman shook her head and looked again at the boy. Then she took her tray and left the room.

"Why won't he wake up?" Ann said. "Howard? I want some answers from these people."

Howard didn't say anything. He sat down again in the chair and crossed one leg over the other. He rubbed his face. He looked at his son and then he settled back in the chair, closed his eyes, and went to sleep.

Ann walked to the window and looked out at the big parking lot. It was night, and cars were driving into and out of the parking lot with their lights on. She stood at the window with her hands gripping the sill and knew in her heart that they were into something now, something hard. She was afraid, and her teeth began to chatter until she tightened her jaws. She saw a big car stop in front of the hospital and someone, a woman in a long coat, got into the car. For a minute she wished she were that woman and somebody, anybody, was driving her away from here to somewhere else, a place where she would find Scotty waiting for her when she stepped out of the car, ready to say *Mom* and let her gather him in her arms.

In a little while Howard woke up. He looked at the boy again, and then he got up from the chair, stretched, and went over to stand beside her at the window. They both stared out into the parking lot and didn't talk. They seemed to feel each other's insides now, as though the worry had made them transparent in a perfectly natural way.

The door opened and Dr. Francis came in. He was wearing a different suit and tie this time, but his hair was the same and he looked as if he had just shaved. He went straight to the bed and examined the boy once more. "He ought to have come around by now. There's just no good reason for this," he said. "But I can tell you we're all convinced he's out of any danger, we'll just feel much better when he wakes up. There's no reason, absolutely none, why he shouldn't come around and soon now. Oh, he'll have himself a dilly of a headache when he does, you can count on that. But all of his signs are fine. They're as normal as can be."

"Is it a coma, then?" Ann asked.

The doctor rubbed his smooth cheek. "We'll call it that for the time being, until he wakes up. But you must be worn out. This is hard to wait out. Feel free to go out for a bite," he said. "It would do you good. I'll put a nurse in here while you're gone, if you'll feel better about going. Go and have yourselves something to eat."

"I couldn't eat," Ann said. "I'm not hungry."

"Do what you need to do, of course," the doctor said. "Anyway, I wanted to tell you that all the signs are good, the tests are positive, nothing at all negative, and just as soon as he wakes up he'll be over the hill."

"Thank you, Doctor," Howard said. He shook hands with the doctor again, and the doctor patted his shoulder and went out.

"I suppose one of us should go home and check on things," Howard said. "Slug needs to be fed, one thing."

"Call one of the neighbors," Ann said. "Call the Morgans. Anyone will feed a dog if you ask them to."

"All right," Howard said. After a while he said, "Honey, why don't you do it? Why don't you go home and check on things, and then come back? It'll do you good. I'll be right here with him. Seriously," he said. "We need to keep up our strength on this. We may want to be here for a while even after he wakes up."

"Why don't you go?" she said. "Feed Slug. Feed yourself."

"I already went," he said. "I was gone for exactly an hour and fifteen minutes. You go home for an hour or so and freshen up, and then come back. I'll stay here."

She tried to think about it, but she was too tired. She closed her eyes and tried to think about it again. After a time she said, "Maybe I will go home for a few minutes. Maybe if I'm not just sitting right here watching him every second he'll wake up and be all right. You know? Maybe he'll wake up if I'm not here. I'll go home and take a bath and put on clean clothes. I'll feed Slug. Then I'll come back."

"I'll be right here," he said. "You go on home, honey, and then come back. I'll be right here keeping an eye on things." His eyes were bloodshot and small, as if he had been drinking for a long time, and his clothes were rumpled. His beard had come out again. She touched his face, and then took her hand back. She understood he wanted to be by himself for a while, to not have to talk or share his worry for a time. She picked up her purse from the nightstand, and he helped her into her coat.

"I won't be gone long," she said.

"Just sit and rest for a little while when you get home," he said. "Eat something. After you get out of the bath, just sit for a while and rest. It'll do you a world of good, you'll see. Then come back down here," he said. "Let's try not to worry ourselves sick. You heard what Dr. Francis said."

She stood in her coat for a minute trying to recall the doctor's exact words, looking for any nuances, any hint of something behind his words other than what he was saying. She tried to remember if his expression had changed any when he bent over to examine Scotty. She remembered the way his features had composed themselves as he rolled back the boy's eyelids and then listened to his breathing.

She went to the door and turned and looked back. She looked at the boy, and then she looked at the father. Howard nodded. She stepped out of the room and pulled the door closed behind her.

She went past the nurses' station and down to the end of the corridor, looking for the elevator. At the end of the corridor she turned to her right where she found a little waiting room with a Negro family sitting in wicker chairs. There was a middle-aged man in a khaki shirt and pants, a baseball cap pushed back on his head. A large woman wearing a house dress and slippers was slumped in one of the chairs. A teenaged girl in jeans, hair done in dozens of little braids, lay stretched out in one of the chairs smoking a cigarette, legs crossed at the ankles. The family swung their eyes to her as she entered the room. The little table was littered with hamburger wrappers and Styrofoam cups.

"Nelson," the large woman said as she roused herself. "Is about Nelson?" Her eyes widened. "Tell me now, lady," the woman said. "Is about Nelson?" She was trying to rise from her chair, but the man had closed his hand over her arm.

"Here, here," he said. "Evelyn."

"I'm sorry," Ann said. "I'm looking for the elevator. My son is in the hospital, and now I can't find the elevator."

"Elevator is down that way, turn left," the man said and aimed a finger down another corridor.

The girl drew on her cigarette and stared at Ann. Her eyes were narrowed to slits, and her broad lips parted slowly as she let the smoke escape. The Negro woman let her head fall down on her shoulder and looked away from Ann, no longer interested.

"My son was hit by a car," Ann said to the man. She seemed to need to explain herself. "He has a concussion and a little skull fracture, but he's going to be all right. He's in shock now, but it might be some kind of coma, too. That's what really worries us, the coma part. I'm going out for a little while, but my husband is with him. Maybe he'll wake up while I'm gone."

"That's too bad," the man said and shifted in the chair. He

shook his head. He looked down at the table, and then he looked back at Ann. She was still standing there. He said, "Our Nelson, he's on the operating table. Somebody cut him. Tried to kill him. There was a fight where he was at. At this party. They say he was just standing and watching. Not bothering nobody. But that don't mean nothing these days. Now he's on the operating table. We're just hoping and praying, that's all we can do now." He gazed at her steadily and then tugged the bill of his cap.

Ann looked at the girl again, who was still watching her, and at the older woman, who kept her head down on her shoulder but whose eyes were now closed. Ann saw the lips moving silently, making words. She had an urge to ask what those words were. She wanted to talk more with these people who were in the same kind of waiting she was in. She was afraid, and they were afraid. They had that in common. She would have liked to have said something else about the accident, told them more about Scotty, that it had happened on the day of his birthday, Monday, that he was still unconscious. Yet she didn't know how to begin and so only stood there looking at them without saying anything more.

She went down the corridor the man had indicated and found the elevator. She stood for a minute in front of the closed doors, still wondering if she was doing the right thing. Then she put out her finger and touched the button.

She pulled into the driveway and cut the engine. Slug ran around from behind the house. In his excitement he began to bark at the car, then ran in circles on the grass. She closed her eyes and leaned her head against the wheel for a minute. She listened to the ticking sounds the engine made as it began to cool. Then she got out of the car. She picked up the little dog, Scotty's dog, and went to the front door, which was unlocked. She turned on lights and put on a kettle of water for tea. She opened some dog food and fed Slug on the back porch. He ate in hungry little smacks, between running back and forth to see that she was going to stay. As she sat down on the sofa with her tea, the telephone rang.

"Yes!" she said as she answered. "Hello!"

"Mrs. Weiss," a man's voice said. It was five o'clock in the morning, and she thought she could hear machinery or equipment of some kind in the background.

"Yes, yes, what is it?" she said carefully into the receiver. "This is Mrs. Weiss. This is she. What is it, please?" She listened to whatever it was in the background. "Is it Scotty, for Christ's sake?"

"Scotty," the man's voice said. "It's about Scotty, yes. It has to do with Scotty, that problem. Have you forgotten about Scotty?" the man said. Then he hung up.

She dialed the hospital's number and asked for the third floor. She demanded information about her son from the nurse who answered the telephone. Then she asked to speak to her husband. It was, she said, an emergency.

She waited, turning the telephone cord in her fingers. She closed her eyes and felt sick at her stomach. She would have to make herself eat. Slug came in from the back porch and lay down near her feet. He wagged his tail. She pulled his ear while he licked her fingers. Howard was on the line.

"Somebody just called here," she said. She twisted the telephone cord and it kinked back into itself. "He said, he said it was about Scotty," she cried.

"Scotty's fine," Howard was telling her. "I mean he's still sleeping. There's been no change. The nurse has been in twice since you've been gone. They're in here every thirty minutes or so. A nurse or a doctor, one. He's all right, Ann."

"Somebody called, he said it was about Scotty," she said.

"Honey, you rest for a little while, you need the rest. Then come back down here. It must be that same caller I had. Just forget it. Come back down here after you've rested. Then we'll have breakfast or something."

"Breakfast," she said. "I couldn't eat anything."

"You know what I mean," he said. "Juice, a muffin, something, I don't know. I don't know anything, Ann. Jesus, I'm not hungry either. Ann, it's hard to talk now. I'm standing here at the desk. Dr. Francis is coming again at eight o'clock this morning. He's going to have something to tell us then, something more definite. That's what one of the nurses said. She didn't know any more than that. Ann? Honey, maybe we'll know something more then, at eight o'clock. Come back here before eight. Meanwhile, I'm right here and Scotty's all right. He's still the same," he added.

"I was drinking a cup of tea," she said, "when the telephone rang. They said it was about Scotty. There was a noise in the background. Was there a noise in the background on that call you had, Howard?"

"I honestly don't remember," he said. "It must have been a drunk or somebody calling, though God knows I don't understand. Maybe the driver of the car, maybe he's a psychopath and found out about Scotty somehow. But I'm here with him. Just rest a little like you were going to do. Take a bath and come back here by seven or so, and we'll talk to the doctor together when he gets here. It's going to be all right, honey. I'm here, and there are doctors and nurses around. They say his condition is stable."

"I'm scared to death," she said.

She ran water, undressed, and got into the tub. She washed and dried quickly, not taking the time to wash her hair. She put on clean underwear, wool slacks, and a sweater. She went into the living room where Slug looked up at her and let his tail thump once against the floor. It was just starting to get light outside when she went out to the car. Driving back to the hospital on the damp, deserted streets, she thought back to the rainy Sunday afternoon nearly two years ago when Scotty had been lost and they'd been afraid he'd drowned.

The sky had darkened that afternoon and rain had begun to fall, and still he hadn't come home. They'd called all his friends, who were at home and safe. She and Howard had gone to look for him at his board-and-rock fort at the far end of the field near the highway, but he wasn't there. Then Howard had run in one direction beside the highway and she had run the other way until she came to what had once been a little stream of water, a drainage ditch, but its banks were filled now with a dark torrent. One of his friends had been with him there when the rain started. They had been making boats out of pieces of scrap wood, and empty beer cans that had been tossed from passing cars. They had been lining up the beer cans on the pieces of wood and sending them out into the stream. The stream ended on this side of the highway at a culvert where the water boiled and could take anything under and into the pipe. The friend had left Scotty there on the bank when the first drops of rain had begun to fall. Scotty had said he was going to stay and build a bigger boat. She had stood on the bank and gazed into the water as it poured into the mouth of the culvert and disappeared under the highway. It was plain to her what must have happened—that he had fallen in, that he must even now be lodged somewhere inside the culvert. The thought was monstrous, so unfair and overwhelming that she couldn't hold it in her mind. But she felt it was true, that he was in there, in the culvert, and knew too it was something that would have to be borne and lived with from here on, a life without Scotty in it. But how to act in the face of this, the fact of the loss, was more than she could comprehend. The horror of the men and equipment working at the mouth of the culvert through the night, that was what she did not know if she could endure, that waiting while the men worked under powerful lights. She would have to somehow get past that to the limitless sweep of emptiness she knew stretched beyond. She was ashamed to know it, but she thought she could live with that. Later, much later, maybe then she would be able to come to terms with that emptiness, after the presence of Scotty had gone out of their lives—then perhaps, she would learn to handle that loss, and the awful absence—she would have to, that's all—but now she did not know how she could get through the waiting part to that other part.

She dropped to her knees. She stared into the current and said that if He would let them have Scotty back, if he could have somehow miraculously—she said it out loud, "miraculously"—escaped the water and the culvert, she knew he hadn't, but if he had, if He could only let them have Scotty back, somehow *not* let him be wedged in the culvert, she promised then that she and Howard would change their lives, change everything, go back to the small town where they had come from, away from this suburban place that could ruthlessly snatch away your only child. She had still been on her knees when she heard Howard calling her name, calling her name from across the field, through the rain. She had raised her eyes and seen them coming toward her, the two of them, Howard and Scotty.

"He was hiding," Howard said, laughing and crying at

once. "I was so glad to see him I couldn't begin to punish him. He'd made a shelter. He'd fixed himself up a place under the overpass, in those bushes. He'd made like a nest for himself," he said. The two of them were still coming toward her as she got to her feet. She doubled her fists. "'Forts leak,' the little nut said. He was dry as a bone when I found him, damn his hide," Howard said, the tears breaking. Then Ann was on Scotty, slapping him on the head and face with a wild fury. "You little devil, you devil you," she shouted as she slapped him. "Ann, stop it," Howard said, grabbing for her arms. "He's all right, that's the main thing. He's all right." She'd picked the boy up while he was still crying and she'd held him. She'd held him. Their clothes soaked, shoes squishing with water, the three of them had begun the walk home. She carried the boy for a while, his arms around her neck, his chest heaving against her breasts. Howard walked beside them saying, "Jesus, what a scare. God almighty, what a fright." She knew Howard had been scared and was now relieved, but he hadn't glimpsed what she had, he couldn't know. The quickness of how she had gone into the death and beyond it had made her suspect herself, that she hadn't loved enough. If she had, she would not have thought the worst so quickly. She shook her head back and forth at this craziness. She grew tired and had to stop and put Scotty down. They walked the rest of the way together, Scotty in the middle, holding hands, the three of them walking home.

But they hadn't moved away and they'd never talked about that afternoon again. From time to time she'd thought about her promise, the prayers she'd offered up, and for a while she'd felt vaguely uneasy, but they had continued to live as they had been living—a comfortably busy life, not a bad or a dishonest life, a life, in fact, with many satisfactions and small pleasures. Nothing more was ever said about that afternoon, and in time she had stopped thinking about it. Now here they were still in the same city and it was two years later, and Scotty was again in peril, an awful peril, and she began to see this circumstance, this accident and the not waking up as punishment. For hadn't she given her word that they'd move away from this city and go back to where they could live a simpler and quieter life, forget the jump in salary and the house which was still so new they hadn't put up the fence or planted grass yet? She imagined them all sitting around each evening in some big living room, in some other town, and listening to Howard read to them.

She drove into the parking lot of the hospital and found a space close to the front door. She felt no inclination to pray now. She felt like a liar caught out, guilty and false, as if she were somehow responsible for what had now happened. She felt she was in some obscure way responsible. She let her thoughts move to the Negro family, and she remembered the name "Nelson" and the table that was covered with hamburger papers, and the teenaged girl staring at her as she drew on her cigarette. "Don't have children," she told the girl's image as she entered the front door of the hospital. "For God's sake, don't."

She took the elevator up to the third floor with two nurses who were just going on duty. It was Wednesday morning, a few minutes before seven. There was a page for a Dr. Madison as the elevator doors slid open on the third floor. She got off behind the nurses, who turned in the other direction and continued the conversation she had interrupted when she'd gotten onto the elevator. She walked down the corridor to the little side room where the Negro family had been waiting. They were gone now, but the chairs were scattered in such a way that it looked as if people had just jumped from them the minute before. She thought the chairs might still be warm. The tabletop was cluttered with the same cups and papers, the ashtray filled with cigarette butts.

She stopped at the nurses' station just down the corridor from the waiting room. A nurse was standing behind the counter, brushing her hair and yawning.

"There was a Negro man in surgery last night," Ann said. "Nelson something was his name. His family was in the waiting room. I'd like to inquire about his condition."

A nurse who was sitting at a desk behind the counter looked up from a chart in front of her. The telephone buzzed and she picked up the receiver, but she kept her eyes on Ann.

"He passed away," said the nurse at the counter. The nurse held the hairbrush and kept on looking at her. "Are you a friend of the family or what?"

"I met the family last night," Ann said. "My own son is in

the hospital. I guess he's in shock. We don't know for sure what's wrong. I just wondered about Mr. Nelson, that's all. Thank you." She went on down the corridor. Elevator doors the same color as the walls slid open and a gaunt, bald man in white pants and white canvas shoes pulled a heavy cart off the elevator. She hadn't noticed these doors last night. The man wheeled the cart out into the corridor and stopped in front of the room nearest the elevator and consulted a clipboard. Then he reached down and slid a tray out of the cart, rapped lightly on the door, and entered the room. She could smell the unpleasant odors of warm food as she passed the cart. She hurried past the other station without looking at any of the nurses and pushed open the door to Scotty's room.

Howard was standing at the window with his hands together behind his back. He turned around as she came in.

"How is he?" she said. She went over to the bed. She dropped her purse on the floor beside the nightstand. She seemed to have been gone a long time. She touched the covers around Scotty's neck. "Howard?"

"Dr. Francis was here a little while ago," Howard said. She looked at him closely and thought his shoulders were bunched a little.

"I thought he wasn't coming until eight o'clock this morning," she said quickly.

"There was another doctor with him. A neurologist."

"A neurologist," she said.

Howard nodded. His shoulders were bunching, she could see that. "What'd they say, Howard? For Christ's sake, what'd they say? What is it?"

"They said, well, they're going to take him down and run more tests on him, Ann. They think they're going to operate, honey. Honey, they are going to operate. They can't figure out why he won't wake up. It's more than just shock or concussion, they know that much now. It's in his skull, the fracture, it has something, something to do with that, they think. So they're going to operate. I tried to call you, but I guess you'd already left the house."

"Oh, God," she said. "Oh, please, Howard, please," she said, taking his arms.

"Look!" Howard said then. "Scotty! Look, Ann!" He turned her toward the bed.

The boy had opened his eyes, then closed them. He opened them again now. The eyes stared straight ahead for a minute, then moved slowly in his head until they rested on Howard and Ann, then traveled away again.

"Scotty," his mother said, moving to the bed.

"Hey, Scott," his father said. "Hey, Son."

They leaned over the bed. Howard took Scotty's left hand in his hands and began to pat and squeeze the hand. Ann bent over the boy and kissed his forehead again and again. She put her hands on either side of his face. "Scotty, honey, it's Mommy and Daddy," she said. "Scotty?"

The boy looked at them again, though without any sign of recognition or comprehension. Then his eyes scrunched closed, his mouth opened, and he howled until he had no more air in his lungs. His face seemed to relax and soften then. His lips parted as his last breath was puffed through his throat and exhaled gently through the clenched teeth.

The doctors called it a hidden occlusion and said it was a one-in-a-million circumstance. Maybe if it could have been detected somehow and surgery undertaken immediately, it could have saved him, but more than likely not. In any case, what would they have been looking for? Nothing had shown up in the tests or in the X-rays. Dr. Francis was shaken. "I can't tell you how badly I feel. I'm so very sorry, I can't tell you," he said as he led them into the doctors' lounge. There was a doctor sitting in a chair with his legs hooked over the back of another chair, watching an early morning TV show. He was wearing a green delivery room outfit, loose green pants and green blouse, and a green cap that covered his hair. He looked at Howard and Ann and then looked at Dr. Francis. He got to his feet and turned off the set and went out of the room. Dr. Francis guided Ann to the sofa, sat down beside her and began to talk in a low, consoling voice. At one point he leaned over and embraced her. She could feel his chest rising and falling evenly against her shoulder. She kept her eyes open and let him hold her. Howard went into the bathroom but left the door open. After a violent fit of weeping, he ran water and washed his face. Then he came out and sat down at a little table that held a telephone. He looked at the telephone as though deciding what to do first. He made some calls. After a time, Dr. Francis used the telephone.

"Is there anything else I can do for the moment?" he asked them.

Howard shook his head. Ann stared at Dr. Francis as if unable to comprehend his words.

The doctor walked them to the hospital's front door. People were entering and leaving the hospital. It was eleven o'clock in the morning. Ann was aware of how slowly, almost reluctantly she moved her feet. It seemed to her that Dr. Francis was making them leave, when she somehow felt they should stay, when it would be more the right thing to do, to stay. She gazed out into the parking lot and then looked back at the front of the hospital from the sidewalk. She began shaking her head. "No, no," she said. "This isn't happening. I can't leave him here, no." She heard herself and thought how unfair it was that the only words that came out were the sorts of words on the TV shows where people were stunned by violent or sudden deaths. She wanted her words to be her own. "No," she said, and for some reason the memory of the Negro woman's head lolling on her shoulder came to her. "No," she said again.

"I'll be talking to you later in the day," the doctor was saying to Howard. "There are still some things that have to be done, things that have to be cleared up to our satisfaction. Some things that need explaining."

"An autopsy," Howard said.

Dr. Francis nodded.

"I understand," Howard said. "Oh, Jesus. No, I don't understand, Doctor. I can't, I can't. I just can't."

Dr. Francis put his arm around Howard's shoulders. "I'm sorry. God, how I'm sorry." Then he let go and held out his hand. Howard looked at the hand, and then he took it. Dr. Francis put his arms around Ann once more. He seemed full of some goodness she didn't understand. She let her head rest on his shoulder, but her eyes were open. She kept looking at the hospital. As they drove out of the parking lot, she looked back at the hospital once more.

At home, she sat on the sofa with her hands in her coat pockets. Howard closed the door to Scotty's room. He got the coffeemaker going and then he found an empty box. He had thought to pick up some of Scotty's things. But instead he sat down beside her on the sofa, pushed the box to one side, and leaned forward, arms between his knees. He began to weep. She pulled his head over into her lap and patted his shoulder. "He's gone," she said. She kept patting his shoulder. Over his sobs she could hear the coffeemaker hissing, out in the kitchen. "There, there," she said tenderly. "Howard, he's gone. He's gone and now we'll have to get used to that. To being alone."

In a little while Howard got up and began moving aimlessly around the room with the box, not putting anything into it, but collecting some things on the floor at one end of the sofa. She continued to sit with her hands in her pockets. Howard put the box down and brought coffee into the living room. Later, Ann made calls to relatives. After each call had been placed and the party had answered, Ann would blurt out a few words and cry for a minute. Then she would quietly explain, in a measured voice, what had happened and tell them about arrangements. Howard took the box out to the garage where he saw Scotty's bicycle. He dropped the box and sat down on the pavement beside the bicycle. He took hold of the bicycle awkwardly, so that it leaned against his chest. He held it, the rubber pedal sticking into his chest and turning the wheel across his trouser leg a little way.

Ann hung up the telephone after talking to her sister. She was looking up another number, when the telephone rang. She picked it up on the first ring.

"Hello," she said, and again she heard something in the background, a humming noise. "Hello! Hello!" she said. "For God's sake," she said. "Who is this? What is it you want? Say something."

"Your Scotty, I got him ready for you," the man's voice said. "Did you forget him?"

"You evil bastard!" she shouted into the receiver. "How can you do this, you evil son of a bitch?"

"Scotty," the man said. "Have you forgotten about Scotty?" Then the man hung up on her.

Howard heard the shouting and came in to find her with her

head on her arms over the table, weeping. He picked up the receiver and listened to the dial tone.

Much later, just before midnight, after they had dealt with many things, the telephone rang again.

"You answer it," she said. "Howard, it's him, I know." They were sitting at the kitchen table with coffee in front of them. Howard had a small glass of whiskey beside his cup. He answered on the third ring.

"Hello," he said. "Who is this? Hello! Hello!" The line went dead. "He hung up," Howard said. "Whoever it was."

"It was him," she said. "That bastard. I'd like to kill him," she said. "I'd like to shoot him and watch him kick," she said.

"Ann, my God," he said.

"Could you hear anything?" she said. "In the background? A noise, machinery, something humming?"

"Nothing, really. Nothing like that," he said. "There wasn't much time. I think there was some radio music. Yes, there was a radio going, that's all I could tell. I don't know what in God's name is going on," he said.

She shook her head. "If I could, could get, my hands, on him." It came to her then. She knew who it was. Scotty, the cake, the telephone number. She pushed the chair away from the table and got up. "Drive me down to the shopping center," she said. "Howard."

"What are you saying?"

"The shopping center. I know who it is who's calling now. I know who it is. It's the baker, the son-of-a-bitching baker, Howard. I had him bake a cake for Scotty's birthday. That's who's calling, that's who has the number and keeps calling us. To harass us about that cake. The baker, that bastard."

They drove out to the shopping center. The sky was clear and stars were out. It was cold, and they ran the heater in the car. They parked in front of the bakery. All of the shops and stores were closed, but there were still cars at the far end of the lot in front of the twin cinemas. The bakery windows were dark, but when they looked through the glass they could see a light in the back room and, now and then, a big man in an apron moving in and out of the white, even light. Through the glass she could see the display cases and some little tables with chairs. She tried the door. She rapped on the glass. But if the baker heard them he gave no sign. He didn't look in their direction.

They drove around behind the bakery and parked. They got out of the car. There was a lighted window too high up for them to see inside. A sign near the back door said, "The Pantry Bakery, Special Orders." She could hear faintly a radio playing inside and something—an oven door?—creaking as it was pulled down. She knocked on the door and waited. Then she knocked again, louder. The radio was turned down and there was a scraping sound now, the distinct sound of something, a drawer, being pulled open and then closed.

The door was unlocked and opened. The baker stood in the light and peered out at them. "I'm closed for business," he said. "What do you want at this hour? It's midnight. Are you drunk or something?"

She stepped into the light that fell through the open door, and he blinked his heavy eyelids as he recognized her. "It's you," he said.

"It's me," she said. "Scotty's mother. This is Scotty's father. We'd like to come in."

The baker said, "I'm busy now. I have work to do."

She had stepped inside the doorway anyway. Howard came in behind her. The baker had moved back. "It smells like a bakery in here. Doesn't it smell like a bakery in here, Howard?"

"What do you want?" the baker said. "Maybe you want your cake? That's it, you decided you wanted your cake. You did order a cake, didn't you?"

"You're pretty smart for a baker," she said. "Howard, this is the man who's been calling us. This is the baker man." She clenched her fists. She stared at him fiercely. There was a deep burning inside her, an anger that made her feel larger than herself, larger than either of these men.

"Just a minute here," the baker said. "You want to pick up your three-day-old cake? That it? I don't want to argue with you, lady. There it sits over there, getting stale. I'll give it to you for half of what I quoted you. No, you want it? You can have it. It's no good to me, no good to anyone now. It cost me time and money to make that cake. If you want it, okay, if you don't, that's okay too. Just forget it and go. I have to get back to work." He looked at them and rolled his tongue behind his teeth.

"More cakes," she said. She knew she was in control of it, of what was increasing her. She was calm.

"Lady, I work sixteen hours a day in this place to earn a living," the baker said. He wiped his hands on his apron. "I work night and day in here, trying to make ends meet." A look crossed Ann's face that made the baker move back and say, "No trouble, now." He reached to the counter and picked up a rolling pin with his right hand and began to tap-tap it against the palm of his other hand. "You want the cake or not? I have to get back to work. Bakers work at night," he said again. His eyes were small, mean looking, she thought, nearly lost in the bristly flesh around his cheeks. His neck around the collar of his T-shirt was thick with fat.

"We know bakers work at night," Ann said. "They make phone calls at night too. You bastard," she said.

The baker continued to tap the rolling pin against his hand. He glanced at Howard. "Careful, careful," he said to them.

"My boy's dead," she said with a cold, even finality. "He was hit by a car Monday afternoon. We've been waiting with him until he died. But, of course, you couldn't be expected to know that, could you? Bakers can't know everything. Can they, Mr. Baker? But he's dead. Dead, you bastard." Just as suddenly as it had welled in her the anger dwindled, gave way to something else, a dizzy feeling of nausea. She leaned against the wooden table that was sprinkled with flour, put her hands over her face and began to cry, her shoulders rocking back and forth. "It isn't fair," she said. "It isn't, isn't fair."

Howard put his hand at the small of her back and looked at the baker. "Shame on you," Howard said to him. "Shame."

The baker put the rolling pin back on the counter. He undid his apron and threw it on the counter. He stood a minute looking at them with a dull, pained look. Then he pulled a chair out from under a card table that held papers and receipts, an adding machine, and a telephone directory. "Please sit down," he said. "Let me get you a chair," he said to Howard. "Sit down now, please." The baker went into the front of the shop and returned with two little wrought-iron chairs. "Please sit down, you people."

Ann wiped her eyes and looked at the baker. "I wanted to kill you," she said. "I wanted you dead."

The baker had cleared a space for them at the table. He shoved the adding machine to one side, along with the stacks of notepaper and receipts. He pushed the telephone directory onto the floor, where it landed with a thud. Howard and Ann sat down and pulled their chairs up to the table. The baker sat down too.

"I don't blame you," the baker said, putting his elbows on the table and shaking his head slowly. "First. Let me say how sorry I am. God alone knows how sorry. Listen to me. I'm just a baker. I don't claim to be anything else. Maybe once, maybe years ago I was a different kind of human being, I've forgotten, I don't know for sure. But I'm not any longer, if I ever was. Now I'm just a baker. That don't excuse my offense, I know. But I'm deeply sorry. I'm sorry for your son, and I'm sorry for my part in this. Sweet, sweet Jesus," the baker said. He spread his hands out on the table and turned them over to reveal his palms. "I don't have any children myself, so I can only imagine what you must be feeling. All I can say to you now is that I'm sorry. Forgive me, if you can," the baker said. "I'm not an evil man, I don't think. Not evil, like you said on the phone. You must understand that what it comes down to is I don't know how to act anymore, it would seem. Please," the man said, "let me ask you if you can find it in your hearts to forgive me?"

It was warm in the bakery and Howard stood up from the table and took off his coat. He helped Ann from her coat. The baker looked at them for a minute and then nodded and got up from the table. He went to the oven and turned off some switches. He found cups and poured them coffee from an electric coffeemaker. He put a carton of cream on the table, and a bowl of sugar.

"You probably need to eat something," the baker said. "I hope you'll eat some of my hot rolls. You have to eat and keep going. Eating is a small, good thing in a time like this," he said.

He served them warm cinnamon rolls just out of the oven, the icing still runny. He put butter on the table and knives to spread the butter. Then the baker sat down at the table with them. He waited. He waited until they each took a roll from the platter and began to eat. "It's good to eat something," he said, watching them. "There's more. Eat up. Eat all you want. There's all the rolls in the world in here."

They ate rolls and drank coffee. Ann was suddenly hungry and the rolls were warm and sweet. She ate three of them, which pleased the baker. Then he began to talk. They listened carefully. Although they were tired and in anguish, they listened to what the baker had to say. They nodded when the baker began to speak of loneliness, and the sense of doubt and limitation that had come to him in his middle years. He told them what it was like to be childless all these years. To repeat the days with the ovens endlessly full and endlessly empty. The party food, the celebrations he'd worked over. Icing knuckle-deep. The wedding couples stuck to each other's arms, hundreds of them, no, thousands by now. Birthdays. Just the candles from all those cakes if you thought you could see them all burning at once. He had a necessary trade. He was a baker. He was glad not to be a florist. It was better to be feeding people. Not giving them something that sat around for a while until it was thrown out. This was a better smell than flowers.

"Here, smell this," the baker said, breaking open a dark loaf. "It's a heavy bread, but rich." They smelled it, then he had them taste it. It had the taste of molasses and coarse grains. They listened to him. They ate what they could. They swallowed the dark bread. It was like daylight under the fluorescent trays of light. They talked on into the early morning, the high pale cast of light in the windows, and they did not think of leaving.

Tell the Women We're Going

BILL JAMISON had always been close with Jerry Roberts. The two grew up in the south area, near the old fairgrounds, went through grade school and junior high together, and then on to Eisenhower where they took as many of the same classes and teachers as they could manage, wore each other's shirts and sweaters and pegged pants, and dated or ganged the same girl—whichever came up as a matter of course.

Summers they took jobs together—swamping peaches, picking cherries, stringing hops, anything they could do that paid a little money to see them through to fall, something where they didn't have to worry about a boss breathing down their necks every five minutes. Jerry didn't like to be told what to do. Bill didn't mind; he liked it that Jerry was the sort of take-charge guy he was. The summer just before their senior year, they chipped in and bought a red '54 Plymouth for $325. Jerry would keep it a week at a time, then Bill. They were used to sharing things, and it worked out fine for a while.

But Jerry got married before the end of the first semester, kept the car, and dropped out of school to go to work steady at Robby's Market. That was the only time there was a strain in their relationship. Bill liked Carol Henderson—he'd known her a couple of years, almost as long as Jerry had—but after Jerry and she got married, things were just never the same between the two friends. He was over there a lot, especially at first—it made him feel older, having married friends—for lunch or dinner, or else late evenings to listen to Elvis Presley, and Bill Haley and the Comets, and there were a couple of Fats Domino records he liked, but it always embarrassed him when Carol and Jerry started kissing and near making out in front of him. Sometimes he'd have to excuse himself and take a walk to Dezorn's service station to get some Coke because there was only the one bed in the apartment, a hideaway that let down right in the middle of the living room. Other times Jerry and Carol would simply head off in a clumsy leg-hugging walk to the bathroom, and Bill would move to the kitchen and

pretend to busy himself looking in the cupboards and refrigerator, trying not to listen.

So he stopped going over so much; and then June he graduated, took a job at the Darigold Milk plant, and joined the
National Guard. In a year he had a milk route of his own and
was going steady with Linda Wilson—a good, clean girl. He
and Linda dropped in at the Roberts' once a week or so, drank
beer and listened to records. Carol and Linda got along fine.
Bill was flattered when Carol said that, confidentially, she
thought Linda was "a real person." Jerry liked Linda too.
"She's a great little chick," he told Bill.

When Bill and Linda married, Jerry was best man, of course;
and at the reception later at the Donnelly Hotel, it was a little
like old times, Jerry and Bill cutting up together and linking
arms and tossing off glasses of spiked punch. But once, in the
midst of his happiness, Bill looked at Jerry and thought how
much older he looked, a lot older than just twenty-two. His
hair was beginning to recede, just like his father's, and he was
getting heavy around the hips. He and Carol had two kids,
and she was pregnant again. He was still with Robby's Market,
though now an assistant manager. Jerry got drunk at the reception and flirted with both bridesmaids, then tried to start a
fight with one of the ushers. Carol had to drive him home
before he made a real scene.

They saw each other every two or three weeks, sometimes
oftener, depending on the weather. If the weather was good,
like now, they might get together on Sunday at Jerry's, barbe-
cue hot dogs or hamburgers, and turn all the kids loose in the
wading pool Jerry had got for next to nothing from one of the
women checkers at the store.

Jerry had a comfortable house. He lived in the country on a
hill overlooking the Naches River. There were a half-dozen
other houses scattered around, but he was by himself, too,
compared to in town anyway. He liked his friends to come to
his place; it was just too much trouble getting all the kids
washed, dressed, and into the car—a red '68 Chevy hardtop.
He and Carol had four kids now, all girls, and Carol was pregnant again. They didn't think they'd have any more after this
one.

Carol and Linda were in the kitchen washing dishes and straightening up. It was around three in the afternoon. Jerry's four little girls were playing with Bill's two boys, down below the house near a corner of the fence. They had a big red plastic ball they kept throwing into the wading pool and, yelling, splashed after. Jerry and Bill sat in reclining lawn chairs on the patio, drinking beer.

Bill had to do most of the talking—things about people they both knew, the power play going on at the Darigold head office in Portland, about a new four-door Pontiac Catalina he and Linda were thinking of buying.

Jerry nodded now and then, but most of the time just stared at the clothesline or at the garage. Bill thought he must be depressed, but then he'd noticed Jerry had gotten deep the last year or so. Bill moved in his chair, lighted a cigarette, finally said, "Anything wrong, man?"

Jerry finished his beer and then mashed the can. He shrugged. "What say we get out for a while? Just drive around a little, stop off and have a beer. Jesus, a guy gets stale just sitting around all his Sundays."

"Sounds good to me. Sure. I'll tell the women we're going."

"By ourselves, remember. By God, no family outing. Say we're going to have a beer or something. I'll wait for you in the car. Take my car."

They hadn't done anything together for a long while. They took the Naches River highway out to Gleed, Jerry driving. The day was warm and sunny, and the air blew through the car and felt good on their necks and arms. Jerry was grinning.

"Where we going?" Bill said. He felt a whole lot better just seeing Jerry brighten up.

"What say we go out to old Riley's, shoot a little rotation?"

"Fine with me. Hey, man, we haven't done anything like this in a long time."

"Guy's got to get out now and then or he gets stale. Know what I mean?" He looked at Bill. "Can't be all work and no play. You know what I mean."

Bill wasn't sure. He liked to get out with the guys from the plant for the Friday night bowling league, and he liked to stop off once or twice a week after work with Jack Broderick and have a few beers, but he liked being at home too. No, he wouldn't say he felt stale exactly. He looked at his watch.

"Still standing," Jerry said, pulling up onto the gravel in front of the Gleed Recreation Center. "Been by here now and then, you know, but I haven't been inside for a year or so. Just no time anymore." He spat.

They went inside, Bill holding the door for Jerry. Jerry punched him lightly in the stomach as he went by.

"Heeey there! How you boys doing? I haven't seen you boys around in I don't know how long. Where you been keeping yourselves?" Riley started around from behind the counter, grinning. He was a heavy bald-headed man wearing a short-sleeved print shirt that hung outside his jeans.

"Ah, dry up you old coot and give us a couple of Olys," Jerry said, winking at Bill. "How you been?"

"Fine, fine, just fine. How you boys doing? Where you been keeping yourselves? You boys getting any on the side? Jerry, the last time I seen you, your old lady was six months pregnant."

Jerry stood a minute and blinked his eyes. "How long's that been, Riley? Has it been that long?"

"How about the Oly?" Bill said. "Riley, you have one with us."

They took stools near the window. Jerry said, "What kind of place is this, Riley, that don't have any girls on a Sunday afternoon?"

Riley laughed. "I guess there just ain't enough to go around, boys."

They had five cans of beer each and took two hours to play three games of rotation and two games of snooker. Riley didn't have anything to do and came around from behind the counter and sat on a stool and talked and watched them play.

Bill kept looking at his watch, then at Jerry. Finally, he said, "You think we should be going now, Jerry? I mean, what d'you think?"

"Yeah, okay. Let's finish this beer, then go." In a little while Jerry drained his can, mashed it, and then sat there on the stool a minute turning the can in his hand. "See you around, Riley."

"You boys come back now, you hear? Take it easy."

Back on the highway Jerry opened it up some—little spurts of eighty-five and ninety—but there were other cars, people returning from the parks and the mountains, and he mostly had to be satisfied with a quick pass now and then, and then a slow creeping along at fifty with the rest.

They'd just passed an old pickup loaded with furniture when they saw two girls on bicycles.

"Look at that!" Jerry said, slowing. "I could do for some of that."

He drove on by, but both of them looked back. The girls saw them and laughed, kept pedaling along the shoulder of the road.

Jerry drove another mile and then pulled off the road at a wide place. "Let's go back. Let's try it."

"Jesus. Well, I don't know, man. We should be getting back. That stuff's too young anyway. Huh?"

"Old enough to bleed, old enough to . . . You know that saying."

"Yeah, but I don't know."

"Christ sake. We'll just have some fun with 'em, give 'em a bad time."

"All right. Sure." He glanced at his watch and then at the sky. "You do the talking."

"Me! I'm driving. You do the talking. Besides, they'll be on your side."

"I don't know, man, I'm rusty."

Jerry hooted as he whipped the car around, started back the way they'd come.

He slowed when he came nearly even with the girls, pulled onto the shoulder across the road from them. "Hey, where you going? Want a lift?"

The girls looked at each other and laughed, but kept riding. The girl on the inside, nearest the road, was seventeen or eighteen, dark-haired, tall and willowy as she leaned over her bicycle. The other girl was the same age, but smaller and with light hair. They both wore shorts and halters.

"Bitches," Jerry said. "We'll get 'em, though." He was waiting for the cars to pass so he could pull a U. "I'll take the brunette, you take the little one. Okay?"

Bill moved his back against the front seat and touched the bridge of his dark glasses. "Hell, we're wasting our time anyway—they're not going to do anything."

"Christ, man! Jesus, don't go in there already defeated."

Bill lighted a cigarette.

Jerry pulled across the road, and in a minute or two drove up behind the girls. "Okay, do your stuff," he said to Bill. "Turn on your charms now. Hustle 'em in for us."

"Hi," Bill said as they drove slowly alongside the girls. "My name's Bill."

"That's nice," the brunette said. The other girl laughed, and then the brunette laughed too.

"Where are you going?"

The girls didn't answer. The little one tittered. They kept riding and Jerry drove along slowly beside them.

"Oh, come on now. Where you going?"

"No place," the little one answered.

"Where's no place?"

"Just no place."

"I told you my name. What's yours? This is Jerry."

The girls looked at each other and laughed again. They kept riding.

A car came up from behind, and the driver leaned on the horn.

"Ah, cram it!" Jerry said. He pulled off a little farther onto the shoulder, though; and after a minute, seeing his chance, the driver of the other car shot around them.

They pulled up alongside the girls again.

"Let us give you a lift," Bill said. "We'll take you wherever you want to go. That's a promise. You must be tired riding those bicycles. You look tired. Too much exercise isn't good for you, you know."

The girls laughed.

"Come on now, tell us your names."

"My name's Barbara, hers is Sharon," the little one said. She laughed again.

"Now we're getting someplace," Jerry said to Bill. "Ask 'em again where they're going."

"Where you girls going? Barbara, . . . where you going, Barb?"

She laughed. "No place," she said, "just down the road."

"Where down the road?"

"D'you want me to tell them?" she said to the other girl.

"I don't care. It doesn't make any difference; I'm not going to go anyplace with them anyway."

"Well, I'm not either," she said. "I didn't mean that."

"Christ sake," Jerry said.

"Where you going?" Bill asked again. "Are you going to Painted Rocks?"

The girls began laughing.

"That's where they're going," Jerry said. "Painted Rocks." He picked up a little speed then and pulled off onto the shoulder ahead of the girls so that they had to come by on his side of the car to get around.

"Don't be that way," Jerry said. "Come on, get in. We're all introduced. What's the matter anyway?"

The girls just laughed as they rode by, and laughed even more when Jerry said, "Come on, we won't bite."

"How do we know?" the little one called back over her shoulder.

"Take my word for it, sister," Jerry said under his breath.

The brunette glanced back, caught Jerry's eyes, and looked away with a frown.

Jerry pulled back onto the highway, dirt and rocks spurting from under the rear tires. "We'll be seeing you," Bill called as they sped by.

"It's in the bag," Jerry said. "See the look that bitch gave me? I tell you, we got it made."

"I don't know," Bill said. "Maybe we should cut for home."

"No, no, we got it made! Just take my word for it."

He pulled off the road under some trees when they came to Painted Rocks. The highway forked here, one road going on to Yakima, the other, the main highway, heading for Naches, Enumclaw, the Chinook Pass, Seattle. A hundred yards off the road was a high sloping black mound of rock, part of a low range of hills honeycombed with footpaths and small caves with a sprinkling of Indian sign-painting here and there on several of the cave walls. The cliff side of the rock, facing the highway, carried announcements and warnings like NACHES 67—GLEED WILDCATS—Jesus Saves—Beat Yakima, flat irregular letters for the most part, in red or white paint.

They sat in the car smoking cigarettes, watching the highway and listening to the intermittent tat-tat of a woodpecker back in the trees. A few mosquitoes flew into the car and hovered over their hands and arms.

Jerry tried to pick up something on the radio and rapped the dashboard sharply. "Wish we had another beer now! Damn, I could sure go for a beer."

"Yeah," Bill said. He looked at his watch. "Almost six, Jerry. How much longer we going to wait?"

"Christ, they'll be along any minute. They'll have to stop when they get where they're going, won't they? I'll bet three bucks, all I got, they'll be here in two or three minutes." He grinned at Bill and bumped his knee. Then he began to tap the head of the gear shift.

When the girls came into view, they were on the opposite side of the highway, facing the traffic.

Jerry and Bill got out of the car and leaned against the front fender, waiting.

When the girls turned off the shoulder into the trees, they saw the men and began to pedal faster. The little one was laughing as she raised up from the seat to push harder.

"Remember," Jerry said, starting away from the car, "I'll take the brunette, you take the little one."

Bill stopped. "What're we going to do? Man, we'd better be careful."

"Hell, we're just having some fun. We'll get 'em to stop and talk awhile, that's all. Who cares? They aren't going to say anything; they're having fun. They like to be paid attention to."

They began sauntering over to the cliff. The girls dropped their bicycles and commenced running up one of the paths. They disappeared around a corner and then reappeared again, a little higher up, where they stopped and looked down.

"What're you guys following us for?" the brunette called down. "Huh? What d'you want?"

Jerry didn't answer, just started up the path.

"Let's run," Barbara said, still laughing and a little out of breath. "Come on."

They turned and started going up the path at a trot.

Jerry and Bill climbed at a walking pace. Bill was smoking a cigarette, stopping every ten feet or so to get a good inhale. He was beginning to wish he were home. It was still warm and clear, but shadows from the overhead rocks and trees were starting to lengthen out over the trail in front of them. Just as the path turned, he looked back and caught a last glimpse of the car. He hadn't realized they were so high.

"Come on," Jerry snapped. "Can't you keep up?"

"I'm coming," Bill said.

"You go right, I'll go straight on. We'll cut 'em off."

Bill angled to the right. He kept climbing. He stopped once and sat down to catch his breath. He couldn't see the car, nor the highway. Over on his left he could see a strip of the Naches River, the size of a ribbon, sparkling beside a stand of miniature white spruce. To the right he could look down the valley and see the apple and pear orchards neatly laid out against the ridge and on down the sides of the ridge into the valley, with here and there a house, or the sun-gleam of an automobile moving on one of the little roads. It was very still and quiet. After a minute he got up, wiped his hands on his pants, and began following the trail again.

He went higher, and then the path began to drop, turning left, toward the valley. When he came around a bend he saw the two girls crouched behind an outcrop of rock, looking down over another path. He stopped, tried casually to light a cigarette, but noticed with a little shock his trembling fingers, and then began to walk toward the girls as nonchalantly as he could.

When they heard a rock turn under his foot, they jerked around, saw him, and jumped up, the little one squealing.

"Come on, wait a minute! Let's sit down and talk this over. I'm tired of walking. Hey!"

Jerry, hearing the voices, came jogging up the path into sight. "Wait, goddamn it!" He tried to cut them off and they broke in another direction, the little one squealing and laughing, both of them running barefoot across the shale and dirt in front of Bill.

Bill wondered where they'd left their shoes. He moved to the right.

The little one turned sharply and cut up the hill; the brunette whirled, paused, and then took off down a path that led toward the valley, along the side of the hill. Jerry went after her.

Bill looked at his watch and then sat down on a rock, took off his dark glasses and looked again at the sky.

The brunette kept running, hopping, until she came to one of the caves, a large overhang of rock with the interior hidden in the shadows. She climbed in as far as she could, sat down and dropped her head, breathing hard.

In a minute or two she heard him coming down the path. He stopped when he came to the overhang. She held her breath. He picked up a piece of shale, sailed it back into the dark. It whacked against the wall just over her head.

"Hey, what d'you want to do—put my eye out? Quit throwing rocks, you damn jerk."

"Thought you might be hiding out in there. Come out with your hands up, or I'm coming in for you."

"Wait a minute," she said.

He jumped up onto a little ledge under the rock and peered into the dark.

"What d'you want?" she said. "Why don't you leave us alone?"

"Well," he said, looking at her, letting his eyes move slowly over her body, "why don't you stop running, and we will."

She came up close to him, and then with a darting movement tried to slip by, but he put his hand out to the wall, blocking her way. He grinned.

She grinned, then bit her lip and tried to go by on the other side.

"You know you're cute when you smile." He tried to grab her around the waist but she turned, slipped away from him.

"Come on! Stop it! Let me out of here."

He moved in front of her again, touched her breast with his fingers. She slapped his hand down, and he grabbed her breast, hard.

"Oh," she said. "You're hurting me. Please, please, you're hurting me."

He relaxed his grip, but didn't let go. "All right," he said. "I'm not going to hurt you." Then he let go.

She pushed him off balance and jumped past onto the path, running downhill.

"Goddamn you," he yelled, "come back here!"

She took a path to the right that began to climb again. He slipped on some bunchgrass, fell, scrambled up and started running again. Then she turned into a narrow defile, a hundred feet long, with light and a view of the valley at the other end. She ran, her bare feet smacking the rock and echoing to him above his own hoarse breathing. At the end she turned and yelled, "Leave me *alone*!" her voice breaking.

He saved his breath. She turned and ducked out of sight. When he got to the end he looked up over his shoulder and saw her climbing steadily on her hands and knees. They were on the valley side, and she was climbing towards the top of a knoll. He knew if she made it he'd probably lose her; he couldn't go much farther. He put everything he had into it, scrabbling up the side, using rocks and bushes for handholds, his heart pounding and his breath coming in sharp cutting gasps.

Just as she reached the top he grabbed her ankle and they crawled onto the little plateau at the same time.

"Damn you," he sobbed. He still had her ankle when she kicked him as hard as she could in the head with her other foot, jarred him so that his ear rang and lights flashed behind his eyes.

"Son, son of a bitch you," his eyes streaming water. He threw himself down over her legs and grabbed her by the arms.

She kept trying to bring her knees up but he turned slightly, kept her pinned down.

They lay like for a while, gasping. The girl's eyes were large and rolling with fear. She kept turning her head from side to side and biting her lips.

"Listen, I'll let you go. You want me to let you go?"

She nodded quickly.

"Okay, I will. First I want it though. Understand? Without any trouble. Okay?"

She lay without speaking.

"Okay? Okay, I said?" he shook her.

After a moment she nodded.

"Okay. Okay."

He turned loose her arms and raised up, began fumbling with her shorts, trying to unzip them and slide them over her hips.

She moved quickly and caught him on the ear with a clenched fist, rolling to the side in the same motion. He lunged after

her. She was yelling now. He jumped onto her back and drove
her face into the ground. He held onto the nape of her neck.
In a minute, when she stopped struggling, he began slipping
her shorts down.

He stood up, turned his back to her and began brushing his
clothes. When he looked at her again she was sitting up, staring
at the scuffed ground and rubbing a few strands of hair against
her forehead.

"You going to tell anybody?"

She did not speak.

He wet his lips. "I wish you wouldn't."

She leaned forward and began to cry, quietly, holding the
back of her hand against her face.

Jerry tried to light a cigarette but dropped the matches and
started to walk off without picking them up. Then he stopped
and looked back. For a minute he couldn't understand what
he was doing there, or who this girl was. He glanced uneasily
across the valley, the sun just starting to sink into the hills. He
felt a slight breeze against his face. The valley was being tipped
in with the dark ground-covering shadows of ridges, rocks,
trees. He looked at the girl again.

"I said I wish you wouldn't say anything. I'm . . . Jesus!
I'm sorry, I really am."

"Just . . . go away."

He came closer. She started to get up. He stepped forward
quickly and hit her on the side of the head with his fist, just as
she got to one knee. She fell back with a scream. When she
tried to get to her feet again, he picked up a rock and slammed
it into her face. He actually heard her teeth and bones crack,
and blood came out between her lips. He dropped the rock.
She went down heavily, and he crouched over her. When she
began moving he picked up the rock and hit her again, not
very hard this time, on the back of the head. Then he dropped
the rock and touched her shoulder. He began to shake her,
and after a minute he turned her over.

Her eyes were open, glassy, and she began turning her head
slowly from side to side, rolling her tongue thickly in her
mouth as she tried to spit out blood and splinters of teeth. As
she moved her head slightly from side to side, her eyes kept

focusing on him, then slipping off. He got up and walked a few feet, then came back. She was trying to sit up. He knelt, put his hands on her shoulders and tried to make her lie down again. But his hands slipped to her throat, and he began to choke her. He couldn't go through with it, though, just enough so that when he released his hands her breath came scraping hysterically up her windpipe. She sank back, and he stood up. Then he bent over and worked loose from the ground a big rock. Loose dirt fell from the bottom of the rock as he raised it up even with his eyes and then over his head. Then he dropped it on the girl's face. It sounded like a slap. He picked up the rock again, trying not to look at her, and dropped it once more. Then he picked up the rock again.

Bill made his way through the defile. It was very late now, almost evening. He saw where somebody had gone up the hill, turned and retraced his steps to go a different, easier way.

He'd caught up with the little one, Barbara, but that was all; he hadn't tried to kiss her, much less anything else. He honestly just hadn't felt like it. Anyway, he was afraid. Maybe she was willing, maybe she wasn't, but he had too much at stake to take a chance. She was down at the bicycles now, waiting for her friend. No, he just wanted to round up Jerry, get back before it got any later. He knew he was going to catch hell from Linda, and she was probably worried sick besides. It was too late, they should have been back hours ago. He was very nervous and sprinted the last few feet up the hill, onto the little plateau.

He saw them both at the same time, Jerry standing to the other side of the girl, holding the rock.

Bill felt himself shrinking, becoming thin and weightless. At the same time he had the sensation of standing against a heavy wind that was cuffing his ears. He wanted to break loose and run, run, but something was moving towards him. The shadows of the rocks as the shape came across them seemed to move with the shape and under it. The ground seemed to have shifted in the odd-angled light. He thought unreasonably of the two bicycles waiting at the bottom of the hill near the car, as though taking one away would change all this, make the girl stop happening to him in that moment he had topped the hill.

But Jerry was standing now in front of him, slung loosely in
his clothes as though the bones had gone out of him. Bill felt
the awful closeness of their two bodies, less than an arm's
length between. Then the head came down on Bill's shoulder.
He raised his hand, and as if the distance now separating them
deserved at least this, he began to pat, to stroke the other,
while his own tears broke.

If It Please You

E DITH PACKER had the tape cassette cord plugged into her ear and was smoking one of his cigarettes. The TV played without any volume as she sat on the sofa with her legs tucked under her and turned the pages of a news magazine. James Packer came out of the guest room which he'd fixed up as an office. He was wearing his nylon windbreaker and looked surprised when he saw her, and then disappointed. She saw him and took the cord from her ear. She put the cigarette in the ashtray and wiggled the toes of one stockinged foot at him.

"Bingo," he said. "Are we going to play bingo tonight or not? We're going to be late, Edith."

"I'm going," she said. "Sure. I guess I got carried away." She liked classical music, and he didn't. He was a retired accountant, but he did tax returns for some old clients and he'd been working tonight. She hadn't wanted to play her music so that he'd hear it and be distracted.

"If we're going, let's go," he said. He looked at the TV, and then went to the set and turned it off.

"I'm going," she said. "Just let me go to the bathroom." She closed the magazine and got up. "Hold your old horses, dear," she said and smiled. She left the room.

He went to make sure the back door was locked and the porch lamp on, then came back to stand in the living room. It was a ten-minute drive to the community center, and he could see they were going to be late for the first game. He liked to be on time, which meant a few minutes early, so he'd have a chance to say hello to people he hadn't seen since last Friday night. He liked to joke with Frieda Parsons as he stirred sugar into his Styrofoam cup of coffee. She was one of the club women who ran the bingo game on Friday nights and during the week worked behind the counter of the town's only drugstore. He liked getting there with a little time to spare so he and Edith could get their coffee from Frieda and take their places at the last table along the wall. He liked that table. They'd occupied the same places at the same table every Friday night for months now. The first Friday night that he'd played

95

bingo there, he'd won a forty-dollar jackpot. He'd told Edith afterwards that now he was hooked forever. "I've been looking for another vice," he'd said and grinned. Dozens of bingo cards were piled on each table, and you were supposed to pick through and find the cards you wanted, the cards that might be winning cards. Then you sat down, scooped a handful of white beans from the bowl on the table, and waited for the game to get under way, for the head of the women's club, stately white-haired Eleanor Bender, to commence turning her basket of numbered poker chips and begin calling numbers. That's the real reason you had to get there early, to get your place and pick out your particular cards. You had cards you favored and even felt you could recognize from week to week, cards whose arrangements of numbers seemed more inviting than those of other cards. Lucky cards, maybe. All of the cards had code numbers printed in the upper right-hand corner, and if you'd won a bingo on a certain card in the past, or even come close, or if you just had a feeling about certain cards, you got there early and went through the piles of cards for your cards. You started referring to them as your cards, and you'd look for them from week to week.

Edith finally came out of the bathroom. She had a puzzled expression on her face. There was no way they were going to be on time.

"What's the matter?" he said. "Edith?"

"Nothing," she said. "Nothing. Well, how do I look, Jimmy?"

"You look fine. Lord, we're just going to a bingo game," he said. "You know about everybody there anyway."

"That's the point," she said. "I want to look nice."

"You look nice," he said. "You always look nice. Can we go now?"

There seemed to be more cars than usual parked on the streets around the center. In the place where he normally parked, there was an old van with psychedelic markings on it. He had to keep going to the end of the block and turn.

"Lots of cars tonight," Edith said.

"There wouldn't be so many if we'd gotten here earlier," he said.

"There'd still be as many, we just wouldn't have seen them," she corrected, teasing. She pinched his sleeve.

"Edith, if we're going to play bingo we ought to try to get there on time," he said. "First rule of life is get where you're going on time."

"Hush," she said. "I feel like something's going to happen tonight. You watch and see. We're going to hit jackpots all night long. We're going to break the bank," she said.

"I'm glad to hear it," he said. "I call that confidence." He finally found a parking space near the end of the block and turned into it. He switched off the engine and cut the lights. "I don't know if I feel lucky tonight or not. I think I felt lucky earlier this evening for about five minutes when I was doing Howard's taxes, but I don't feel very lucky right now. It's not lucky if we have to start out walking half a mile just to play bingo."

"You stick close to me," she said. "We'll do fine."

"I don't feel lucky," he said. "Lock your door."

They began walking. There was a cold breeze and he zipped the windbreaker to his neck. She pulled her coat closer. He could hear the surf breaking on the rocks at the bottom of the cliff down behind the community center.

She said, "I'll take one of your cigarettes, Jimmy, before we get inside."

They stopped under the streetlamp at the corner. The wires supporting the old streetlamp swayed in the wind, and the light threw their shadows back and forth over the pavement. He could see the lights of the center at the end of the block. He cupped his hands and held the lighter for her. Then he lit his own cigarette. "When are you going to stop?" he said.

"When you stop," she said. "When I'm ready to stop. Maybe just like when you were ready to stop drinking. I'll just wake up some morning and stop. Like that. Like you. Then I'll find a hobby."

"I can teach you to knit," he said.

"I guess I don't think I have the patience for that," she said. "Besides, one knitter in the house is enough."

He smiled. He took her arm and they kept walking.

When they reached the steps in front of the center, she threw down her cigarette and stepped on it. They went up the

steps and into the foyer. There was a sofa in the room, along
with a scarred wooden table and several folding chairs. On the
walls of the room hung old photographs of fishing boats and a
naval vessel, a frigate from before the First World War, that had
capsized off the point and been driven ashore onto the sandy
beaches below the town. One photograph that always in-
trigued him showed a boat turned upside down on the rocks at
low tide, a man standing on the keel and waving at the camera.
There was a sea chart in an oak frame, and several paintings of
pastoral scenes done by club members: rugged mountains
behind a pond and a grove of trees, and paintings of the sun
going down over the ocean. They passed through the room,
and he took her arm again as they entered the hall. Several of
the club women sat to the right of the entrance behind a long
table. There were thirty or so other tables set up on the floor,
along with folding chairs. Most of the chairs were filled. At the
far end of the hall was a stage where Christmas programs were
put on, and sometimes amateur theatrical productions. The
bingo game was in progress. Eleanor Bender, holding a micro-
phone, was calling numbers.

They didn't stop for coffee but walked quickly along the
wall toward the back, toward their table. Heads bent over the
tables. No one looked up at them. People watched their cards
and waited for the next number to be called. He headed them
toward their table, but tonight starting out the way it had
already, he knew someone would have their places, and he was
right.

It was a couple of hippies, he realized with a start, a man and
a young woman, a girl really. The girl had on an old faded
jeans outfit, pants and jacket, and a man's denim shirt, and was
wearing rings and bracelets and long dangling earrings that
moved when she moved. She moved now, turned to the long-
haired fellow in the buckskin jacket beside her and pointed at a
number on his card, then pinched his arm. The fellow had his
hair pulled back and tied behind his head, and a scruffy bunch
of hair on his face. He wore little steel-frame spectacles and
had a tiny gold ring in his ear.

"Jesus," James said and stopped. He guided them to another table. "Here's two chairs. We'll have to take these places
and take our chances. There's hippies in our place." He glared

over in their direction. He took off his windbreaker and helped Edith with her coat. Then he sat down and looked again at the pair sitting in their place. The girl scanned her cards as the numbers were called. Then she leaned over next to the bushy fellow and looked his cards over, as if, James thought, she were afraid he might not have sense enough to mark his own numbers. James picked up a stack of bingo cards from the table and gave half to Edith. "Pick some winners for yourself," he said. "I'm just going to take these first three on top. I don't think it matters tonight which cards I choose. I don't feel very lucky tonight, and there's nothing I can do to change the feeling. What the hell's that pair doing here? They're kind of off their beaten path, if you ask me."

"Don't pay them any attention, Jimmy," she said. "They're not hurting anybody. They're just young, that's all."

"This is regular Friday night bingo for the people of this community," he said. "I don't know what they want here."

"They want to play bingo," she said, "or they wouldn't be here. Jimmy, dear, it's a free country. I thought you wanted to play bingo. Let's play, shall we? Here, I've found the cards I want." She gave him the stack of cards, and he put them with the other cards they wouldn't use in the center of the table. He noticed a pile of discards in front of the hippie. Well, he'd come here to play bingo and by God he was going to play. He fished a handful of beans from the bowl.

The cards were twenty-five cents each, or three cards for fifty cents. Edith had her three. James peeled a dollar bill from a roll of bills he kept for this occasion. He put the dollar next to his cards. In a few minutes one of the club women, a thin woman with bluish hair and a spot on her neck—he knew her only as Alice—would come around with a coffee can picking up quarters, dollar bills, dimes, and nickels, making change from the can when necessary. It was this woman, or another woman named Betty, who collected the money and paid off jackpots.

Eleanor Bender called "I-25," and a woman at a table in the middle of the room yelled, "Bingo!"

Alice made her way between the tables. She bent over the woman's card as Eleanor Bender read out the winning numbers. "It's a bingo," Alice said.

"That bingo, ladies and gentlemen, is worth twelve dollars,"

Eleanor Bender said. "Congratulations to you!" Alice counted out some bills for the woman, smiled vaguely, and moved away.

"Get ready now," Eleanor Bender said. "Next game in two minutes. I'll set the lucky numbers in motion right now." She began turning the basket of poker chips.

They played four or five games to no purpose. Once James was close on one of his cards, one number away from a bingo. But Eleanor Bender called five numbers in succession, none of them his, and even before someone else in the hall had found the right number and called out, he knew she wouldn't be calling the number he needed. Not for anything, he was convinced, would she have called his number.

"You were close that time, Jimmy," Edith said. "I was watching your card."

"Close doesn't count," he said. "It may as well have been a mile. She was teasing me, that's all." He turned the card up and let the beans slide into his hand. He closed his hand and made a fist. He shook the beans in his fist. Something came to him about a kid who'd thrown some beans out of a window. It had something to do with a carnival, or a fair. A cow was in there too, he thought. The memory reached to him from a long way and was somehow disturbing.

"Keep playing," Edith said. "Something's going to happen. Change cards, maybe."

"These cards are as good as any others," he said. "It just isn't my night, Edith, that's all."

He looked over at the hippies again. They were laughing at something the fellow had said. He could see the girl rubbing his leg under the table. They didn't seem to be paying attention to anyone else in the room. Alice came around collecting money for the next game. But just after Eleanor Bender had called the first number, James happened to glance in the direction of the hippies again. He saw the fellow put a bean down on a card he hadn't paid for, a card that was supposed to be with the discard pile. But the card lay so that the fellow could see it and play it along with his other cards. Eleanor Bender called another number, and the fellow placed another bean on the same card. Then he pulled the card over to him with the intention of playing it. James was amazed at the act. Then he got mad. He couldn't concentrate on his own cards. He kept looking up to see what the hippie was doing. No one else seemed to have noticed.

"James, look at your cards," Edith said. "Watch your cards, dear. You missed number thirty-four. Here." She placed one of her beans on his number. "Pay attention, dear."

"That hippie over there who has our place is cheating. Doesn't that beat all?" James said. "I can't believe my eyes."

"Cheating? What's he doing?" she said. "How's he cheating at bingo, Jimmy?" She looked around, a little distracted, as if she'd forgotten where the hippie was sitting.

"He's playing a card that he hasn't paid for," he said. "I can see him doing it. My God, there's nothing they won't stop at. A bingo game! Somebody ought to report him."

"Not you, dear. He's not hurting us," Edith said. "One card more or less in such a roomful of cards and people. Let him play as many cards as he wants. There're some people here playing six cards." She spoke slowly and tried to keep her eyes on her cards. She marked a number.

"But they've paid for them," he said. "I don't mind that. That's different. This damned fellow is cheating, Edith."

"Jimmy, forget it, dear," she said. She extracted a bean from her palm and placed it on a number. "Leave him alone. Dear, play your cards. You have me confused now, and I've missed a number. Please play your cards."

"I have to say it's a hell of a bingo game when they can get away with murder," he said. "I resent that. I do."

He looked back at his cards, but he knew he might as well write this game off. The remaining games as well, for that matter. Only a few numbers on his cards had beans. There was no way of telling how many numbers he'd missed, how far behind he'd fallen. He clenched the beans in his fist. Without hope, he squeezed a bean out onto the number just called, G-60. Someone yelled, "Bingo!"

"Christ," he said.

Eleanor Bender said they would take a ten-minute break for people to get up and move around. The game after the break would be a blackout, one dollar a card, winner take all. This week's pot, Eleanor announced, was ninety-eight dollars. There was whistling and clapping. He looked over at the hippies. The fellow was touching the ring in his ear and looking around the room. The girl had her hand on his leg again.

"I have to go to the bathroom," Edith said. "Give me your cigarettes. Maybe you'd get us one of those nice raisin cookies we saw, and a cup of coffee."

"I'll do that," he said. "And, by God, I am going to change cards. These cards I'm playing are born losers."

"I'll go to the bathroom," she said. She put his cigarettes into her purse and stood up from the table.

He waited in line for cookies and coffee. He nodded at Frieda Parsons when she made some light remark, paid, then walked back to where the hippies were sitting. They already had their coffee and cookies. They were eating and drinking and conversing like normal people. He stopped behind the fellow's chair.

"I see what you're doing," James said to him.

The man turned around. His eyes widened behind his spectacles. "Pardon me?" he said and stared at James. "What am I doing?"

"You know," James said. The girl seemed frightened. She held her cookie and fixed her eyes on James. "I don't have to spell it out for you," James said to the man. "A word to the wise, that's all. I can see what you're doing."

He walked back to his table. He was trembling. Damn all the hippies in this world, he thought. It was enough of an encounter so that it made him feel he'd like to have a drink. Imagine wanting to drink over something happening at a bingo game. He put the coffee and cookies down on the table. Then he raised his eyes to the hippie, who was watching him. The girl was watching him too. The hippie grinned. The girl took a bite of her cookie.

Edith came back. She handed him the cigarettes and sat down. She was quiet. Very quiet. In a minute James recovered himself and said, "Is there anything the matter with you, Edith? Are you all right?" He looked at her closely. "Edith, has something happened?"

"I'm all right," she said and picked up her coffee. "No, I guess I should tell you, Jimmy. I don't want to worry you, though." She took a sip of her coffee and waited. Then she said, "I'm spotting again."

"Spotting?" he said. "What do you mean, Edith?" But he knew what she meant, that at this age and happening with the kind of pain she'd said it did, it might mean what they most feared. "Spotting," he said quietly.

"You know," she said, picking up some cards and beginning to sort through them. "I'm menstruating a little. Oh dear," she said.

"I think we should go home. I think we'd better leave," he said. "That isn't good, is it?" He was afraid she wouldn't tell him if the pain started. He'd had to ask her before, watching to see how she looked. She'd have to go in now. He knew it.

She sorted through some more cards and seemed flustered and a little embarrassed. "No, let's stay," she said after a minute. "Maybe it's nothing to worry about. I don't want you to worry. I *feel* all right, Jimmy," she said.

"Edith."

"We'll stay," she said. "Drink your coffee, Jimmy. It'll be all right, I'm sure. We came here to play bingo," she said and smiled a little.

"This is the worst bingo night in history," he said. "I'm ready to go anytime. I think we should go now."

"We'll stay for the blackout, and then it's just forty-five minutes or so. Nothing can happen in that time. Let's play bingo," she said, trying to sound cheerful.

He swallowed some coffee. "I don't want my cookie," he said. "You can have my cookie." He cleared away the cards he was using and took two cards from the stack of bingo cards that weren't in use. He looked over angrily at the hippies as if they were somehow to blame for this new development. But the fellow was gone from the table and the girl had her back to him. She had turned in her chair and was looking toward the stage.

They played the blackout game. Once he glanced up and the hippie was still at it, playing a card he hadn't paid for. James still felt he should call the matter to someone's attention, but he couldn't leave his cards, not at a dollar a card. Edith's lips were tight. She wore a look that could have been determination, or worry.

James had three numbers to cover on one card and five numbers on another card, a card he'd already given up on, when the hippie girl began screaming. "Bingo! Bingo! Bingo! I have a bingo!"

The man clapped and shouted with her. "She's got a bingo! She's got a bingo, folks! A bingo!" He kept clapping.

Eleanor Bender herself went to the girl's table to check her card against the master list of numbers. Then she said, "This young woman has just won herself a ninety-eight-dollar jackpot. Let's give her a round of applause. Let's hear it for her."

Edith clapped along with the rest of the players, but James kept his hands on the table. The hippie fellow hugged the girl. Eleanor Bender handed the girl an envelope. "Count it if you want to," she said with a smile. The girl shook her head.

"They'll probably use the money to buy drugs," James said.

"James, please," Edith said. "It's a game of chance. She won fair and square."

"Maybe she did," he said. "But her partner there is out to take everyone for all he can get."

"Dear, do you want to play the same cards again?" Edith said. "They're about to start the next game."

They stayed for the rest of the games. They stayed until the last game was played, a game called Progressive. It was a bingo game whose jackpot was increased each week if no one had bingoed on a fixed amount of numbers. If no one had hit a bingo when the last number was called, that game was declared closed and more money, five dollars, was added to the pot for the next week's game, along with another number. The first week the game had started, the jackpot was seventy-five dollars and thirty numbers. This week it was a hundred and twenty-five dollars and forty numbers. Bingos were rare before forty numbers had been called, but after forty numbers you could expect someone to bingo at any time. James put his money down and played his cards without any hope or intention of winning. He felt close to despair. It wouldn't have surprised him if the hippie had won this game.

When the forty numbers had been called and no one had cried out, Eleanor Bender said, "That's bingo for tonight. Thank you all for coming. God bless you, and if He's willing we'll see you again next Friday. Good night and have a nice weekend."

James and Edith filed out of the hall along with the rest of the players, but somehow they managed to get behind the hippie couple, who were still laughing and talking about her big jackpot. The girl patted her coat pocket and laughed again. She had an arm around the fellow's waist under his buckskin jacket, fingers just touching his hip.

"Let those people get ahead of us, for God's sake," James said to Edith. "They're a plague."

Edith kept quiet, but she hung back a little with James to give the couple time to move ahead.

"Good night, James. Good night, Edith," Henry Kuhlken said. Kuhlken was a graying heavyset man who'd lost a son in a boating accident years before. His wife had left him for another man not long afterwards. He'd turned to serious drinking after a time and later wound up in AA, where James had first met him and heard his stories. Now he owned one of the two service stations in town and sometimes did mechanical work on their car. "See you next week."

"'Night, Henry," James said. "I guess so. But I feel pretty bingoed out tonight."

Kuhlken laughed. "I know just exactly what you mean," he said and moved on.

The wind was up and James thought he could hear the surf over the sound of automobile engines starting. He saw the hippie couple stop at the van. He might have known. He should have put two and two together. The fellow pulled open his door and then reached across and opened the door on the woman's side. He started the van just as they walked by on the shoulder of the road. The fellow turned on his headlamps, and James and Edith were illumined against the walls of the nearby houses.

"That dumbbell," James said.

Edith didn't answer. She was smoking and had the other hand in her coat pocket. They kept walking along the shoulder. The van passed them and shifted gears as it reached the corner. The streetlamp was swinging in the wind. They walked on to their car. James unlocked her door and went around to his side. Then they fastened the seat belts and drove home.

—

Edith went into the bathroom and shut the door. James took off his windbreaker and threw it across the back of the sofa. He turned on the TV and sat down and waited.

In a little while Edith came out of the bathroom. She didn't say anything. James waited some more and tried to keep his eyes on the TV. She went to the kitchen and ran water. He heard her turn off the faucet. In a minute she came to the kitchen doorway and said, "I guess I'll have to see Dr. Crawford in the morning, Jimmy. I guess something's happening down there." She looked at him. Then she said, "Oh, damn it, damn it, the lousy, lousy luck," and began to cry.

"Edith," he said and moved to her.

She stood there shaking her head. She covered her eyes and leaned into him as he put his arms around her. He held her.

"Edith, dearest Edith," he said. "Good Lord." He felt helpless and terrified. He stood with his arms around her.

She shook her head a little. "I think I'll go to bed, Jimmy. I am just exhausted, and I really *don't* feel well. I'll go to see Dr. Crawford first thing in the morning. It'll be all right, I think, dear. You try not to worry. If anyone needs to worry tonight, let me. Don't you. You worry enough as it is. I think it'll be all right," she said and stroked his back. "I just put some water on for coffee, but I think I'll go to bed now. I feel worn out. It's these bingo games," she said and tried to smile.

"I'll turn everything off and go to bed too," he said. "I don't want to stay up tonight either, no sir."

"Jimmy, dear, I'd rather be alone right now, if you don't mind," she said. "It's hard to explain. It's just that right now I want to be alone. Dear, maybe that doesn't make any sense. You understand, don't you?"

"Alone," he repeated. He squeezed her wrist.

She reached up to his face and held him and studied his features for a minute. Then she kissed him on the lips. She went into the bedroom and turned on the light. She looked back at him, and then she shut the door.

He went to the refrigerator. He stood in front of the open door and drank tomato juice while he surveyed its lighted interior. Cold air blew out at him. The little packages and cartons of foodstuffs on the shelves, a chicken covered in plastic wrap, the neat foil-wrapped bundles of leftovers, all of this suddenly repelled him. He thought for some reason of Alice, that spot on her neck, and he shivered. He shut the door and spit the last of the juice into the sink. Then he rinsed his mouth and made himself a cup of instant coffee which he carried into the living room where the TV was still playing. It was an old Western. He sat down and lit a cigarette. After watching the screen for a few minutes, he felt he'd seen the movie before, years ago. The characters seemed faintly recognizable in their roles, and some of the things they said sounded familiar, as things to come often did in movies you'd forgotten. Then the hero, a movie star who'd recently died, said something—asked a hard question of another character, a stranger who'd just ridden into the little town; and all at once things fell into place, and James knew the very words that the stranger would pick out of the air to answer the question. He knew how things would turn out, but he kept watching the movie with a rising sense of apprehension. Nothing could stop what had been set in motion. Courage and fortitude were displayed by the hero and the townsmen-turned-deputies, but these virtues were not enough. It took only one lunatic and a torch to bring everything to ruin. He finished the coffee and smoked and watched the movie until its violent and inevitable conclusion. Then he turned off the set. He went to the bedroom door and listened, but there was no way of telling if she was awake. At least there was no light showing under the door. He hoped she was asleep. He kept listening. He felt vulnerable and somehow unworthy. Tomorrow she'd go to Dr. Crawford. Who knew what he would find? There'd be tests. Why Edith? he wondered. Why us? Why not someone else, why not those hippies tonight? They were sailing through life free as birds, no responsibilities, no doubts about the future. Why not them then, or someone else like them? It didn't add up. He moved away from the bedroom door. He thought about going out for a walk, as he did sometimes at night, but the wind had picked up and he could hear branches cracking in the birch tree behind the house. It'd be too cold anyway, and somehow the idea of a solitary walk tonight at this hour was dispiriting.

He sat in front of the TV again, but he didn't turn on the set. He smoked and thought of the way the hippie had grinned at him across the room. That sauntering, arrogant gait as he moved down the street toward his van, the girl's arm around his waist. He remembered the sound of the heavy surf, and he thought of great waves rolling in to break on the beach in the dark at this very minute. He recalled the fellow's earring and pulled at his own ear. What would it be like to want to saunter around like that fellow sauntered, a hippie girl's arm around your waist? He ran his fingers through his hair and shook his head at the injustice. He recalled the way the girl looked as she yelled her bingo, how everyone had turned enviously to look at her in her youth and excitement. If they only knew, she and her friend. If he could only tell them.

He thought of Edith in there in bed, the blood moving through her body, trickling, looking for a way out. He closed his eyes and opened them. He'd get up early in the morning and fix a nice breakfast for them. Then, when his office opened, she would call Dr. Crawford, set a time for seeing him, and he would drive her to the office and sit in the waiting room and page through magazines while he waited. About the time Edith came out with her news, he imagined that the hippies would be having their own breakfast, eating with appetite after a long night of lovemaking. It wasn't fair. He wished they were here now in the living room, in the noontime of their lives. He'd tell them what they could expect, he'd set them straight. He would stop them in the midst of their arrogance and laughter and tell them. He'd tell them what was waiting for them after the rings and bracelets, the earrings and long hair, the loving.

He got up and went into the guest room and turned on the lamp over the bed. He glanced at his papers and account books and at the adding machine on his desk and experienced a welling of dismay and anger. He found a pair of old pajamas in one of the drawers and began undressing. He turned back the covers on the bed at the other end of the room from his desk. Then he walked back through the house, turning off lights and checking doors. For the first time in four years he wished he had some whiskey in the house. Tonight would be the night for it, all right. He was aware that twice now in the course of this evening he had wanted something to drink, and he found this so discouraging that his shoulders slumped. They said in

AA never to become too tired, or too thirsty, or too hungry—
or too smug, he might add. He stood looking out the kitchen
window at the tree shaking under the force of the wind. The
window rattled at its edges. He recalled the pictures down at
the center, the boats going aground on the point, and hoped
nothing was out on the water tonight. He left the porch lamp
on. He went back to the guest room and took his basket of
embroidery from under the desk and settled himself into the
leather chair. He raised the lid of the basket and took out the
metal hoop with the white linen stretched tight and secured
within the hoop. Holding the tiny needle to the light, he
threaded the eye with one end of the blue silk thread. Then he
set to work where he'd left off on the floral design a few nights
before.

When he'd first stopped drinking he'd laughed at the suggestion he'd heard one night at AA from a middle-aged busi-
nessman who said he might want to look into needlework. It
was, he was told by the man, something he might want to do
with the free time he'd now have on his hands, the time previously given over to drinking. It was implied that needlework
was something he might find good occupation in day or night,
along with a sense of satisfaction. "Stick to your knitting," the
man had said and winked. James had laughed and shaken his
head. But after a few weeks of sobriety when he did find himself with more time than he could profitably employ, and an
increasing need for something to do with his hands and mind,
he'd asked Edith if she'd shop for the materials and instruction
booklets he needed. He was never all that good at it, his fingers were becoming increasingly slow and stiff, but he had
done a few things that gave him satisfaction after the pillow-
cases and dishcloths for the house. He'd done crocheting too
—the caps and scarves and mittens for the grandchildren.
There was a sense of accomplishment when a piece of work, no
matter how commonplace, lay finished in front of him. He'd
gone from scarves and mittens to create little throw rugs
which lay on the floor of every room in the house now. He'd
also made two woolen ponchos which he and Edith wore
when they walked on the beach; and he'd knitted an afghan,
his most ambitious project to date, something that had kept
him busy for the better part of six months. He'd worked on it

every evening, piling up the small squares, and had been happy with the feeling of regular industry. Edith was sleeping under that afghan right now. Late nights he liked the feel of the hoop, its taut holding of the white cloth. He kept working the needle in and out of the linen, following the outline of the design. He tied little knots and clipped off bits of thread when he had to. But after a while he began to think about the hippie again, and he had to stop work. He got mad all over again. It was the principle of the thing, of course. He realized it hadn't helped the hippie's chances, except maybe by a fraction, just by cheating on a single card. He hadn't won, that was the point, the thing to bear in mind. You couldn't win, not really, not where it counted. He and the hippie were in the same boat, he thought, but the hippie just didn't know it yet.

James put the embroidery back into the basket. He stared down at his hands for a minute after he did so. Then he closed his eyes and tried to pray. He knew it would give him some satisfaction to pray tonight, if he could just find the right words. He hadn't prayed since he was trying to kick the drink, and he had never once imagined then that the praying would do any good, it just seemed to be one of the few things he could do under the circumstances. He'd felt at the time that it couldn't hurt anyway, even if he didn't believe in anything, least of all in his ability to stop drinking. But sometimes he felt better after praying, and he supposed that was the important thing. In those days he'd prayed every night that he could remember to pray. When he went to bed drunk, especially then, if he could remember, he prayed; and sometimes just before he had his first drink in the morning he prayed to summon the strength to stop drinking. Sometimes, of course, he felt worse, even more helpless and in the grip of something most perverse and horrible, after he'd say his prayers and then find himself immediately reaching for a drink. He had finally quit drinking, but he did not attribute it to prayer and he simply hadn't thought about prayer since then. He hadn't prayed in four years. After he'd stopped drinking, he just hadn't felt any need for it. Things had been fine since then, things had gotten good again after he'd stopped drinking. Four years ago he'd awakened one morning with a hangover, but instead of pouring himself a glass of orange juice and vodka, he decided he wouldn't. The vodka had still been in the house, too, which made the situation all the more remarkable. He just didn't drink that morning, nor that afternoon or evening. Edith had noticed, of course, but hadn't said anything. He shook a lot. The next day and the next were the same: he didn't drink and he stayed sober. On the fourth day, in the evening, he found the courage to say to Edith that it had been several days now since he'd had a drink. She had said simply, "I know that, dear." He remembered that now, the way she'd looked at him and touched his face, much in the manner she'd touched his face tonight. "I'm proud of you," she'd said, and that was all she'd said. He started going to the AA meetings, and it was soon after that he took up needlework.

Before the drinking had turned bad on him and he'd prayed to be able to stop, he'd prayed on occasions some years before that, after his youngest son had gone off to Vietnam to fly jet planes. He'd prayed off and on then, sometimes during the day if he thought about his son in connection with reading something in the newspaper about that terrible place; and sometimes at night lying in the dark next to Edith, turning over the day's events, his thoughts might come to rest on his son. He'd pray then, idly, like most men who are not religious pray. But nevertheless he'd prayed that his son would survive and come home in one piece. And he had returned safely too, but James hadn't ever for a minute really attributed his return to prayer—of course not. Now he suddenly remembered much farther back to a time when he'd prayed hardest of all, a time when he was twenty-one years old and still believed in the power of prayer. He'd prayed one entire night for his father, that he would recover from his automobile accident. But his father had died anyway. He'd been drunk and speeding and had hit a tree, and there was nothing that could be done to save his life. But even now he still remembered sitting outside the emergency room until sunlight entered the windows and praying and praying for his father, making all kinds of promises through his tears, if only his father would pull through. His mother had sat next to him and cried and held his father's shoes which had unaccountably come along in the ambulance beside him when they'd brought him to the hospital.

He got up and put his basket of embroidery away for the

night. He stood at the window. The birch tree behind the house was fixed in the little area of yellow light from the back porch lamp, the treetop lost in the overhead darkness. The leaves had been gone for months, but the bare branches switched in the gusts of wind. As he stood there he began to feel frightened, and then it was on him, a real terror welling in his chest. He could believe that something heavy and mean was moving around out there tonight, and that at any minute it might charge or break loose and come hurtling through the window at him. He moved back a few steps and stood where a corner of light from the porch lamp caused the room to brighten under him. His mouth had gone dry. He couldn't swallow. He raised his hands toward the window and let them drop. He suddenly felt he had lived nearly his whole life without having ever once really stopped to think about anything, and this came to him now as a terrible shock and increased his feeling of unworthiness.

He was very tired and had little strength left in his limbs. He pulled up the waist of his pajamas. He barely had energy to get into bed. He pushed up from the bed and turned off the lamp. He lay in the dark for a while. Then he tried praying again, slowly at first, forming the words silently with his lips, and then beginning to mutter words aloud and to pray in earnest. He asked for enlightenment on these matters. He asked for help in understanding the situation. He prayed for Edith, that she would be all right, that the doctor wouldn't find anything seriously wrong, not, please not, cancer, that's what he prayed for strongest. Then he prayed for his children, two sons and a daughter, scattered here and there across the continent. He included his grandchildren in these prayers. Then his thoughts moved to the hippie again. In a little while he had to sit up on the side of the bed and light a cigarette. He sat on the bed in the dark and smoked. The hippie woman, she was just a girl, not much younger or different-looking than his own daughter. But the fellow, him and his little spectacles, he was something else. He sat there for a while longer and turned things over. Then he put out his cigarette and got back under the covers. He settled onto his side and lay there. He rolled over onto his other side. He kept turning until he lay on his back, staring at the dark ceiling.

The same yellow light from the back porch lamp shone against the window. He lay with his eyes open and listened to the wind buffet the house. He felt something stir inside him again, but it was not anger this time. He lay without moving for a while longer. He lay as if waiting. Then something left him and something else took its place. He found tears in his eyes. He began praying again, words and parts of speech piling up in a torrent in his mind. He went slower. He put the words together, one after the other, and prayed. This time he was able to include the girl and the hippie in his prayers. Let them have it, yes, drive vans and be arrogant and laugh and wear rings, even cheat if they wanted. Meanwhile, prayers were needed. They could use them too, even his, especially his, in fact. "If it please you," he said in the new prayers for all of them, the living and the dead.

So Much Water So Close to Home

M Y husband eats with good appetite but seems tired, edgy. He chews slowly, arms on the table, and stares at something across the room. He looks at me and looks away again, and wipes his mouth on the napkin. He shrugs, goes on eating. Something has come between us though he would like to believe otherwise.

"What are you staring at me for?" he asks. "What is it?" he says and lays his fork down.

"Was I staring?" I say and shake my head stupidly, stupidly.

The telephone rings. "Don't answer it," he says.

"It might be your mother," I say. "Dean—it might be something about Dean."

"Watch and see," he says.

I pick up the receiver and listen for a minute. He stops eating. I bite my lip and hang up.

"What did I tell you?" he says. He starts to eat again, then throws the napkin onto his plate. "Goddamn it, why can't people mind their own business? Tell me what I did wrong and I'll listen! It's not fair. She was dead, wasn't she? There were other men there besides me. We talked it over and we all decided. We'd only just got there. We'd walked for hours. We couldn't just turn around, we were five miles from the car. It was opening day. What the hell, I don't see anything wrong. No, I don't. And don't look at me that way, do you hear? I won't have you passing judgment on me. Not you."

"You know," I say and shake my head.

"What do I know, Claire? Tell me. Tell me what I know. I don't know anything except one thing; you hadn't better get worked up over this." He gives me what he thinks is a meaningful look. "She was dead, dead, dead, do you hear?" he says after a minute. "It's a damn shame, I agree. She was a young girl and it's a shame, and I'm sorry, as sorry as anyone else, but she was dead, Claire, dead. Now let's leave it alone. Please, Claire. Let's leave it alone now."

"That's the point," I say. "She was dead—but don't you see? She needed help."

"I give up," he says and raises his hands. He pushes his chair away from the table, takes his cigarettes and goes out to the patio with a can of beer. He walks back and forth for a minute and then sits in a lawn chair and picks up the paper once more. His name is there on the first page along with the names of his friends, the other men who made the "grisly find."

I close my eyes for a minute and hold onto the drainboard. I must not dwell on this any longer. I must get over it; put it out of sight, out of mind, etc., and "go on." I open my eyes. Despite everything, knowing all that may be in store, I rake my arm across the drainboard and send the dishes and glasses smashing and scattering across the floor.

He doesn't move. I know he has heard, he raises his head as if listening, but he doesn't move otherwise, doesn't turn around to look. I hate him for that, for not moving. He waits a minute, then draws on his cigarette and leans back in the chair. I pity him for listening, detached, and then settling back and drawing on his cigarette. The wind takes the smoke out of his mouth in a thin stream. Why do I notice that? He can never know how much I pity him for that, for sitting still and listening, and letting the smoke stream out of his mouth . . .

He planned his fishing trip into the mountains last Sunday, a week before the Memorial Day weekend. He and Gordon Johnson, Mel Dorn, Vern Williams. They play poker, bowl, and fish together. They fish together every spring and early summer, the first two or three months of the season, before family vacations, Little League baseball, and visiting relatives can intrude. They are decent men, family men, responsible at their jobs. They have sons and daughters who go to school with our son, Dean. On Friday afternoon these four men left for a three-day fishing trip to the Naches River. They parked the car in the mountains and hiked several miles to where they wanted to fish. They carried their bedrolls, food and cooking utensils, their playing cards, their whiskey. The first evening at the river, even before they could set up camp, Mel Dorn found the girl floating face down in the river, nude, lodged near the shore against some branches. He called the other men and they all came to look at her. They talked about what to do. One of the men—Stuart didn't say which—perhaps it was Vern Williams, he is a heavyset, easy man who laughs often—one of them thought they should start back to the car at once. The others stirred the sand with their shoes and said they felt inclined to stay. They pleaded fatigue, the late hour, the fact that the girl "wasn't going anywhere." In the end they all decided to stay. They went ahead and set up the camp and built a fire and drank their whiskey. They drank a lot of whiskey and when the moon came up they talked about the girl. Someone thought they should do something to prevent the body from floating away. Somehow they thought that this might create a problem for them if she floated away during the night. They took flashlights and stumbled down to the river. The wind was up, a cold wind, and waves from the river lapped the sandy bank. One of the men, I don't know who, it might have been Stuart, he could have done it, waded into the water and took the girl by the fingers and pulled her, still face down, closer to shore, into shallow water, and then took a piece of nylon cord and tied it around her wrist and then secured the cord to tree roots, all the while the flashlights of the other men played over the girl's body. Afterwards, they went back to camp and drank more whiskey. Then they went to sleep. The next morning, Saturday, they cooked breakfast, drank lots of coffee, more whiskey, and then split up to fish, two men upriver, two men down.

That night, after they had cooked their fish and potatoes and had more coffee and whiskey, they took their dishes down to the river and washed them a few yards from where the girl lay in the water. They drank again and then they took out their cards and played and drank until they couldn't see their cards any longer. Vern Williams went to sleep but the others told coarse stories and spoke of vulgar or dishonest escapades out of their past, and no one mentioned the girl until Gordon Johnson, who'd forgotten for a minute, commented on the firmness of the trout they'd caught, and the terrible coldness of the river water. They'd stopped talking then but continued to drink until one of them tripped and fell cursing against the lantern, and then they climbed into their sleeping bags.

The next morning they got up late, drank more whiskey, fished a little as they kept drinking whiskey, and then, at one o'clock in the afternoon, Sunday, a day earlier than they'd planned, decided to leave. They took down their tents, rolled their sleeping bags, gathered their pans, pots, fish and fishing gear, and hiked out. They didn't look at the girl again before they left. When they reached the car they drove the highway in silence until they came to a telephone. Stuart made the call to the sheriff's office while the others stood around in the hot sun and listened. He gave the man on the other end of the line all of their names—they had nothing to hide, they weren't ashamed of anything—and agreed to wait at the service station until someone could come for more detailed directions and individual statements.

He came home at eleven o'clock that night. I was asleep but woke when I heard him in the kitchen. I found him leaning against the refrigerator drinking a can of beer. He put his heavy arms around me and rubbed his hands up and down my back, the same hands he'd left with two days before, I thought.

In bed he put his hands on me again and then waited, as if thinking of something else. I turned slightly and then moved my legs. Afterwards, I know he stayed awake for a long time, for he was awake when I fell asleep; and later, when I stirred for a minute, opening my eyes at a slight noise, a rustle of sheets, it was almost daylight outside, birds were singing, and he was on his back smoking and looking at the curtained window. Half-asleep, I said his name, but he didn't answer. I fell asleep again.

He was up that morning before I could get out of bed, to see if there was anything about it in the paper, I suppose. The telephone began to ring shortly after eight o'clock.

"Go to hell," I heard him shout into the receiver. The telephone rang again a minute later, and I hurried into the kitchen. "I have nothing else to add to what I've already said to the sheriff. That's right!" He slammed down the receiver.

"What is going on?" I said, alarmed.

"Sit down," he said slowly. His fingers scraped, scraped against his stubble of whiskers. "I have to tell you something. Something happened while we were fishing." We sat across from each other at the table, and then he told me.

I drank coffee and stared at him as he spoke. I read the account in the newspaper that he shoved across the table . . . unidentified girl eighteen to twenty-four years of age . . . body three to five days in the water . . . rape a possible

motive . . . preliminary results show death by strangulation
. . . cuts and bruises on her breasts and pelvic
area . . . autopsy . . . rape, pending further investigation.

"You've got to understand," he said. "Don't look at me like
that. Be careful now, I mean it. Take it easy, Claire."

"Why didn't you tell me last night?" I asked.

"I just . . . didn't. What do you mean?" he said.

"You know what I mean," I said. I looked at his hands, the
broad fingers, knuckles covered with hair, moving, lighting a
cigarette now, fingers that had moved over me, into me last
night.

He shrugged. "What difference does it make, last night, this
morning? You were sleepy, I thought I'd wait until this
morning to tell you." He looked out to the patio; a robin flew
from the lawn to the picnic table and preened its feathers.

"It isn't true," I said. "You didn't leave her there like that?"

He turned quickly and said, "What'd I do? Listen to me
carefully now, once and for all. Nothing happened. I have
nothing to be sorry for or feel guilty about. Do you hear me?"

I got up from the table and went to Dean's room. He was
awake and in his pajamas, putting together a puzzle. I helped
him find his clothes and then went back to the kitchen and put
his breakfast on the table. The telephone rang two or three
more times and each time Stuart was abrupt while he talked
and angry when he hung up. He called Mel Dorn and Gordon
Johnson and spoke with them, slowly, seriously, and then he
opened a beer and smoked a cigarette while Dean ate, asked
him about school, his friends, etc., exactly as if nothing had
happened.

Dean wanted to know what he'd done while he was gone,
and Stuart took some fish out of the freezer to show him.

"I'm taking him to your mother's for the day," I said.

"Sure," Stuart said and looked at Dean, who was holding
one of the frozen trout. "If you want to and he wants to, that
is. You don't have to, you know. There's nothing wrong."

"I'd like to anyway," I said.

"Can I go swimming there?" Dean asked and wiped his fingers on his pants.

"I believe so," I said. "It's a warm day so take your suit, and
I'm sure Grandmother will say it's okay."

Stuart lighted another cigarette and looked at us.

Dean and I drove across town to Stuart's mother's. She lives in an apartment building with a pool and a sauna bath. Her name is Catherine Kane. Her name, Kane, is the same as mine, which seems impossible. Years ago, Stuart has told me, she used to be called Candy by her friends. She is a tall, cold woman with white-blond hair. She gives me the feeling that she is always judging, judging. I explain briefly in a low voice what has happened (she hasn't yet read the newspaper) and promise to pick Dean up that evening. "He brought his swimming suit," I say. "Stuart and I have to talk about some things," I add vaguely. She looks at me steadily from over her glasses. Then she nods and turns to Dean, saying, "How are you, my little man?" She stoops and puts her arms around him. She looks at me again as I open the door to leave. She has a way of looking at me without saying anything.

When I returned home Stuart was eating something at the table and drinking beer . . .

After a time I sweep up the broken dishes and glassware and go outside. Stuart is lying on his back on the grass now, the newspaper and can of beer within reach, staring at the sky. It is breezy but warm out and birds call.

"Stuart, could we go for a drive?" I say. "Anywhere."

He rolls over and looks at me and nods. "We'll pick up some beer," he says. "I hope you're feeling better about this. Try to understand, that's all I ask." He gets to his feet and touches me on the hip as he goes past. "Give me a minute and I'll be ready."

We drive through town without speaking. Before we reach the country he stops at a roadside market for beer. I notice a great stack of papers just inside the door. On the top step a fat woman in a print dress holds out a licorice stick to a little girl. In a few minutes we cross Everson Creek and turn into a picnic area a few feet from the water. The creek flows under the bridge and into a large pond a few hundred yards away. There are a dozen or so men and boys scattered around the banks of the pond under the willows, fishing.

So much water so close to home, why did he have to go miles away to fish?

"Why did you have to go there of all places?" I say.

"The Naches? We always go there. Every year, at least once."
We sit on a bench in the sun and he opens two cans of beer
and gives one to me. "How the hell was I to know anything
like that would happen?" He shakes his head and shrugs, as if
it had all happened years ago, or to someone else. "Enjoy the
afternoon, Claire. Look at this weather."

"They said they were innocent."

"Who? What are you talking about?"

"The Maddox brothers. They killed a girl named Arlene
Hubly near the town where I grew up, and then cut off her
head and threw her into the Cle Elum River. She and I went to
the same high school. It happened when I was a girl."

"What a hell of a thing to be thinking about," he says.
"Come on, get off it. You're going to get me riled in a minute.
How about it now? Claire?"

I look at the creek. I float toward the pond, eyes open, face
down, staring at the rocks and moss on the creek bottom until
I am carried into the lake where I am pushed by the breeze.
Nothing will be any different. We will go on and on and on
and on. We will go on even now, as if nothing had happened. I
look at him across the picnic table with such intensity that his
face drains.

"I don't know what's wrong with you," he says. "I don't—"

I slap him before I realize. I raise my hand, wait a fraction of
a second, and then slap his cheek hard. This is crazy, I think as
I slap him. We need to lock our fingers together. We need to
help one another. This is crazy.

He catches my wrist before I can strike again and raises his
own hand. I crouch, waiting, and see something come into his
eyes and then dart away. He drops his hand. I drift even faster
around and around in the pond.

"Come on, get in the car," he says. "I'm taking you home."

"No, no," I say, pulling back from him.

"Come on," he says, "Goddamn it."

"You're not being fair to me," he says later in the car. Fields
and trees and farmhouses fly by outside the window. "You're
not being fair. To either one of us. Or to Dean, I might add.
Think about Dean for a minute. Think about me. Think about
someone else besides yourself for a change."

There is nothing I can say to him now. He tries to concentrate on the road, but he keeps looking into the rearview mirror. Out of the corner of his eye, he looks across the seat to where I sit with my knees doubled under me. The sun blazes against my arm and the side of my face. He opens another beer while he drives, drinks from it, then shoves the can between his legs and lets out breath. He knows. I could laugh in his face. I could weep.

2.

Stuart believes he is letting me sleep this morning. But I was awake long before the alarm sounded, thinking, lying on the far side of the bed, away from his hairy legs and his thick, sleeping fingers. He gets Dean off for school, and then he shaves, dresses, and leaves for work himself soon after. Twice he looks into the bedroom and clears his throat, but I keep my eyes closed.

In the kitchen I find a note from him signed "Love." I sit in the breakfast nook in the sunlight and drink coffee and make a coffee ring on the note. The telephone has stopped ringing, that is something. No more calls since last night. I look at the paper and turn it this way and that on the table. Then I pull it close and read what it says. The body is still unidentified, unclaimed, apparently unmissed. But for the last twenty-four hours men have been examining it, putting things into it, cutting, weighing, measuring, putting back again, sewing up, looking for the exact cause and moment of death. And the evidence of rape. I'm sure they hope for rape. Rape would make it easier to understand. The paper says she will be taken to Keith & Keith Funeral Home pending arrangements. People are asked to come forward with information, etc.

Two things are certain: 1) people no longer care what happens to other people, and 2) nothing makes any real difference any longer. Look at what has happened. Yet nothing will change for Stuart and me. Really change, I mean. We will grow older, both of us, you can see it in our faces already, in the bathroom mirror, for instance, mornings when we use the bathroom at the same time. And certain things around us will change, become easier or harder, one thing or the other, but nothing will ever really be any different. I believe that. We have made our decisions, our lives have been set in motion, and they will go on and on until they stop. But if that is true, what then? I mean, what if you believe that, but you keep it covered up, until one day something happens that should change something, but then you see nothing is going to change after all. What then? Meanwhile, the people around you continue to talk and act as if you were the same person as yesterday, or last night, or five minutes before, but you are really undergoing a crisis, your heart feels damaged . . .

The past is unclear. It is as if there is a film over those early years. I cannot be sure that the things I remember happening really happened to me. There was a girl who had a mother and father—the father ran a small café where the mother acted as waitress and cashier—who moved as if in a dream through grade school and high school and then, in a year or two, into secretarial school. Later, much later—what happened to the time in between?—she is in another town working as a receptionist for an electronic parts firm and becomes acquainted with one of the engineers who asks her for a date. Eventually, seeing that's his aim, she lets him seduce her. She had an intuition at the time, an insight about the seduction that later, try as she might, she couldn't recall. After a short while they decide to get married, but already the past, her past, is slipping away. The future is something she can't imagine. She smiles, as if she has a secret, when she thinks about the future. Once during a particularly bad argument, over what she can't now remember, five years or so after they were married, he tells her that someday this affair (his words: "this affair") will end in violence. She remembers this. She files this away somewhere and begins repeating it aloud from time to time. Sometimes, she spends the whole morning on her knees in the sandbox behind the garage playing with Dean and one or two of his friends. But every afternoon at four o'clock her head begins to hurt. She holds her forehead and feels dizzy with the pain. Stuart asks her to see a doctor and she does, secretly pleased at the doctor's solicitous attention. She goes away for a while to a place the doctor recommends. His mother comes out from Ohio in a hurry to care for the child. But she, Claire, Claire spoils everything and returns home in a few weeks. His mother moves out of the house and takes an apartment across town and perches there, as if waiting. One night in bed when they are both near sleep, Claire tells him that she heard some women patients at DeWitt discussing fellatio. She thinks this is something he might like to hear. She smiles in the dark. Stuart is pleased at hearing this. He strokes her arm. Things are going to be okay, he says. From now on everything is going to be different and better for them. He has received a promotion and a substantial raise. They have even bought another car, a station wagon, her car. They're going to live in the here and now. He says he feels able to relax for the first time in years. In the dark, he goes on stroking her arm . . . He continues to bowl and play cards regularly. He goes fishing with three friends of his.

That evening three things happen: Dean says that the children at school told him that his father found a dead body in the river. He wants to know about it.

Stuart explains quickly, leaving out most of the story, saying only that, yes, he and three other men did find a body while they were fishing.

"What kind of a body?" Dean asks. "Was it a girl?"

"Yes, it was a girl. A woman. Then we called the sheriff." Stuart looks at me.

"What'd he say?" Dean asks.

"He said he'd take care of it."

"What did it look like? Was it scary?"

"That's enough talk," I say. "Rinse your plate, Dean, and then you're excused."

"But what'd it look like?" he persists. "I want to know."

"You heard me," I say. "Did you hear me, Dean? Dean!" I want to shake him. I want to shake him until he cries.

"Do what your mother says," Stuart tells him quietly. "It was just a body, and that's all there is to tell."

I am clearing the table when Stuart comes up behind and touches my arm. His fingers burn. I start, almost losing a plate.

"What's the matter with you?" he says, dropping his hand. "Tell me, Claire, what is it?"

"You scared me," I say.

"That's what I mean. I should be able to touch you without you jumping out of your skin." He stands in front of me with a little grin, trying to catch my eyes, and then he puts his arm around my waist. With his other hand he takes my free hand and puts it on the front of his pants.

"Please, Stuart." I pull away and he steps back and snaps his fingers.

"Hell with it, then," he says. "Be that way if you want. But just remember."

"Remember what?" I say quickly. I look at him and hold my breath.

He shrugs. "Nothing, nothing," he says and cracks his knuckles.

The second thing that happens is that while we are watching television that evening, he in his leather reclining chair, I on the couch with a blanket and magazine, the house quiet except for the television, a voice cuts into the program to say that the murdered girl has been identified. Full details will follow on the eleven o'clock news.

We look at each other. In a few minutes he gets up and says he is going to fix a nightcap. Do I want one?

"No," I say.

"I don't mind drinking alone," he says. "I thought I'd ask."

I can see he is obscurely hurt, and I look away, ashamed and yet angry at the same time.

He stays in the kitchen for a long while, but comes back with his drink when the news begins.

First the announcer repeats the story of the four local fishermen finding the body, then the station shows a high school graduation photograph of the girl, a dark-haired girl with a round face and full, smiling lips, then a film of the girl's parents entering the funeral home to make the identification. Bewildered, sad, they shuffle slowly up the sidewalk to the front steps to where a man in a dark suit stands waiting and holding the door. Then, it seems as if only a second has passed, as if they have merely gone inside the door and turned around and come out again, the same couple is shown leaving the mortuary, the woman in tears, covering her face with a handkerchief, the man stopping long enough to say to a reporter, "It's her, it's Susan. I can't say anything right now. I hope they get the person or persons who did it before it happens again. It's all this violence . . ." He motions feebly at the television camera.

Then the man and woman get into an old car and drive away into the late afternoon traffic.

The announcer goes on to say that the girl, Susan Miller, had gotten off work as a cashier in a movie theater in Summit, a town 120 miles north of our town. A green late-model car pulled up in front of the theater and the girl, who according to witnesses looked as if she'd been waiting, went over to the car and got in, leading authorities to suspect that the driver of the car was a friend, or at least an acquaintance. The authorities would like to talk to the driver of the green car.

Stuart clears his throat, then leans back in the chair and sips his drink.

The third thing that happens is that after the news Stuart stretches, yawns, and looks at me. I get up and begin making a bed for myself on the couch.

"What are you doing?" he says, puzzled.

"I'm not sleepy," I say, avoiding his eyes. "I think I'll stay up awhile longer and then read something until I fall asleep."

He stares as I spread a sheet over the couch. When I start to go for a pillow, he stands at the bedroom door, blocking the way.

"I'm going to ask you once more," he says. "What the hell do you think you're going to accomplish?"

"I need to be by myself tonight," I say. "I just need to have time to think."

He lets out breath. "I'm thinking you're making a big mistake by doing this. I'm thinking you'd better think again about what you're doing. Claire?"

I can't answer. I don't know what I want to say. I turn and begin to tuck in the edges of the blanket. He stares at me a minute longer and then I see him raise his shoulders. "Suit yourself, then. I could give a fuck less what you do," he says and turns and walks down the hall scratching his neck.

This morning I read in the paper that services for Susan Miller are to be held in Chapel of the Pines, Summit, at two o'clock the next afternoon. Also, that police have taken statements from three people who saw her get into the green Chevrolet, but they still have no license number for the car. They are getting warmer, though, the investigation is continuing. I sit for a long while holding the paper, thinking, then I call to make an appointment at the hairdresser's.

I sit under the dryer with a magazine on my lap and let Millie do my nails.

"I'm going to a funeral tomorrow," I say after we have talked a bit about a girl who no longer works there.

Millie looks up at me and then back at my fingers. "I'm sorry to hear that, Mrs. Kane. I'm real sorry."

"It's a young girl's funeral," I say.

"That's the worst kind. My sister died when I was a girl, and I'm still not over it to this day. Who died?" she says after a minute.

"A girl. We weren't all that close, you know, but still."

"Too bad. I'm real sorry. But we'll get you fixed up for it, don't worry. How's that look?"

"That looks . . . fine. Millie, did you ever wish you were somebody else, or else just nobody, nothing, nothing at all?"

She looks at me. "I can't say I ever felt that, no. No, if I was somebody else I'd be afraid I might not like who I was." She holds my fingers and seems to think about something for a minute. "I don't know, I just don't know . . . Let me have your other hand now, Mrs. Kane."

At eleven o'clock that night I make another bed on the couch and this time Stuart only looks at me, rolls his tongue behind his lips, and goes down the hall to the bedroom. In the night I wake and listen to the wind slamming the gate against the fence. I don't want to be awake, and I lie for a long while with my eyes closed. Finally I get up and go down the hall with my pillow. The light is burning in our bedroom and Stuart is on his back with his mouth open, breathing heavily. I go into Dean's room and get into bed with him. In his sleep he moves over to give me space. I lie there for a minute and then hold him, my face against his hair.

"What is it, Mama?" he says.

"Nothing, honey. Go back to sleep. It's nothing, it's all right."

I get up when I hear Stuart's alarm, put on coffee and prepare breakfast while he shaves.

He appears in the kitchen doorway, towel over his bare shoulder, appraising.

"Here's coffee," I say. "Eggs will be ready in a minute."

He nods.

I wake Dean and the three of us have breakfast. Once or twice Stuart looks at me as if he wants to say something, but each time I ask Dean if he wants more milk, more toast, etc.

"I'll call you today," Stuart says as he opens the door.

"I don't think I'll be home today," I say quickly. "I have a lot of things to do today. In fact, I may be late for dinner."

"All right. Sure." He wants to know, he moves his briefcase from one hand to the other. "Maybe we'll go out for dinner tonight? How would you like that?" He keeps looking at me. He's forgotten about the girl already. "Are you . . . all right?"

I move to straighten his tie, then drop my hand. He wants to kiss me good-bye. I move back a step. "Have a nice day, then," he says finally. Then he turns and goes down the walk to his car.

I dress carefully. I try on a hat that I haven't worn in several years and look at myself in the mirror. Then I remove the hat, apply a light makeup, and write a note for Dean.

> Honey, Mommy has things to do this afternoon,
> but will be home later. You are to stay in the house
> or in the backyard until one of us comes home.
>
>   Love

I look at the word "Love" and then I underline it. As I am writing the note I realize I don't know whether backyard is one word or two. I have never considered it before. I think about it and then I draw a line and make two words of it.

I stop for gas and ask directions to Summit. Barry, a forty-year-old mechanic with a moustache, comes out from the rest-room and leans against the front fender while the other man, Lewis, puts the hose into the tank and begins to slowly wash the windshields.

"Summit," Barry says, looking at me and smoothing a finger down each side of his moustache. "There's no best way to get to Summit, Mrs. Kane. It's about a two-, two-and-a-half-hour drive each way. Across the mountains. It's quite a drive for a woman. Summit? What's in Summit, Mrs. Kane?"

"I have business," I say, vaguely uneasy. Lewis has gone to wait on another car.

"Ah. Well, if I wasn't all tied up there"—he gestures with his thumb toward the bay—"I'd offer to drive you to Summit and back again. Road's not all that good. I mean it's good enough, there's just a lot of curves and so on."

"I'll be all right. But thank you." He leans against the fender. I can feel his eyes as I open my purse.

Barry takes the credit card. "Don't drive it at night," he says. "It's not all that good a road, like I said, and while I'd be willing to bet you wouldn't have car trouble with this, I know this car, you can never be sure about blowouts and things like that. Just to be on the safe side I'd better check these tires." He taps one of the front tires with his shoe. "We'll run it onto the hoist. Won't take long."

"No, no, it's all right. Really, I can't take any more time. The tires look fine to me."

"Only takes a minute," he says. "Be on the safe side."

"I said no. No! They look fine to me. I have to go now, Barry . . ."

"Mrs. Kane?"

"I have to go now."

I sign something. He gives me the receipt, the card, some stamps. I put everything in my purse. "You take it easy," he says. "Be seeing you."

Waiting to pull into traffic, I look back and see him watching. I close my eyes, then open them. He waves.

I turn at the first light, then turn again and drive until I come to the highway and read the sign: SUMMIT 117 miles. It is ten thirty and warm.

The highway skirts the edge of town, then passes through farm country, through fields of oats and sugar beets and apple orchards, with here and there a small herd of cattle grazing in open pastures. Then everything changes, the farms become fewer and fewer, more like shacks now than houses, and stands of timber replace the orchards. All at once I'm in the mountains and on the right, far below, I catch glimpses of the Naches River.

In a little while a green pickup truck comes up behind me and stays behind for miles. I keep slowing at the wrong times, hoping he will pass, and then increasing my speed, again at the wrong times. I grip the wheel until my fingers hurt. Then on a long clear stretch he does pass, but he drives along beside for a minute, a crew-cut man in a blue workshirt in his early thirties, and we look at each other. Then he waves, toots the horn twice, and pulls ahead of me.

I slow down and find a place, a dirt road off of the shoulder, pull over and shut off the ignition. I can hear the river somewhere down below the trees. Ahead of me the dirt road goes into the trees. Then I hear the pickup returning.

I start the engine just as the truck pulls up behind me. I lock the doors and roll up the windows. Perspiration breaks on my face and arms as I put the car in gear, but there is no place to drive.

"You all right?" the man says as he comes up to the car. "Hello. Hello in there." He raps the glass. "Are you okay?" He leans his arms on the door then and brings his face close to the window.

I stare at him and can't find any words.

"After I passed I slowed up some," he says, "but when I didn't see you in the mirror I pulled off and waited a couple of minutes. When you still didn't show I thought I'd better drive back and check. Is everything all right? How come you're locked up in there?"

I shake my head.

"Come on, roll down your window. Hey, are you sure you're okay? Huh? You know it's not good for a woman to be batting around the country by herself." He shakes his head and looks at the highway and then back at me. "Now come on, roll down the window, how about it? We can't talk this way."

"Please, I have to go."

"Open the door, all right?" he says, as if he isn't listening. "At least roll down the window. You're going to smother in there." He looks at my breasts and legs. The skirt has pulled up over my knees. His eyes linger on my legs, but I sit still, afraid to move.

"I want to smother," I say. "I am smothering, can't you see?"

"What in the hell?" he says and moves back from the door. He turns and walks back to his truck. Then, in the side mirror, I watch him returning, and close my eyes.

"You don't want me to follow you toward Summit, or anything? I don't mind. I got some extra time this morning."

I shake my head again.

He hesitates and then shrugs. "Have it your way, then," he says.

I wait until he has reached the highway, and then I back out. He shifts gears and pulls away slowly, looking back at me in his rearview mirror. I stop the car on the shoulder and put my head on the wheel.

The casket is closed and covered with floral sprays. The organ begins soon after I take a seat near the back of the chapel. People begin to file in and find chairs, some middle-aged and older people, but most of them in their early twenties or even younger. They are people who look uncomfortable in their suits and ties, sports coats and slacks, their dark dresses and leather gloves. One boy in flared pants and a yellow short-sleeved shirt takes the chair next to mine and begins to bite his lips. A door opens at one side of the chapel and I look up and for a minute the parking lot reminds me of a meadow, but then the sun flashes on car windows. The family enters in a group and moves into a curtained area off to the side. Chairs creak as they settle themselves. In a few minutes a thick, blond man in a dark suit stands and asks us to bow our heads. He speaks a brief prayer for us, the living, and when he finishes he asks us to pray in silence for the soul of Susan Miller, departed. I close my eyes and remember her picture in the newspaper and on television. I see her leaving the theater and getting into the green Chevrolet. Then I imagine her journey down the river, the nude body hitting rocks, caught at by branches, the body floating and turning, her hair streaming in the water. Then the hands and hair catching in the overhanging branches, holding, until four men come along to stare at her. I can see a man who is drunk (Stuart?) take her by the wrist. Does anyone here know about that? What if these people knew that? I look around at the other faces. There is a connection to be made of these things, these events, these faces, if I can find it. My head aches with the effort to find it.

He talks about Susan Miller's gifts: cheerfulness and beauty, grace and enthusiasm. From behind the closed curtain someone clears his throat, someone else sobs. The organ music begins. The service is over.

Along with the others I file slowly past the casket. Then I

move out onto the front steps and into the bright, hot afternoon light. A middle-aged woman who limps as she goes down the stairs ahead of me reaches the sidewalk and looks around, her eyes falling on me. "Well, they got him," she says. "If that's any consolation. They arrested him this morning. I heard it on the radio before I came. A guy right here in town. A longhair, you might have guessed." We move a few steps down the hot sidewalk. People are starting cars. I put out my hand and hold on to a parking meter. Sunlight glances off polished hoods and fenders. My head swims. "He's admitted having relations with her that night, but he says he didn't kill her." She snorts. "You know as well as I do. But they'll probably put him on probation and then turn him loose."

"He might not have acted alone," I say. "They'll have to be sure. He might be covering up for someone, a brother, or some friends."

"I have known that child since she was a little girl," the woman goes on, and her lips tremble. "She used to come over and I'd bake cookies for her and let her eat them in front of the TV." She looks off and begins shaking her head as the tears roll down her cheeks.

3.

Stuart sits at the table with a drink in front of him. His eyes are red and for a minute I think he has been crying. He looks at me and doesn't say anything. For a wild instant I feel something has happened to Dean, and my heart turns.

Where is he? I say. Where is Dean?

Outside, he says.

Stuart, I'm so afraid, so afraid, I say, leaning against the door.

What are you afraid of, Claire? Tell me, honey, and maybe I can help. I'd like to help, just try me. That's what husbands are for.

I can't explain, I say. I'm just afraid. I feel like, I feel like, I feel like . . .

He drains his glass and stands up, not taking his eyes from me. I think I know what you need, honey. Let me play doctor, okay? Just take it easy now. He reaches an arm around my waist and with his other hand begins to unbutton my jacket, then my blouse. First things first, he says, trying to joke.

Not now, please, I say.

Not now, please, he says, teasing. Please nothing. Then he steps behind me and locks an arm around my waist. One of his hands slips under my brassiere.

Stop, stop, stop, I say. I stamp on his toes.

And then I am lifted up and then falling. I sit on the floor looking up at him and my neck hurts and my skirt is over my knees. He leans down and says, You go to hell, then, do you hear, bitch? I hope your cunt drops off before I touch it again. He sobs once and I realize he can't help it, he can't help himself either. I feel a rush of pity for him as he heads for the living room.

He didn't sleep at home last night.

This morning, flowers, red and yellow chrysanthemums. I am drinking coffee when the doorbell rings.

Mrs. Kane? the young man says, holding his box of flowers.

I nod and pull the robe tighter at my throat.

The man who called, he said you'd know. The boy looks at my robe, open at the throat, and touches his cap. He stands with his legs apart, feet firmly planted on the top step, as if asking me to touch him down there. Have a nice day, he says.

A little later the telephone rings and Stuart says, Honey, how are you? I'll be home early, I love you. Did you hear me? I love you, I'm sorry, I'll make it up to you. Good-bye, I have to run now.

I put the flowers into a vase in the center of the dining room table and then I move my things into the extra bedroom.

Last night, around midnight, Stuart breaks the lock on my door. He does it just to show me that he can, I suppose, for he does not do anything when the door springs open except stand there in his underwear looking surprised and foolish while the anger slips from his face. He shuts the door slowly and a few minutes later I hear him in the kitchen opening a tray of ice cubes.

He calls today to tell me that he's asked his mother to come stay with us for a few days. I wait a minute, thinking about this, and then hang up while he is still talking. But in a while I dial his number at work. When he finally comes on the line I say, It doesn't matter, Stuart. Really, I tell you it doesn't matter one way or the other.

I love you, he says.

He says something else and I listen and nod slowly. I feel sleepy. Then I wake up and say, For God's sake, Stuart, she was only a child.

Dummy

My father was very nervous and disagreeable for a long time after Dummy's death, and I believe it somehow marked the end of a halcyon period in his life, too, for it wasn't much later that his own health began to fail. First Dummy, then Pearl Harbor, then the move to my grandfather's farm near Wenatchee, where my father finished out his days caring for a dozen apple trees and five head of cattle.

For me, Dummy's death signaled the end of my extraordinarily long childhood, sending me forth, ready or not, into the world of men—where defeat and death are more in the natural order of things.

First my father blamed it on the woman, Dummy's wife. Then he said, no, it was the fish. If it hadn't been for the fish it wouldn't have happened. I know he felt some to blame for it, because it was Father showed Dummy the advertisement in the classified section of *Field and Stream* for "live black bass shipped anywhere in the U.S." (It may be there now, for all I know.) That was at work one afternoon and Father asked Dummy why not order some bass and stock that pond in back of his house. Dummy wet his lips, Father said, and studied the advertisement a long while before laboriously copying the information down on the back of a candy wrapper and stuffing the wrapper down the front of his coveralls. It was later, after he received the fish, he began acting peculiarly. They changed his whole personality, Father claimed.

I never knew his real name. If anyone else did, I never heard it called. Dummy it was then, and Dummy I remember him by now. He was a little wrinkled man in his late fifties, bald headed, short but very muscular arms and legs. If he grinned, which was seldom, his lips furled back over yellow, broken teeth and gave him an unpleasant, almost crafty expression; an expression I still remember very clearly, though it's been twenty-five years ago. His small watery eyes always watched your lips when you were speaking, though sometimes they'd roam familiarly over your face, or your body. I don't know why, but I had the impression he was never really deaf. At least, not as deaf as he made out. But that isn't important. He couldn't speak, that was certain enough. He worked at the sawmill where my father worked, the Cascade Lumber Company in Yakima, Washington, and it was the men there who had given him the nickname "Dummy." He had worked there ever since the early 1920s. He was working as a cleanup man when I knew him, though I guess at one time or another he'd done every kind of common-labor job around the plant. He wore a grease-spotted felt hat, a khaki work shirt, and a light denim jacket over a bulging pair of coveralls. In his top front pockets he nearly always carried two or three rolls of toilet paper, as one of his jobs was to clean and supply the men's toilets; and the men on nights used to walk off after their shift with a roll or two in their lunchboxes. He also carried a flashlight, even though he worked days, as well as wrenches, pliers, screw-drivers, friction tape, all the things the millwrights carried. Some of the newer men like Ted Slade or Johnny Wait might kid him pretty heavily in the lunchroom about something, or tell him dirty jokes to see what he'd do, just because they knew he didn't like dirty jokes; or Carl Lowe, the sawyer, might reach down and snag Dummy's hat as he walked under the platform, but Dummy seemed to take it all in stride, as if he expected to be kidded and had gotten used to it.

Once, though, one day when I took Father his lunch at noon, four or five of the men had Dummy off in a corner at one of the tables. One of the men was drawing a picture and, grin-ning, was trying to explain something to Dummy, touching here and there on the paper with his pencil. Dummy was frowning. His neck crimsoned as I watched, and he suddenly drew back and hit the table with his fist. After a moment's stunned silence, everyone at the table broke up with laughter.

My father didn't approve of the kidding. He never kidded Dummy, to my knowledge. Father was a big, heavy-shouldered man with a crew haircut, a double chin, and a paunch—which, given the chance, he was fond of showing off. He was easy to make laugh, just as easy, only in a different way, to get riled. Dummy would stop in the filing room where he worked and sit on a stool and watch Father use the big emery-wheel grinders on the saws, and, if he wasn't too busy, he'd talk to Dummy as he worked. Dummy seemed to like my father, and

Father liked him too, I'm certain. In his own way, Father was probably as good a friend as Dummy had.

Dummy lived in a small tarpaper-covered house near the river, five or six miles from town. A half mile behind the house, at the end of a pasture, lay a big gravel pit that the state had dug years before when they were paving the roads in that area. Three good-sized holes had been scooped out and over the years they had filled with water. Eventually, the three separate ponds had formed one really large pond, with a towering pile of rocks at one side, and two smaller piles on the other. The water was deep with a blackish-green look to it; clear enough at the surface, but murky down toward the bottom.

Dummy was married to a woman fifteen or twenty years younger than he, who had the reputation of going around with Mexicans. Father said later it was busybodies at the mill that helped get Dummy so worked up at the end by telling him things about his wife. She was a small stout woman with glittery, suspicious eyes. I'd seen her only twice; once when she came to the window the time Father and I arrived at Dummy's to go fishing, and one other time when Pete Jensen and I stopped there on our bicycles to get a glass of water.

It wasn't just the way she made us wait out on the porch in the hot sun without asking us in that made her seem so distant and unfriendly. It was partly the way she said, "What do you want?" when she opened the door, before we could say a word. Partly the way she scowled, and partly the house, I suppose, the dry musty smell that came through the open door and reminded me of my aunt Mary's cellar.

She was a lot different than other grown women I'd met. I just stared for a minute, before I could say anything.

"I'm Del Fraser's son. He works with, with your husband. We were just on our bicycles and thought we'd stop for a drink . . ."

"Just a minute," she said. "Wait here."

Pete and I looked at each other.

She returned with a little tin cup of water in each hand. I downed mine in a single gulp and then ran my tongue around the cool rim. She didn't offer us any more.

I said, "Thanks," handing back the cup and smacking my lips.

"Thanks a lot!" Pete said.

She watched us without saying anything. Then, as we started to get on our bicycles, she walked over to the edge of the porch.

"You little fellas had a car now, I might catch a ride into town with you." She grinned; her teeth looked shiny white and too large for her mouth from where I stood. It was worse than seeing her scowl. I turned the handle grips back and forth and stared at her uneasily.

"Let's go," Pete said to me. "Maybe Jerry'll give us a pop if his dad ain't there."

He started away on his bicycle and looked back a few seconds later at the woman standing on the porch, still grinning to herself at her little joke.

"I wouldn't take you to town if I had a car!" he called.

I pushed off hurriedly and followed him down the road without looking back.

There weren't many places you could fish for bass in our part of Washington: rainbow trout, mostly, a few brook trout and Dolly Varden in some of the high mountain streams, and silvers in Blue Lake and Lake Rimrock; that was mostly it, except for the migratory runs of steelhead and salmon in several of the freshwater rivers in the late fall. But if you were a fisherman, it was enough to keep you occupied. No one I knew fished for bass. A lot of people I knew had never seen a real bass, only pictures now and then in some of the outdoor magazines. But my father had seen plenty of bass when he was growing up in Arkansas and Georgia: back home, as he always referred to the South. Now, though, he just liked to fish and didn't care much what he caught. I don't think he minded if he caught anything; I believe he just liked the idea of staying out all day, eating sandwiches and drinking beer with friends while sitting in a boat, or else walking by himself up or down a riverbank and having time to think, if that's what he felt like doing that particular day.

Trout, then, all kinds of trout, salmon and steelhead in the fall, and whitefish in the winter on the Columbia River. Father would fish for anything, at any time of the year, and with pleasure, but I think he was especially pleased that Dummy was going to stock his pond with black bass, for of course, Father assumed that when the bass were large enough, he'd be able to

fish there as often as he wished, Dummy being a friend. His
eyes gleamed when he told me one evening that Dummy had
sent off in the mail for a supply of black bass.

"Our own private pond!" Father said. "Wait till you tie into
a bass, Jack! You'll be all done as a trout fisherman."

Three or four weeks later the fish arrived. I'd gone swimming at the city pool that afternoon and Father told me about
it later. He'd just gotten home from work and changed clothes
when Dummy pulled up in the driveway. With hands trembling he showed Father the wire from the parcel post he'd
found at home that said three tanks of live fish from Baton
Rouge, Louisiana, were waiting to be picked up. Father was
excited too, and he and Dummy went down right then in
Dummy's pickup.

The tanks—barrels, really—were each crated in white, clean-
smelling new pine boards, with large rectangular openings cut
on the sides and at the top of each crate. They were standing in
the shade around at the back of the train depot, and it took my
father and Dummy both to lift each crate into the back of the
truck.

Dummy drove very carefully through town and then twenty-
five miles an hour all the way to his house. He drove through
his yard without stopping, down to within fifty feet of the
pond. By that time it was nearly dark, and he had his head-
lights on. He had a hammer and tire iron under the seat and
jumped out with them in his hand as soon as they stopped.
They lugged all three tanks down close to the water before
Dummy started to open the first crate. He worked in the head-
lights from his truck, and once caught his thumb with the claw
side of the hammer. The blood oozed thickly out over the
white boards, but he didn't seem to notice. After he'd pried
the boards off the first tank, he found the barrel inside covered
thickly with burlap and a kind of rattan material. A heavy
board lid had a dozen nickel-sized holes scattered around.
They raised the lid and both of them moved up over the tank
as Dummy took out his flashlight. Inside, scores of little bass
fingerlings finned darkly in the water in the tank. The beam of
light didn't bother them, they just swam and circled darkly
without seeming to go anywhere. Dummy moved his light

around the tank several minutes before he snapped it off and dropped it back in his pocket. He picked up the barrel with a grunt, started down to the water.

"Wait a minute, Dummy, let me help you," Father called to him.

Dummy set the tank at the water's edge, again removed the lid, and slowly poured the contents into the pond. He took out his flashlight and shined it into the water. Father went down, but there was nothing to be seen; the fish had scattered. Frogs croaked hoarsely on all sides, and in the overhead dark, nighthawks wheeled and darted after insects.

"Let me get the other crate, Dummy," Father said, reaching as if to take the hammer from Dummy's coveralls.

Dummy pulled back and shook his head. He undid the two crates himself, leaving dark drops of blood on the boards, stopping long enough with each tank to shine his light through the clear water to where the little bass swam slowly and darkly from one side to the other. Dummy breathed heavily through his open mouth the whole time, and when he was through he gathered up all the boards and the burlap mesh and the barrels and threw everything noisily into the back of the truck.

From that night, Father maintained, Dummy was a different person. The change didn't come about all at once, of course, but after that night, gradually, ever gradually, Dummy moved closer to the abyss. His thumb was swollen and still bleeding some, and his eyes had a protruding, glassy look to them in the light from the dashboard, as he bounced the truck across the pasture, and then drove the road taking Father home.

That was the summer I was twelve.

Dummy wouldn't let anyone go there now, not after Father and I tried to fish there one afternoon two years later. In those two years Dummy had fenced all the pasture behind his house, then fenced the pond itself with electrically charged barbed wire. It cost him over five hundred dollars for materials alone, Father said to my mother in disgust.

Father wouldn't have any more to do with Dummy. Not since that afternoon we were out there, toward the end of July. Father had even stopped speaking to Dummy, and he wasn't the sort to cut anyone.

One evening just before fall, when Father was working late and I took him his dinner, a plate of hot food covered with aluminum foil, and a mason jar of ice tea, I found him standing in front of the window talking with Syd Glover, the millwright. Father gave a short, unnaturally harsh laugh just as I came in and said, "You'd guess that fool was married to them fish, the way he acts. I just wonder when the men in white coats will come to take him away."

"From what I hear," Syd said, "he'd do better to put that fence round his house. Or his bedroom, to be more exact."

Father looked around and saw me then, raised his eyebrows slightly. He looked back at Syd. "But I told you how he acted, didn't I, the time me and Jack was out to his house?" Syd nodded, and Father rubbed his chin reflectively, then spat out the open window into the sawdust, before turning to me with a greeting.

A month before, Father had finally prevailed upon Dummy to let the two of us fish the pond. Bulldozed him might be the better word, for Father said he decided he simply wasn't going to take any more excuses. He said he could see Dummy stiffen up when he kept insisting one day, but he went on talking fast, joking to Dummy about thinning out the weakest bass, doing the rest of the bass a favor, and so on. Dummy just stood there pulling at his ear and staring at the floor. Father finally said we'd see him tomorrow afternoon, then, right after work. Dummy turned and walked away.

I was excited. Father had told me before that the fish had multiplied crazily and it would be like dropping your line into a hatchery pond. We sat at the kitchen table that night long after Mother had gone to bed, talking and eating snacks and listening to the radio.

Next afternoon when Father pulled into the drive, I was waiting on the front lawn. I had his half-dozen old bass plugs out of their boxes, testing the sharpness of the treble hooks with my forefinger.

"You ready?" he called to me, jumping out of the car. "I'll go to the toilet in a hurry, you put the stuff in. You can drive us out there, if you want."

"You bet!" I said. Things were starting out great. I'd put everything in the backseat and started toward the house when

Father came out the front door wearing his canvas fishing hat and eating a piece of chocolate cake with both hands.

"Get in, get in," he said between bites. "You ready?"

I got in on the driver's side while he went around the car. Mother looked at us. A fair-skinned, severe woman, her blond hair pulled into a bun at the back of her head and fastened down with a rhinestone clip. Father waved to her.

I let off the hand brake and backed out slowly onto the road. She watched us until I shifted gears, and then waved, still unsmiling. I waved, and Father waved again. He'd finished his cake, and he wiped his hands on his pants. "We're off!" he said.

It was a fine afternoon. We had all the windows down in the 1940 Ford station wagon, and the air was cold and blew through the car. The telephone wires alongside the road made a humming noise, and after we crossed the Moxee Bridge and swung west onto Slater Road, a big rooster pheasant and two hens flew low across the road in front of us and pitched into an alfalfa field.

"Look at that!" Father said. "We'll have to come out here this fall. Harland Winters has bought a place out here somewheres, I don't know exactly where, but he said he'd let us hunt when the season opens."

On either side of us, green wavy alfalfa fields, with now and then a house, or a house with a barn and some livestock behind a rail fence. Farther on, to the west, a huge yellow-brown cornfield and behind that, a stand of white birch trees that grew beside the river. A few white clouds moved across the sky.

"It's really great, isn't it, Dad? I mean, I don't know, but everything's just fun we do, isn't it?"

Father sat in the seat cross-legged, tapping his toe against the floorboards. He put his arm out the window and let the wind take it. "Sure, it is. Everything." Then, after a minute, he said, "Sure, you bet it's fun! Great to be alive!"

In a few minutes we pulled up in front of Dummy's, and he came out of the house wearing his hat. His wife looked out the window.

"You have your frying pan out, Dummy?" Father called to him as he came down the porch steps. "Fillet of bass and fried potatoes."

Dummy came up to where we stood beside the car. "What a

day for it!" Father went on. "Where's your pole, Dummy? Ain't you going to fish?"

Dummy jerked his head back and forth, No. He moved his weight from one bandy leg to the other and looked at the ground and then at us. His tongue rested on his lower lip, and he began working his right foot into the dirt. I shouldered the wicker creel and immediately felt Dummy's eyes on me, watching, as I gave Father his pole and picked up my own.

"We ready?" Father said. "Dummy?"

Dummy took off his hat and, with the same hand, wiped his wrist over his bald head. He turned abruptly, and we followed him over to the fence, about a hundred feet behind his house. Father winked at me.

We walked slowly across the spongy pasture. There was a fresh, clean smell in the air. Every twenty feet or so snipe flew up from the clumps of grass at the edge of the old furrows, and once a hen mallard jumped off a tiny, almost invisible puddle of water, and flew off quacking loudly.

"Probably got her nest there," Father said. A few feet farther on he began whistling, but then stopped after a minute.

At the end of the pasture the ground sloped gently and became dry and rocky with a few nettle bushes and scrub oak trees scattered here and there. Ahead of us, behind a tall stand of willows, the first pile of rocks rose fifty or seventy-five feet in the air. We cut to the right, following an old set of car tracks, going through a field of milkweed that came up to our waists. The dry pods at the tops of the stalks rattled as we pushed through. Dummy was walking ahead, I followed two or three steps behind, and Father was behind me. Suddenly I saw the sheen of water over Dummy's shoulder, and my heart jumped. "There it is!" I blurted out. "There it is!" Father said after me, craning his neck to see. Dummy began walking even slower and kept bringing his hand up nervously and moving his hat back and forth over his head.

He stopped. Father came up beside him and said, "What do you think, Dummy? Is one place as good as another? Where should we come onto it?"

Dummy wet his lower lip and looked around at us as if frightened.

"What's the matter with you, Dummy?" Father said sharply. "This is your pond, ain't it? You act like we was trespassing or something."

Dummy looked down and picked an ant off the front of his coveralls.

"Well, hell," Father said, letting out his breath. He took out his watch. "If it's still all right with you, Dummy, we can fish for forty-five minutes or an hour. Before it gets dark. Huh? What about it?"

Dummy looked at him and then put his hands in his front pockets and turned toward the pond. He started walking again. Father looked at me and shrugged. We trailed along behind. Dummy acting the way he was took some of the edge off our excitement. Father spat two or three times without clearing his throat.

We could see the whole pond now, and the water was dimpled with rising fish. Every minute or so a bass would leap clear of the water and come down hugely in a great splash, sending the water across the pond in ever-widening circles. As we came closer we could hear the ker-splat-splat as they hit the water. "My God," Father said under his breath.

We came up to the pond at an open place, a gravel beach fifty feet long. Some shoulder-high water tules grew on the left, but the water was clear and open in front of us. The three of us stood there side by side a minute, watching the fish come up out toward the center.

"Get down!" Father said as he dropped into an awkward crouch. I dropped down too and peered into the water in front of us, where he was staring.

"Honest to God," he whispered.

A school of bass cruised slowly by, twenty or thirty of them, not one under two pounds.

The fish veered off slowly. Dummy was still standing, watching them. But a few minutes later the same school returned, swimming thickly under the dark water, almost touching one another. I could see their big, heavy-lidded eyes watching us as they finned slowly by, their shiny sides rippling under the water. They turned again, for the third time, and then went on, followed by two or three stragglers. It didn't make any difference if we sat down or stood up; the fish just weren't frightened of us. Father said later he felt sure Dummy came down there afternoons and fed them, because, instead of shying away from us as fish should do, these turned in even closer to the bank. "It was a sight to behold," he said afterwards.

We sat there for ten minutes, Father and I, watching the bass come swimming up out of the deep water and fin idly by in front of us. Dummy just stood there pulling at his fingers and looking around the pond as if he expected someone. I could look straight down the pond to where the tallest rock pile shelved into the water, the deepest part, Father said. I let my eyes roam around the perimeter of the pond—the grove of willows, the birch trees, the great tule bed at the far end, a block away, where blackbirds flew in and out, calling in their high, warbling summer voices. The sun was behind our backs now, pleasantly warm on my neck. There was no wind. All over the pond the bass were coming up to nuzzle the water, or jumping clear of the water and falling on their sides, or coming up to the surface to cruise with their dorsal fins sticking out of the water like black hand-fans.

We finally got up to cast and I was shaky with excitement. I could hardly take the plug hooks from the cork handle of the rod. Dummy suddenly gripped my shoulder with his big fingers, and I found his pinched face a few inches from mine. He bobbed his chin two or three times at my father. He wanted only one of us to cast, and that was Father.

"Shh-Jesus!" Father said, looking at us both. "Jesus Kayrist!" He laid his pole on the gravel after a minute. He took off his hat and then put it back on and glared at Dummy before he moved over to where I stood. "Go ahead, Jack," he said. "That's all right, go ahead, Son."

I looked at Dummy just before I cast; his face had gone rigid and there was a thin line of drool on his chin.

"Come back hard on the son of a bitch when he strikes," Father said. "Make sure you set the hooks; their mouths are as hard as a doorknob."

I flipped off the drag lever and threw back my arm, lurched forward and heaved the rattling yellow plug out as far as I could. It splatted the water forty feet away. Before I could begin winding to pick up the slack, the water boiled.

"Hit him!" Father yelled. "You got him! Hit him! Hit him again!"

I came back hard, twice. I had him, all right. The steel casting rod bowed over and sprung wildly back and forth. Father kept yelling, "Let him go, let him go! Let him run with it! Give him more line, Jack! Now wind in! Wind in! No, let him run! Woo-ee! Look at him go!"

The bass jump-jumped around the pond and every time it came up out of the water it shook its head, and we could hear the plug rattle. And then the bass would take off on another run. In ten minutes I had the fish on its side, a few feet from shore. It looked enormous, six or seven pounds, maybe, and it lay on its side, whipped, mouth open and gills working slowly. My knees felt so weak I could hardly stand, but I held the rod up, the line tight. Father waded out over his shoes.

Dummy began sputtering behind me, but I was afraid to take my eyes away from the fish. Father kept moving closer, leaning forward now, his arm reaching lower, trying to gill it. Dummy suddenly stepped in front of me and began shaking his head and waving his hands. Father glanced at him.

"Why, what the hell's the matter with you, you son of a bitch? This boy's got hold the biggest bass I've seen; he ain't going to throw him back. What's wrong with you?"

Dummy kept shaking his head and gesturing toward the pond.

"I'm not about to let this boy's fish go. You've got another think coming if you think I'm going to do that."

Dummy reached for my line. Meanwhile the bass had gained strength and turned over and started swimming back out again. I yelled and then, I lost my head, I guess; I slammed down the brake on the reel and started winding. The bass made a last, furious run, and the plug flew over our heads and caught in a tree branch.

"Come on, Jack," Father said, grabbing up his pole. "Let's get out of here before we're crazy as this son of a bitch. Come on, goddam him, before I knock him down."

We started away from the pond, Father snapping his jaws he was so angry. We walked fast. I wanted to cry but kept swallowing rapidly, trying to hold back the tears. Once Father stumbled over a rock and ran forward a few feet to keep from falling. "Goddam the son of a bitch," he muttered. The sun was almost down and a breeze had come up. I looked back over my shoulder and saw Dummy still down at the pond, only now he'd moved over by the willows and had one arm wrapped around a tree, was leaning over and looking down into the water. He looked very dark and tiny beside the water.

Father saw me look back, and he stopped and turned. "He's talking to them," he said. "He's telling them he's sorry. He's crazy as a coot, that son of a bitch! Come on."

That February the river flooded.

It had snowed heavily throughout our part of the state during the first weeks of December, and then the weather had turned very cold just before Christmas, the ground froze, and the snow remained fast on the ground. Toward the end of January the Chinook wind struck. I woke up one morning to hear the house being buffeted by the wind, and the steady drizzle of water running off the roof.

It blew for five days, and on the third day the river began to rise.

"It's up to fifteen feet," Father said one evening, looking up from the newspaper. "Three feet over flood level. Old Dummy's going to lose his fish."

I wanted to go down to the Moxee Bridge to see how high the water was running, but Father shook his head.

"A flood is nothing to see. I've seen all the floods I want to see."

Two days later the river crested, and after that the water slowly began to subside.

Orin Marshall and Danny Owens and I bicycled the five or six miles out to Dummy's one Saturday morning a week later. We parked the bicycles off the road before we got there and walked across pastureland that bordered Dummy's property.

It was a damp, blustery day, the clouds dark and broken, moving fast across the gray sky. The ground was soppy wet and we kept coming to puddles in the thick grass that we couldn't go around and so waded through. Danny was just learning how to cuss and filled the air with a wild string of profanities every time he stepped in over his shoes. We could see the swollen river at the end of the pasture, the water still high and out of its channel, surging around the trunks of trees and eating away at the edge of the land. Out toward the middle, the water moved heavily and swiftly, and now and then a bush floated by, or a tree with its branches sticking up.

We came to Dummy's fence and found a cow wedged in against the wire. She was bloated and her skin was slick-looking and gray. It was the first dead thing of any size any of us had seen. Orin took a stick and touched the open jelly eyes, then raised the tail and touched here and there with the stick.

We moved on down the fence, toward the river. We were afraid to touch the wire because we thought it might still carry an electric shock. But at the edge of what looked like a deep canal, the fence came to an abrupt end. The ground had simply dropped into the water here, and this part of the fence as well. We crossed through the wire and followed the swift channel that cut directly into Dummy's land and headed straight for his pond. Coming closer we saw that the channel had cut lengthwise into the pond, forced an outlet for itself at the other end, then twisted and turned several times, and re-joined the river a quarter of a mile away. The pond itself now looked like a part of the main river, broad and turbulent. There was no doubt that most of Dummy's fish had been carried away, and those that might remain would be free to come and go as they pleased when the water dropped.

Then I caught sight of Dummy. It scared me, seeing him, and I motioned to the other guys and we all got down. He was standing at the far side of the pond, near where the water rushed out, gazing into the rapids. In a while he looked up and saw us. We broke suddenly and fled the way we'd come, running like frightened rabbits.

"I can't help but feel sorry for old Dummy, though," Father said at dinner one night a few weeks later. "Things are going all to hell for him, that's for sure. He brought it on himself, but you can't help feeling sorry for him anyway."

Father went on to say George Laycock saw Dummy's wife sitting in the Sportsman's Club with a big Mexican fellow last Friday night. "And that ain't the half of it—"

Mother looked up at him sharply and then at me, but I just went on eating like I hadn't heard anything.

"Damn it to hell, Bea, the boy's old enough to know the facts of life! Anyway," he said after a minute, to no one in particular, "there's liable to be some trouble there."

He'd changed a lot, Dummy had. He was never around any of the men now, if he could help it. He didn't take his breaks at the same time, nor did he eat his lunch with them anymore. No one felt like joking with him any longer, either, since he chased Carl Lowe with a two-by-four stud after Carl knocked his hat off. He was missing a day or two a week from work on the average, and there was some talk of his being laid off.

"He's going off the deep end," Father said. "Clear crazy if he don't watch out."

Then on a Sunday afternoon in May, just before my birthday, Father and I were cleaning the garage. It was a warm, still day and the dust hung in the air in the garage. Mother came to the back door and said, "Del, there's a call for you. I think it's Vern."

I followed him inside to wash up, and I heard him take the phone and say, "Vern? How are you? What? Don't tell me that, Vern. No! God, that ain't true, Vern. All right. Yes. Good-bye."

He put the phone down and turned to us. His face was pale and he put his hand on the table.

"Some bad news . . . It's Dummy. He drowned himself last night and killed his wife with a hammer. Vern just heard it on the radio."

We drove out there an hour later. Cars were parked in front of the house, and between the house and the pasture. Two or three sheriff's cars, a highway patrol car, and several other cars. The gate to the pasture stood open, and I could see tire marks that led toward the pond.

The screen door was propped open with a box, and a thin, pock-faced man in slacks and sports shirt and wearing a shoulder holster stood in the doorway. He watched us get out of the station wagon.

"What happened?" Father asked.

The man shook his head. "Have to read about it in the paper tomorrow night."

"Did they . . . find him?"

"Not yet. They're still dragging."

"All right if we walk down? I knew him pretty well."

"Don't matter to me. They might chase you off down there, though."

"You want to stay here, Jack?" Father asked.

"No," I said, "I guess I'll go along."

We walked across the pasture, following the tire marks, taking pretty much the same route as we had the summer before.

As we got closer we could hear the motorboats, could see the dirty fluffs of exhaust smoke hanging over the pond. There was only a small trickle of water coming in and leaving the pond now, though you could see where the high water had cut away the ground and carried off rocks and trees. Two small boats with two uniformed men in each cruised slowly back and forth over the water. One man steered from the front, and the other man sat in the back, handling the rope for the hooks.

An ambulance was parked on the gravel beach where we'd fished that evening so long ago, and two men in white lounged against the back, smoking cigarettes.

The door was open on the sheriff's car parked a few feet the other side of the ambulance, and I could hear a loud crackling voice coming over the speaker.

"What happened?" Father asked the deputy, who was standing near the water, hands on hips, watching one of the boats. "I knew him pretty well," he added. "We worked together."

"Murder and suicide, it appears," the man said, taking an unlit cigar from his mouth. He looked us over and then looked back at the boat again.

"How'd it happen?" Father persisted.

The deputy hooked his fingers under his belt, shifted the large revolver a little more comfortably on his broad hip. He spoke from the side of his mouth, around his cigar.

"He took the wife out of a bar last night and beat her to death in the truck with a hammer. There was witnesses. Then . . . whatever his name is . . . he drove to this here pond with the woman in the truck still, and just jumped in over his head. Beats all. I don't know, couldn't swim, I guess, but I don't know that . . . But they say it's hard for a man to drown himself, just give up and drown without even trying, if he knows how to swim. A fellow named Garcy or Garcia followed them home. Had been chasing after the woman, from what we gather, but he claims he saw the man jump in from off that rock pile, and then he found the woman in the truck, dead." He spat. "A hell of a mix-up, ain't it?"

One of the motors suddenly cut. We all looked up. The man in back of one of the boats stood up, began pulling heavily on his rope.

"Let's hope they got him," the deputy said. "I'd like to get home."

In a minute or two I saw an arm emerge out of the water; the hooks had evidently struck him in the side, or the back. The arm submerged a minute later and then reappeared, along with a shapeless bundle of something. It's not him, I thought for an instant, it's something else that has been in the pond for months.

The man in the front of the boat moved to the back, and together they hauled the dripping bundle over the side.

I looked at Father, who'd turned away, lips trembling. His face was lined, set. He looked older, suddenly, and terrified. He turned to me and said, "Women! That's what the wrong kind of woman can do for you, Jack."

But he stammered when he said it and moved his feet uncomfortably, and I don't think he really believed it. He just didn't know what else to say at the time. I'm not sure what he believed, I only know he was frightened with the sight, as I was. But it seemed to me life became more difficult for him after that, that he was never able to act happy and carefree anymore. Not like he used to act, anyway. For myself, I knew I wouldn't forget the sight of that arm emerging out of the water. Like some kind of mysterious and terrible signal, it seemed to herald the misfortune that dogged our family in the coming years.

But that was an impressionable period, from twelve to twenty. Now that I'm older, as old as my father was then, have lived awhile in the world—been around some, as they say—I know it now for what it was, that arm. Simply, the arm of a drowned man. I have seen others.

"Let's go home," my father said.

Pie

HER car was there, no others, and Burt gave thanks for that. He pulled into the drive and stopped beside the pie he'd dropped last night. It was still there, the aluminum pan upside down, the pumpkin splattered on the pavement. It was Friday, almost noon, the day after Christmas.

He'd come on Christmas Day to visit his wife and children. But Vera told him before he came that he had to be gone before six o'clock when her friend and his children were coming for dinner. They had sat in the living room and solemnly opened the presents he had brought. The lights on the Christmas tree blinked. Packages wrapped in shiny paper and secured with ribbons and bows lay stuffed under the tree waiting for six o'clock. He watched the children, Terri and Jack, open their gifts. He waited while Vera's fingers carefully undid the ribbon and tape on her present. She unwrapped the paper. She opened the box and took out a beige cashmere sweater.

"It's nice," she said. "Thank you, Burt."

"Try it on," Terri said to her mother.

"Put it on, Mom," Jack said. "All *right*, Dad."

Burt looked at his son, grateful for this show of support. He could ask Jack to ride his bicycle over some morning during these holidays and they'd go out for breakfast.

She did try it on. She went into the bedroom and came out running her hands up and down the front of the sweater. "It's nice," she said.

"It looks great on you," Burt said and felt a welling in his chest.

He opened his gifts: from Vera a certificate for twenty dollars at Sondheim's men's store; a matching comb and brush set from Terri; handkerchiefs, three pair of socks, and a ballpoint pen from Jack. He and Vera drank rum and Coke. It grew dark outside and became five-thirty. Terri looked at her mother and got up and began to set the dining room table. Jack went to his room. Burt liked it where he was, in front of the fireplace, a glass in his hand, the smell of turkey in the air. Vera went into the kitchen. Burt leaned back on the sofa.

Christmas carols came to him from the radio in Vera's bedroom. From time to time Terri walked into the dining room
with something for the table. Burt watched as she placed linen
napkins in the wine glasses. A slender vase with a single red
rose appeared. Then Vera and Terri began talking in low voices
in the kitchen. He finished his drink. A little wax and sawdust
log burned on the grate, giving off red, blue, and green
flames. He got up from the sofa and put eight logs, the entire
carton, into the fireplace. He watched until they began to
flame. Then, making for the patio door, he caught sight of the
pies lined up on the sideboard. He stacked them up in his
arms; there were five of them, pumpkin and mincemeat—she
must think she was feeding a soccer team. He got out of the
house with the pies. But in the drive, in the dark, he'd dropped
a pie as he fumbled with the car door.

Now he walked around the broken pie and headed for the
patio door. The front door was permanently closed since that
night his key had broken off inside the lock. It was an overcast
day, the air damp and sharp. Vera was saying he'd tried to burn
the house down last night. That's what she'd told the children,
what Terri had repeated to him when he called the house this
morning to apologize. "Mom said you tried to burn the house
down last night," Terri had said and laughed. He wanted to
set the record straight. He also wanted to talk about things in
general.

There was a wreath made out of pinecones on the patio
door. He rapped on the glass. Vera looked out at him and
frowned. She was in her bathrobe. She opened the door a little.

"Vera, I want to apologize for last night," he said. "I'm
sorry I did what I did. It was stupid. I want to apologize to the
kids, too."

"They're not here," she said. "Terri is off with her boyfriend, that son of a bitch and his motorcycle, and Jack is playing
football." She stood in the doorway and he stood on the patio
next to the philodendron plant. He pulled at some lint on his
coat sleeve. "I can't take any more scenes after last night," she
said. "I've had it, Burt. You literally tried to burn the house
down last night."

"I did not."

"You did. Everybody here was a witness. You ought to see the fireplace. You almost caught the wall on fire."

"Can I come in for a minute and talk about it?" he said. "Vera?"

She looked at him. She pulled the robe together at her throat and moved back inside.

"Come in," she said. "But I have to go somewhere in an hour. And please try to restrain yourself. Don't pull anything again, Burt. Don't for God's sake try to burn my house down again."

"Vera, for heaven's sake."

"It's true."

He didn't answer. He looked around. The Christmas tree lights blinked off and on. There was a pile of soft tissue papers and empty boxes at the end of the sofa. A turkey carcass filled a platter in the center of the dining room table. The bones were picked clean and the leathery remains sat upright in a bed of parsley as if in a kind of horrible nest. The napkins were soiled and had been dropped here and there on the table. Some of the dishes were stacked, and the cups and wine glasses had been moved to one end of the table, as if someone had started to clean up but thought better of it. It was true, the fireplace had black smoke stains reaching up the bricks toward the mantel. A mound of ash filled the fireplace, along with an empty Shasta cola can.

"Come out to the kitchen," Vera said. "I'll make some coffee. But I have to leave pretty soon."

"What time did your friend leave last night?"

"If you're going to start that you can go right now."

"Okay, okay."

He pulled a chair out and sat down at the kitchen table in front of the big ashtray. He closed his eyes and opened them. He moved the curtain aside and looked out at the backyard. A bicycle without a front wheel rested on its handlebars and seat. Weeds grew along the redwood fence.

"Thanksgiving?" she said. She ran water into a saucepan. "Do you remember Thanksgiving? I said then that was the last holiday you'd ever ruin for us. Eating bacon and eggs instead of turkey at ten o'clock at night. People can't live like that, Burt."

"I know it. I said I'm sorry, Vera. I meant it."

"Sorry isn't good enough anymore. It just isn't."

The pilot light was out again. She was at the stove trying to light the gas burner under the pan of water. "Don't burn yourself," he said. "Don't catch yourself on fire."

She didn't answer. She lit the ring.

He could imagine her robe catching fire and himself jumping up from the table, throwing her down onto the floor and rolling her over and over into the living room where he would cover her with his own body. Or should he run to the bedroom first for a blanket to throw over her?

"Vera?"

She looked at him.

"Do you have anything to drink around the house? Any of that rum left? I could use a drink this morning. Take the chill off."

"There's some vodka in the freezer, and there is rum around here somewhere, if the kids didn't drink it up."

"When did you start keeping vodka in the freezer?"

"Don't ask."

"Okay, I won't."

He took the vodka from the freezer, looked for a glass, then poured some into a cup he found on the counter.

"Are you just going to drink it like that, out of a cup? Jesus, Burt. What'd you want to talk about, anyway? I told you I have someplace to go. I have a flute lesson at one o'clock. What is it you want, Burt?"

"Are you still taking flute?"

"I just said so. What is it? Tell me what's on your mind, and then I have to get ready."

"I just wanted to say I was sorry about last night, for one thing. I was upset. I'm sorry."

"You're always upset at something. You were just drunk and wanted to take it out on us."

"That's not true."

"Why'd you come over here then, when you knew we had plans? You could have come the night before. I told you about the dinner I planned yesterday."

"It was Christmas. I wanted to drop off my gifts. You're still my family."

She didn't answer.

"I think you're right about this vodka," he said. "If you have any juice I'll mix this with some juice."

She opened the refrigerator and moved things around. "There's cran-apple juice, that's all."

"That's fine," he said. He got up and poured cran-apple juice into his cup, added more vodka, and stirred the drink with his little finger.

"I have to go to the bathroom," she said. "Just a minute."

He drank the cup of cran-apple juice and vodka and felt better. He lit a cigarette and tossed the match into the big ashtray. The bottom of the ashtray was covered with cigarette stubs and a layer of ash. He recognized Vera's brand, but there were some unfiltered cigarettes as well, and another brand—lavender-colored stubs heavy with lipstick. He got up and dumped the mess into the sack under the sink. The ashtray was a heavy piece of blue stoneware with raised edges they'd bought from a bearded potter on the mall in Santa Cruz. It was as big as a plate and maybe that's what it'd been intended for, a plate or a serving dish of some sort, but they'd immediately started using it as an ashtray. He put it back on the table and ground out his cigarette in it.

The water on the stove began to bubble just as the phone rang. She opened the bathroom door and called to him through the living room: "Answer that, will you? I'm just about to get into the shower."

The kitchen phone was on the counter in a corner behind the roasting pan. It kept ringing. He picked the receiver up cautiously.

"Is Charlie there?" a flat, toneless voice asked him.

"No," he said. "You must have the wrong number. This is 323-4464. You have the wrong number."

"Okay," the voice said.

But while he was seeing to the coffee, the phone rang again. He answered.

"Charlie?"

"You have the wrong number. Look here, you'd better check your numbers again. Look at your prefix." This time he left the receiver off the hook.

Vera came back into the kitchen wearing jeans and a white sweater and brushing her hair. He added instant coffee to the cups of hot water, stirred the coffee, and then floated vodka onto his coffee. He carried the cups over to the table.

She picked up the receiver, listened, and said, "What's this about? Who was on the phone?"

"Nobody," he said. "It was a wrong number. Who smokes lavender-colored cigarettes?"

"Terri. Who else would smoke such things?"

"I didn't know she was smoking these days," he said. "I haven't seen her smoking."

"Well, she is. I guess she doesn't want to do it in front of you yet," she said. "That's a laugh, if you think about it." She put down the hairbrush. "But that son of a bitch she's going out with, that's something else. He's trouble. He's been in and out of scrapes ever since he dropped out of high school."

"Tell me about it."

"I just did. He's a creep. I worry about it, but I don't know what I can do. My God, Burt, I've got my hands full. It makes you wonder sometimes."

She sat across the table from him and drank her coffee. They smoked and used the ashtray. There were things he wanted to say, words of devotion and regret, consoling things.

"Terri also steals my dope and smokes that too," Vera said, "if you really want to know what goes on around here."

"God almighty. She smokes dope?"

Vera nodded.

"I didn't come over here to hear that."

"What did you come over here for then? You didn't get all the pie last night?"

He recalled stacking pie on the floorboards of the car before driving away last night. Then he'd forgotten all about pie. The pies were still in the car. For a minute he thought he should tell her.

"Vera," he said. "It's Christmas, that's why I came."

"Christmas is over, thank God. Christmas has come and gone," she said. "I don't look forward to holidays anymore. I'll never look forward to another holiday as long as I live."

"What about me?" he said. "I don't look forward to holidays either, believe me. Well, there's only New Year's now to get through."

"You can get drunk," she said.

"I'm working on it," he said and felt the stirrings of anger.

The phone rang again.

"It's someone wanting Charlie," he said.

"What?"

"Charlie," he said.

Vera picked up the phone. She kept her back to Burt as she talked. Then she turned to him and said, "I'll take this call on the phone in the bedroom. Would you please hang up this phone after I've picked it up in there? I can tell, so hang it up when I say."

He didn't answer, but he took the receiver. She left the kitchen. He held the receiver to his ear and listened, but he couldn't hear anything at first. Then someone, a man, cleared his throat at the other end of the line. He heard Vera pick up the other phone and call to him: "Okay, you can hang it up now, Burt. I have it. Burt?"

He replaced the receiver in its cradle and stood looking at it. Then he opened the silverware drawer and pushed things around inside. He tried another drawer. He looked in the sink, then went into the dining room and found the carving knife on the platter. He held it under hot water until the grease broke. He wiped the blade dry on his sleeve. Then he moved to the phone, doubled the cord in his hand, and sawed through the plastic coating and the copper wire without any difficulty. He examined the ends of the cord. Then he shoved the phone back into its corner near the canisters.

Vera came in and said, "The phone went dead while I was talking. Did you do anything to the phone, Burt?" She looked at the phone and then picked it up from the counter. Three feet of green cord trailed from the phone.

"Son of a bitch," she said. "Well, that does it. Out, out, out, where you belong." She was shaking the phone at him. "That's it, Burt. I'm going to get a restraining order, that's what I'm going to get. Get out right now, before I call the police." The phone made a *ding* as she banged it down on the counter. "I'll go next door and call them if you don't leave now. You're destructive is what you are."

He had picked up the ashtray and was stepping back from

the table. He held the ashtray by its edge, his shoulders bunched. He was poised as if he were going to hurl it, like a discus.

"Please," she said. "Leave now. Burt, that's our ashtray. Please. Go now."

He left through the patio door after telling her good-bye. He wasn't certain, but he thought he'd proved something. He hoped he'd made it clear that he still loved her, and that he was jealous. But they hadn't talked. They'd soon have to have a serious talk. There were matters that needed sorting out, important things that still had to be discussed. They'd talk again. Maybe after these holidays were over and things were back to normal.

He walked around the pie in the drive and got into his car. He started the car and put it into reverse. He backed out into the street. Then he put the car in low gear and went forward.

The Calm

IT was Saturday morning. The days were short and there was chill in the air. I was getting a haircut. I was in the chair and three men were sitting along the wall across from me, waiting. Two of the men I'd never seen before, but one of them I recognized though couldn't place. I kept looking at him as the barber worked on my hair. He was moving a toothpick around in his mouth. He was heavyset, about fifty years old and had short wavy hair. I tried to place him, and then I saw him in a cap and uniform, wearing a gun, little eyes watchful behind the glasses as he stood in the bank lobby. He was a guard. Of the two other men, one was considerably the older, but with a full head of curly gray hair. He was smoking. The other, though not so old, was nearly bald on top, and the hair at the sides of his head hung in dark lanks over his ears. He had on logging boots and his pants were shiny with machine oil.

The barber put a hand on top of my head to turn me for a better look. Then he said to the guard, "Did you get your deer, Charles?"

I liked this barber. We weren't acquainted well enough to call each other by name, but when I came in for a haircut he knew me and knew I used to fish, so we'd talk fishing. I don't think he hunted, but he could talk on any subject and was a good listener. In this regard he was like some bartenders I've known.

"Bill, it's a funny story. The damnedest thing," the guard said. He removed the toothpick and laid it in the ashtray. He shook his head. "I did and yet I didn't. So yes and no to your question."

I didn't like his voice. For a big man the voice didn't fit. I thought of the word "wimpy" my son used to use. It was somehow feminine, the voice, and it was smug. Whatever it was it wasn't the kind of voice you'd expect, or want to listen to all day. The two other men looked at him. The older man was turning the pages of a magazine, smoking, and the other fellow was holding a newspaper. They put down what they were looking at and turned to listen.

"Go on, Charles," the barber said. "Let's hear it." He turned my head again, held the clippers a minute, then went back to work.

"We were up on Fikle Ridge, my old man and me and the kid. We were hunting those draws. My old man was stationed at the head of one draw, and me and the kid were on another. The kid had a hangover, goddamn his hide. It was in the afternoon and we'd been out since daybreak. The kid, he was pale around the gills and drank water all day, mine and his both. But we were in hopes of some of the hunters down below moving a deer up in our direction. We were sitting behind a log watching the draw. We'd heard shooting down in the valley."

"There's orchards down there," said the fellow with the newspaper. He fidgeted a lot and kept crossing a leg, swinging his boot for a time, and then crossing the other leg. "Those deer hang out around those orchards."

"That's right," the guard said. "They'll go in there at night, the bastards, and eat those green apples. Well, we'd heard shooting earlier in the day, as I said, and we were just sitting there on our hands when this big old buck comes up out of the underbrush not a hundred feet in front of us. The kid saw him the same time I did, of course, and threw down and started banging at him, the knothead. The old buck wasn't in any danger from the kid as it turns out, but at first he couldn't tell where the shots were coming from. He didn't know which way to jump. Then I got off a shot, but in all the commotion I just stunned him."

"Stunned him," the barber said.

"You know, stunned him," the guard said. "It was a gut shot. It just stunned him, like. He dropped his head and began trembling. He trembled all over. The kid was still shooting. I felt like I was back in Korea. I shot again but missed. Then old Mr. Buck moves off into the brush once more, but now, by God, he didn't have any what you'd call bounce left in him. The kid had emptied his gun by this time to no purpose, but I'd hit him. I'd rammed one right in his guts and that took the wind out of his sails. That's what I meant by stunning him."

"Then what?" The fellow had rolled his newspaper and was tapping it against his knee. "What then? You must have trailed him. Invariably, they'll find a hard place to die."

I looked at this fellow again. I still recall those words. The older man had been listening all the while, watching as the guard told his story. The guard was relishing his limelight.

"But you trailed him?" the older man asked, though it wasn't really a question.

"I did. Me and the kid, we trailed him. But the kid wasn't good for much. He got sick on the trail. Slowed us down, that knothead." He had to laugh now, thinking about that situation. "Drinking beer and chasing all night, then thinking he can hunt deer the next day. He knows better now, by God. But we trailed him. A good trail, too. There was blood on the ground and blood on the leaves and honeysuckle. Blood everywhere. There was even blood on those pine trees he leant against, resting up. Never seen an old buck with so much blood. I don't know how he kept going. But it started to get dark on us, and we had to go back. I was worried about the old man, too, but I needn't have worried, as it turns out."

"Sometimes they'll just go forever. But invariably they'll find them a hard place to die," the fellow with the newspaper said, repeating himself for good measure.

"I chewed the kid out good for missing his shot in the first place, and when he started to say something back, I cuffed him I was so mad. Right here." He pointed to the side of his head and grinned. "I boxed his ears for him, that damn kid. He's not too old. He needed it."

"Well, the coyotes'll have that deer now," the fellow said. "Them and the crows and buzzards." He unrolled his newspaper, smoothed it out and put it off to one side. He crossed a leg again. He looked around at the rest of us and shook his head. But it didn't look like it mattered much one way or the other to him.

The older man had turned in his chair and was looking out the window at the dim morning sun. He lit a cigarette.

"I figure so," the guard said. "It's a pity. He was a big old son of a bitch. I wish I had his horns over my garage. But so, in answer to your question, Bill, I both got my deer and didn't get him. But we had venison on the table anyway, it turns out. The old man had got himself a little spike in the meantime. He already had him back to camp, hanging up and gutted slick as a whistle. Had the liver, heart, and kidneys wrapped in waxed paper and placed in the cooler already. He heard us coming down and met us just outside of camp. He held out his hands just all covered with dried blood. Didn't say a word. Old fart scared me at first. I didn't know for a minute what'd happened. Old hands looked like they'd been painted. 'Looky,' he said"—and here the guard held out his own plump hands—"'Looky here at what I've done.' Then we stepped into the light and I seen his little deer hanging there. A little spike. Just a little bastard, but the old man, he was tickled to death. Me and the kid didn't have anything to show for our day, except the kid, he was still hungover and pissed off and had a sore ear." He laughed and looked around the shop, as if remembering. Then he picked up his toothpick and stuck it back into his mouth.

The older man put his cigarette out and turned to Charles. He drew a breath and said, "You ought to be out there right now looking for that deer instead of in here getting a haircut. That's a disgusting story." Nobody said anything. A look of wonderment passed over the guard's features. He blinked his eyes. "I don't know you and I don't want to know you, but I don't think you or your kid or your old man ought to be allowed out in the woods with other hunters."

"You can't talk like that," the guard said. "You old asshole. I've seen you someplace."

"Well, I haven't seen you before. I'd recollect if I'd seen your fat face before."

"Boys, that's enough. This is my barbershop. It's my place of business. I can't have this."

"I ought to box *your* ears," the older man said. I thought for a minute he was going to pull up out of his chair. But his shoulders were rising and falling, and he was having a visible difficulty with his breathing.

"You ought to try it," the guard said.

"Charles, Albert's a friend of mine," the barber said. He had put his comb and scissors on the counter and had his hands on my shoulders now, as if I was thinking to spring from the chair into the middle of it. "Albert, I've been cutting Charles's head of hair, and his boy's too, for years now. I wish you wouldn't pursue this." He looked from one man to the other and kept his hands on my shoulders.

"Take it outside," the Invariably fellow said, flushed and hoping for something.

"That'll be enough," the barber said. "I don't want to have to be calling the law. Charles, I don't want to hear anything more on the subject. Albert, you're next in line, so if you'll just hold on a minute until I'm finished with this man. Now," he turned to Invariably, "I don't know you from Adam, but it would help things if you'd not put your oar in again."

The guard got up and said, "I think I'll come back for my cut later, Bill. Right now the company leaves something to be desired." He went out without looking at anybody and pulled the door closed, hard.

The older man sat there smoking his cigarette. He looked out the window for a minute, and then he examined something on the back of his hand. Then he got up and put on his hat.

"I'm sorry, Bill. That guy pushed a button, I guess. I can wait a few more days for a haircut. I don't have any engagements but one. I'll be seeing you next week."

"You come around next week then, Albert. You take it easy now. You hear? That's all right, Albert."

The man went outside, and the barber stepped over to the window to watch him go. "Albert's about dead from emphysema," he said from the window. "We used to fish together. He taught me everything there is to know about salmon fishing. The women. They used to just flock after him, that old boy. He's picked up a temper, though, in his later years. But I can't say, in all honesty, if there wasn't some provocation this morning." We watched him through the window get into his truck and shut the door. Then he started the engine and drove away.

Invariably couldn't sit still. He was on his feet and moving around the shop now, stopping to examine everything, the old wooden hat rack, photos of Bill and his friends holding stringers of fish, the calendar from the hardware store showing pictures of outdoor scenes for each month of the year—he flipped every page and came back to October—even going so far as to stand and scrutinize the barber's license, which was up on the wall at the end of the counter. He stood first on one foot and then the other, reading the fine print. Then he turned to the barber and said, "I think I'm going to get going too and come back later. I don't know about you, but I need a beer." He went out quickly, and we heard his car start.

"Well, do you want me to finish barbering this hair or not?" the barber said to me in a rough manner, as if I was the cause of this.

Somebody else came in then, a man wearing a jacket and tie. "Hello, Bill. What's happening?"

"Hello, Frank. Nothing worth repeating. What's new with you?"

"Nothing," the man said. He hung his jacket on the hat rack and loosened his tie. Then he sat down in a chair and picked up Invariably's newspaper.

The barber turned me in the chair to face the mirror. He put a hand on either side of my head and positioned me a last time. He brought his head down next to mine and we looked into the mirror together, his hands still encircling my head. I looked at myself, and he also looked at me. But if he saw something, he didn't ask any questions or offer any comment. He began then to run his fingers back and forth through my hair, slowly, as if thinking of something else the while. He ran his fingers through my hair as intimately, as tenderly, as a lover's fingers.

That was in Crescent City, California, up near the Oregon border. I left soon after. But today I was thinking of that place, Crescent City, and my attempt at a new life there with my wife, and how even then, in the chair that morning, I had made up my mind to leave and not look back. I recalled the calm I felt when I closed my eyes and let the fingers move through my hair, the sadness in those fingers, the hair already starting to grow again.

Mine

DURING the day the sun had come out and the snow melted into dirty water. Streaks of water ran down from the little, shoulder-high window that faced the backyard. Cars slushed by on the street outside. It was getting dark, outside and inside.

He was in the bedroom pushing clothes into a suitcase when she came to the door.

I'm glad you're leaving, I'm glad you're leaving! she said. Do you hear?

He kept on putting his things into the suitcase and didn't look up.

Son of a bitch! I'm so glad you're leaving! She began to cry. You can't even look me in the face, can you? Then she noticed the baby's picture on the bed and picked it up.

He looked at her and she wiped her eyes and stared at him before turning and going back to the living room.

Bring that back.

Just get your things and get out, she said.

He did not answer. He fastened the suitcase, put on his coat, and looked at the bedroom before turning off the light. Then he went out to the living room. She stood in the doorway of the little kitchen, holding the baby.

I want the baby, he said.

Are you crazy?

No, but I want the baby. I'll get someone to come by for his things.

You can go to hell! You're not touching this baby.

The baby had begun to cry and she uncovered the blanket from around his head.

Oh, oh, she said, looking at the baby.

He moved towards her.

For God's sake! she said. She took a step back into the kitchen.

I want the baby.

Get out of here!

She turned and tried to hold the baby over in a corner behind the stove as he came up.

He reached across the stove and tightened his hands on the baby.

Let go of him, he said.

Get away, get away! she cried.

The baby was red-faced and screaming. In the scuffle they knocked down a little flowerpot that hung behind the stove.

He crowded her into the wall then, trying to break her grip, holding onto the baby and pushing his weight against her arm.

Let go of him, he said.

Don't, she said, you're hurting him!

He didn't talk again. The kitchen window gave no light. In the near-dark he worked on her fisted fingers with one hand and with the other hand he gripped the screaming baby up under an arm near the shoulder.

She felt her fingers being forced open and the baby going from her. No, she said, just as her hands came loose. She would have it, this baby whose chubby face gazed up at them from the picture on the table. She grabbed for the baby's other arm. She caught the baby around the wrist and leaned back.

He would not give. He felt the baby going out of his hands and he pulled back hard. He pulled back very hard.

In this manner they decided the issue.

Distance

SHE'S in Milan for Christmas and wants to know what it was like when she was a kid. Always that on the rare occasions when he sees her.

Tell me, she says. Tell me what it was like then. She sips Strega, waits, eyes him closely.

She is a cool, slim, attractive girl. The father is proud of her, pleased and grateful she has passed safely through her adolescence into young womanhood.

That was a long time ago. That was twenty years ago, he tells her. They're in his apartment in the Via Fabroni near the Cascina Gardens.

You can remember, she says. Go on, tell me.

What do you want to hear? he asks. What else can I tell you? I could tell you about something that happened when you were a baby. Do you want to hear about their first real argument? It involves you, he says and smiles at her.

Tell me, she says and claps her hands with anticipation. But first get us another drink, please, so you won't have to interrupt halfway through.

He comes back from the kitchen with drinks, settles into his chair, begins slowly:

They were kids themselves, but they were crazy in love, this eighteen-year-old boy and his seventeen-year-old girlfriend when they married, and not all that long afterwards they had a daughter.

The baby came along in late November during a severe cold spell that just happened to coincide with the peak of the waterfowl season in that part of the country. The boy loved to hunt, you see, that's part of it.

The boy and girl, husband and wife now, father and mother, lived in a three-room apartment under a dentist's office. Each night they cleaned the upstairs in exchange for their rent and utilities. In summer they were expected to maintain the lawn and the flowers, and in winter the boy shoveled snow from the walks and spread rock salt on the pavement. Are you still with me?

167

I am, she says. A nice arrangement for everyone, dentist included.

That's right, he says. Except when the dentist found out they were using his letterhead stationery for their personal correspondence. But that's another story.

The two kids, as I've told you, were very much in love. On top of this they had great ambitions and they were wild dreamers. They were always talking about the things they were going to do and the places they were going to go.

He gets up from his chair and looks out the window for a minute over the slate rooftops at the snow that falls steadily through the weak late afternoon light.

Tell the story, she reminds gently.

The boy and girl slept in the bedroom and the baby slept in a crib in the living room. The baby was about three weeks old at this time and had only just begun to sleep through the night.

On this one Saturday night after finishing his work upstairs, the boy went into the dentist's private office, put his feet up on his desk, and called Carl Sutherland, an old hunting and fishing friend of his father's.

Carl, he said when the man picked up the receiver, I'm a father. We had a baby girl.

Congratulations, boy, Carl said. How is the wife?

She's fine, Carl. The baby's fine too, the boy said. We named her Catherine. Everybody's fine.

That's good, Carl said. I'm glad to hear it. Well, you give my regards to the wife. If you called about going hunting, I'll tell you something. The geese are flying down there to beat the band. I don't think I've ever seen so many of them and I've been going there for years. I shot five today, two this morning and three this afternoon. I'm going back in the morning and you come along if you want to.

I want to, the boy said. That's why I called.

You be here at five thirty then and we'll go, Carl said. Bring lots of shells. We'll get some shooting in all right, don't worry. I'll see you in the morning.

The boy liked Carl Sutherland. He had been a friend of the boy's father, who was dead now. After the father's death, maybe trying to replace a loss they both felt, the boy and Sutherland had started hunting together. Sutherland was a bluff, heavyset, balding man who lived alone and was not given to casual talk. Once in a while when they were together the boy felt uncomfortable, wondered if he had said or done something wrong because he was not used to being around people who kept still for long periods of time. But when he did talk the older man was often opinionated, and frequently the boy didn't agree with the opinions. Yet the man had a toughness about him and a woods knowledge that the boy liked and admired.

The boy hung up the telephone and went downstairs to tell the girl about going hunting the next morning. He was happy about going hunting, and he laid out his things a few minutes later: hunting coat and shell bag, boots, woolen socks, brown canvas hunting cap with fur earmuffs, 12-gauge pump shotgun, long john woolen underwear.

What time will you be back? the girl asked.

Probably around noon, he said, but maybe not until after five or six o'clock. Would that be too late?

It's fine, she said. Catherine and I will get along just fine. You go and have some fun, you deserve it. Maybe tomorrow evening we'll dress Catherine up and go visit Claire.

Sure, that sounds like a good idea, he said. Let's plan on that.

Claire was the girl's sister, ten years older. She was a striking woman. I don't know if you've seen pictures of her. (She hemorrhaged to death in a hotel in Seattle when you were about four.) The boy was a little in love with her, just as he was a little in love with Betsy, the girl's younger sister who was only fifteen then. Joking once he'd said to the girl, if we weren't married I could go for Claire.

What about Betsy? the girl had said. I hate to admit it but I truly feel she's better looking than Claire or me. What about her?

Betsy too, the boy said and laughed. Of course Betsy. But not in the same way I could go for Claire. Claire is older, but I don't know, there's something about her you could fall for. No, I believe I'd prefer Claire over Betsy, I think, if I had to make a choice.

But who do you really love? the girl asked. Who do you love most in all the world? Who's your wife?

You're my wife, the boy said.

And will we always love each other? the girl asked, enormously enjoying this conversation, he could tell.

Always, the boy said. And we'll always be together. We're like the Canadian geese, he said, taking the first comparison that came to mind, for they were often on his mind in those days. They only marry once. They choose a mate early in life, and then the two of them stay together always. If one of them dies or something the other one will never remarry. It will live off by itself somewhere, or even continue to live with the flock, but it will stay single and alone amongst all the other geese.

That's a sad fate, the girl said. It's sadder for it to live that way, I think, alone but with all the others, than just to live off by itself somewhere.

It is sad, the boy said, but it's a part of nature like everything else.

Have you ever killed one of those marriages? she asked. You know what I mean.

He nodded. Two or three times I've shot a goose, he said, then a minute or two later I'd see another one turn back from the rest and begin to circle and call over the goose that lay on the ground.

Did you shoot it too? she asked with concern.

If I could, he answered. Sometimes I missed.

And it didn't bother you? she asked.

Never, he said. You can't think about it when you're doing it. I love everything there is about hunting geese. And I love to just watch them even when I'm not hunting them. But there are all kinds of contradictions in life. You can't think about all the contradictions.

After dinner he turned up the furnace and helped her bathe the baby. He marveled again at the infant who had half his features, the eyes and mouth, and half the girl's, the chin, the nose. He powdered the tiny body and then powdered in between the fingers and toes. He watched the girl put the baby into its diaper and pajamas.

He emptied the bath into the shower basin and went upstairs. It was overcast and cold outside. His breath steamed in the air. The grass, what there was of it, reminded him of canvas, stiff and gray under the streetlight. Snow lay in piles beside the walk. A car went by and he heard sand grinding under the tires. He let himself imagine what it might be like tomorrow, geese milling in the air over his head, shotgun plunging against his shoulder.

Then he locked the door and went downstairs.

In bed they tried to read but both of them fell asleep, she first, letting the magazine sink to the quilt after a few minutes. His eyes closed, but he roused himself, checked the alarm, turned off the lamp.

He woke to the baby's cries. The light was on out there, and the girl was standing beside the crib rocking the baby in her arms. In a minute she put the baby down, turned out the light, and returned to bed.

It was two o'clock in the morning and the boy fell asleep again.

But half an hour later he heard the baby once more. This time the girl continued to sleep. The baby cried fitfully for a few minutes and stopped. The boy listened, then began to doze.

Again the baby's cries woke him. The living room light was burning. He sat up and turned on the lamp.

I don't know what's wrong, the girl said, walking back and forth with the baby. I've changed her and given her something more to eat, but she keeps crying. She won't stop crying. I'm so tired I'm afraid I might drop her.

You come back to bed, the boy said. I'll hold her for a while.

He got up and took the baby, and the girl went to lie down again.

Just rock her for a few minutes, the girl said from the bedroom. Maybe she'll go back to sleep.

The boy sat on the couch and held the baby, jiggling it in his lap until its eyes closed. His own eyes were near closing. He rose carefully and put the baby back in the crib.

It was quarter to four and he still had forty-five minutes. He crawled into bed and dropped off.

But a few minutes later the baby began to cry once more, and this time they both got up, and the boy swore.

For God's sake, what's the matter with you? the girl said to him. Maybe she's sick or something. Maybe we shouldn't have given her the bath.

The boy picked up the baby. The baby kicked its feet and

smiled. Look, he said, I really don't think there's anything wrong with her.

How do you know that? the girl said. Here, let me have her. I know that I ought to give her something, but I don't know what.

Her voice had an edginess that caused the boy to look at her closely.

After a few minutes and the baby had not cried, the girl put her down again. He and the girl looked at the baby, then looked at each other as the baby opened its eyes once more and began to cry.

The girl took the baby. Baby, baby, she said with tears in her eyes.

Probably it's something on her stomach, the boy said.

The girl didn't answer. She went on rocking the baby in her arms, paying no attention now to the boy.

The boy waited a minute longer, then went to the kitchen and put on water for coffee. He drew on his woolen underwear over his shorts and T-shirt, buttoned up, then got into his clothes.

What are you doing? the girl said to him.

Going hunting, he said.

I don't think you should, she said. Maybe you could go later on in the day if the baby is all right then, but I don't think you should go this morning. I don't want to be left alone with her like this.

Carl's planning on me going, the boy said. We've planned it.

I don't give a damn about what you and Carl have planned, she flared. And I don't give a damn about Carl either. I don't even know the man. I don't want you to go is all. I don't think you should even consider wanting to go under the circumstances.

You've met Carl before, you know him, the boy said. What do you mean you don't know him?

That's not the point and you know it, the girl said. The point is I don't intend to be left alone with a sick baby. If you weren't being selfish you'd realize that.

Now wait a minute, that's just not true, he said. You don't understand.

No, you don't understand, she said. I'm your wife. This is

your baby. She's sick or something, look at her. Why else is she crying? You can't leave us to go hunting.

Don't get hysterical about it, he said.

I'm saying you can go hunting anytime, she said. Something's wrong with this baby and you want to leave us to go hunting.

She began to cry then. She put the baby back in the crib, but the baby started again. The girl dried her eyes hastily on the sleeve of her nightgown and picked her up once more.

The boy laced his boots slowly, put on his shirt, sweater, and coat. The kettle whistled on the stove in the kitchen.

You're going to have to choose, the girl said. Carl or us, I mean it, you've got to choose.

What do you mean? the boy said slowly.

You heard what I said, the girl answered. If you want a family you're going to have to choose. If you go out that door you're not coming back, I'm serious.

They stared at each other. Then the boy took his hunting gear and went upstairs. He started the car after some difficulty, went around to the car windows and, making a job of it, scraped away the ice.

The temperature had dropped during the night, but the weather had cleared so that stars had come out, and now they gleamed in the sky over his head. Driving, the boy glanced up once at the stars and was moved when he considered their bright distance.

Carl's porch light was on, his station wagon parked in the drive with the motor idling. Carl came outside as the boy pulled to the curb. The boy had decided.

You might want to park off the street, Carl said as the boy came up the walk. I'm all ready, just let me hit the lights. I feel like hell, I really do, he went on. I thought maybe you had overslept so I just this minute finished calling your place. Your wife said you had left. I feel like hell calling.

It's okay, the boy said, trying to pick his words. He leaned his weight on one leg and turned up his collar. He put his hands in his coat pockets. She was already up, Carl. We've both been up for a while. I guess there's something wrong with the baby, I don't know. She keeps crying, I mean. The thing is, I guess I can't go this time. He shivered against the cold and looked away.

You should have stepped to the phone and called me, boy, Carl said. It's okay. Shoot, you know you didn't have to come over here to tell me. What the hell, this hunting business you can take it or leave it. It's not that important. You want a cup of coffee?

No thanks, I'd better get back, the boy said.

Well, since I'm already up and ready I expect I'll go ahead and go, Carl said. He looked at the boy and lit a cigarette.

The boy kept standing on the porch, not saying anything.

The way it's cleared up, Carl said, I don't look for much action this morning anyway. It sure is cold though.

The boy nodded. I'll see you, Carl, he said.

So long, Carl said. Hey, don't let anybody ever tell you otherwise, Carl called after him. You're a lucky boy and I mean that.

The boy started his car and waited, watched Carl go through the house and turn off all the lights. Then the boy put the car in gear and pulled away.

The living room light was on, but the girl was asleep on the bed and the baby was asleep beside her.

The boy took off his boots, pants, and shirt and, in his socks and woolen underwear, sat on the couch and read the Sunday paper.

Soon it began to turn light outside. The girl and the baby slept on. After a while the boy went to the kitchen and began to fry bacon.

The girl came out in her robe a few minutes later and put her arms around him without saying anything.

Hey, don't catch your robe on fire, the boy said. She was leaning against him but touching the stove too.

I'm sorry about earlier, she said. I don't know what got into me, why I said those things.

It's all right, he said. Here, honey, let me get this bacon.

I didn't mean to snap like that, she said. It was awful.

It was my fault, he said. How's Catherine?

She's fine now. I don't know what was the matter with her earlier. I changed her again after you left, and then she was fine. She was just fine then and went right off to sleep. I don't know what it was. Don't be mad with us though.

The boy laughed. I'm not mad with you, don't be silly, he said. Here, let me do something with this pan.

You sit down, the girl said. I'll fix the breakfast. How does a waffle sound with this bacon?

Sounds great, he said. I'm starved.

She took the bacon out of the pan and then made waffle batter. He sat at the table, relaxed now, and watched her move around the kitchen.

She left to close their bedroom door, then stopped in the living room to put on a record that they both liked.

We don't want to wake that one up again, the girl said.

She put a plate in front of him with bacon, a fried egg, and a waffle. She put another plate on the table for herself. It's ready, she said.

It looks swell, he said. He spread butter and poured syrup over the waffle, but as he started to cut into the waffle he turned the plate into his lap.

I don't believe it, he said, jumping up from the table.

The girl looked at him, then at the expression on his face, and she began to laugh.

If you could see yourself in the mirror, she said and kept laughing.

He looked down at the syrup that covered the front of his woolen underwear, at the pieces of waffle, bacon, and egg that clung to the syrup. He began to laugh.

I was starved, he said, shaking his head.

You were starved, she said, still laughing.

He peeled off the woolen underwear and threw it at the bathroom door. Then he opened his arms and she moved into them. They began to move very slowly to the recorded music, she in her robe, he in his shorts and T-shirt.

We won't fight anymore, will we? she said. It's not worth it, is it?

That's right, he said. Look how it makes you feel after.

We'll not fight anymore, she said.

When the record ended he kissed her for a long while on the lips. This was about eight o'clock in the morning, a cold Sunday in December.

He gets up from his chair and refills their glasses.

That's it, he says. End of story. I admit it's not much of one.

I was interested, she says. It was very interesting, if you want to know. But what happened? she asks. Later, I mean.

He shrugs and carries his drink over to the window. It's dark now but still snowing.

Things change, he says. Kids grow up. I don't know what happened. But things do change and without your realizing it or wanting them to.

Yes, that's true, only— But she does not finish.

She drops the subject then. In the window's reflection he sees her study her nails. Then she raises her head, asks brightly if he is, after all, going to show her something of the city.

Absolutely, he says. Put your boots on and let's get under way.

But he continues to stand at the window, remembering that gone life. After that morning there would be those hard times ahead, other women for him and another man for her, but that morning, that particular morning, they had danced. They danced, and then they held to each other as if there would always be that morning, and later they laughed about the waffle. They leaned on each other and laughed about it until tears came, while outside everything froze, for a while anyway.

Beginners

MY friend Herb McGinnis, a cardiologist, was talking. The four of us were sitting around his kitchen table drinking gin. It was Saturday afternoon. Sunlight filled the kitchen from the big window behind the sink. There were Herb and I and his second wife, Teresa—Terri, we called her— and my wife, Laura. We lived in Albuquerque, but we were all from somewhere else. There was an ice bucket on the table. The gin and the tonic water kept going around, and we somehow got on the subject of love. Herb thought real love was nothing less than spiritual love. When he was young he'd spent five years in a seminary before quitting to go to medical school. He'd left the Church at the same time, but he said he still looked back to those years in the seminary as the most important in his life.

Terri said the man she lived with before she lived with Herb loved her so much he tried to kill her. Herb laughed after she said this. He made a face. Terri looked at him. Then she said, "He beat me up one night, the last night we lived together. He dragged me around the living room by my ankles, all the while saying, 'I love you, don't you see? I love you, you bitch.' He went on dragging me around the living room, my head knocking on things." She looked around the table at us and then looked at her hands on her glass. "What do you do with love like that?" she said. She was a bone-thin woman with a pretty face, dark eyes, and brown hair that hung down her back. She liked necklaces made of turquoise, and long pendant earrings. She was fifteen years younger than Herb, had suffered periods of anorexia, and during the late sixties, before she'd gone to nursing school, had been a dropout, a "street person" as she put it. Herb sometimes called her, affectionately, his hippie.

"My God, don't be silly. That's not love, and you know it," Herb said. "I don't know what you'd call it—madness is what I'd call it—but it's sure as hell not love."

"Say what you want to, but I know he loved me," Terri said. "I know he did. It may sound crazy to you, but it's true just the same. People are different, Herb. Sure, sometimes he may have acted crazy. Okay. But he loved me. In his own way, maybe, but he loved me. There *was* love there, Herb. Don't deny me that."

Herb let out breath. He held his glass and turned to Laura and me. "He threatened to kill *me* too." He finished his drink and reached for the gin bottle. "Terri's a romantic. Terri's of the 'Kick-me-so-I'll-know-you-love-me' school. Terri, hon, don't look that way." He reached across the table and touched her cheek with his fingers. He grinned at her.

"Now he wants to make up," Terri said. "After he tries to dump on me." She wasn't smiling.

"Make up what?" Herb said. "What is there to make up? I know what I know, and that's all."

"What would you call it then?" Terri said. "How'd we get started on this subject anyway?" She raised her glass and drank. "Herb always has love on his mind," she said. "Don't you, honey?" She smiled now, and I thought that was the last of it.

"I just wouldn't call Carl's behavior love, that's all I'm saying, honey," Herb said. "What about you guys?" he said to Laura and me. "Does that sound like love to you?"

I shrugged. "I'm the wrong person to ask. I didn't even know the man. I've only heard his name mentioned in passing. Carl. I wouldn't know. You'd have to know all the particulars. Not in my book it isn't, but who's to say? There're lots of different ways of behaving and showing affection. That way doesn't happen to be mine. But what you're saying, Herb, is that love is an absolute?"

"The kind of love I'm talking about is," Herb said. "The kind of love I'm talking about, you don't try to kill people."

Laura, my sweet, big Laura, said evenly, "I don't know anything about Carl, or anything about the situation. Who can judge anyone else's situation? But, Terri, I didn't know about the violence."

I touched the back of Laura's hand. She gave me a quick smile, then turned her gaze back to Terri. I picked up Laura's hand. The hand was warm to the touch, the nails polished, perfectly manicured. I encircled the broad wrist with my fingers, like a bracelet, and held her.

"When I left he drank rat poison," Terri said. She clasped

her arms with her hands. "They took him to the hospital in Santa Fe where we lived then and they saved his life, and his gums separated. I mean they pulled away from his teeth. After that his teeth stood out like fangs. My God," she said. She waited a minute, then let go of her arms and picked up her glass.

"What people won't do!" Laura said. "I'm sorry for him and I don't even think I like him. Where is he now?"

"He's out of the action," Herb said. "He's dead." He handed me the saucer of limes. I took a section of lime, squeezed it over my drink, and stirred the ice cubes with my finger.

"It gets worse," Terri said. "He shot himself in the mouth, but he bungled that too. Poor Carl," she said. She shook her head.

"Poor Carl nothing," Herb said. "He was dangerous." Herb was forty-five years old. He was tall and rangy with wavy, graying hair. His face and arms were brown from the tennis he played. When he was sober, his gestures, all his movements, were precise and careful.

"He did love me though, Herb, grant me that," Terri said. "That's all I'm asking. He didn't love me the way you love me, I'm not saying that. But he loved me. You can grant me that, can't you? That's not much to ask."

"What do you mean, 'He bungled it'?" I asked. Laura leaned forward with her glass. She put her elbows on the table and held her glass in both hands. She glanced from Herb to Terri and waited with a look of bewilderment on her open face, as if amazed that such things happened to people you knew. Herb finished his drink. "How'd he bungle it when he killed himself?" I said again.

"I'll tell you what happened," Herb said. "He took this twenty-two pistol he'd bought to threaten Terri and me with —oh, I'm serious, he wanted to use it. You should have seen the way we lived in those days. Like fugitives. I even bought a gun myself, and I thought I was a nonviolent sort. But I bought a gun for self-defense and carried it in the glove compartment. Sometimes I'd have to leave the apartment in the middle of the night, you know, to go to the hospital. Terri and I weren't married then and my first wife had the house and kids, the dog, everything, and Terri and I were living in this apartment. Sometimes, as I say, I'd get a call in the middle of the night and have to go in to the hospital at two or three in the morning. It'd be dark out there in the parking lot and I'd break into a sweat before I could even get to my car. I never knew if he was going to come up out of the shrubbery or from behind a car and start shooting. I mean, he was crazy. He was capable of wiring a bomb to my car, anything. He used to call my answering service at all hours and say he needed to talk to the doctor, and when I'd return the call he'd say, 'Son of a bitch, your days are numbered.' Little things like that. It was scary, I'm telling you."

"I still feel sorry for him," Terri said. She sipped her drink and gazed at Herb. Herb stared back.

"It sounds like a nightmare," Laura said. "But what exactly happened after he shot himself?" Laura is a legal secretary. We'd met in a professional capacity, lots of other people around, but we'd talked and I'd asked her to have dinner with me. Before we knew it, it was a courtship. She's thirty-five, three years younger than I am. In addition to being in love, we like each other and enjoy one another's company. She's easy to be with. "What happened?" Laura asked again.

Herb waited a minute and turned the glass in his hand. Then he said, "He shot himself in the mouth in his room. Someone heard the shot and told the manager. They came in with a passkey, saw what had happened, and called an ambulance. I happened to be there when they brought him in to the emergency room. I was there on another case. He was still alive, but beyond anything anyone could do for him. Still, he lived for three days. I'm serious though, his head swelled up to twice the size of a normal head. I'd never seen anything like it, and I hope I never do again. Terri wanted to go in and sit with him when she found out about it. We had a fight over it. I didn't think she'd want to see him like that. I didn't think she should see him, and I still don't."

"Who won the fight?" Laura said.

"I was in the room with him when he died," Terri said. "He never regained consciousness, and there was no hope for him, but I sat with him. He didn't have anyone else."

"He was dangerous," Herb said. "If you call that love, you can have it."

"It was love," Terri said. "Sure it was abnormal in most people's eyes, but he was willing to die for it. He did die for it."

"I sure as hell wouldn't call it love," Herb said. "You don't know what he died for. I've seen a lot of suicides, and I couldn't say anyone close to them ever knew for sure. And when they claimed to be the cause, well I don't know." He put his hands behind his neck and leaned on the back legs of his chair. "I'm not interested in that kind of love. If that's love, you can have it."

After a minute, Terri said, "We were afraid. Herb even made a will out and wrote to his brother in California who used to be a Green Beret. He told him who to look for if something happened to him mysteriously. Or not so mysteriously!" She shook her head and laughed at it now. She drank from her glass. She went on. "But we did live a little like fugitives. We *were* afraid of him, no question. I even called the police at one point, but they were no help. They said they couldn't do anything to him, they couldn't arrest him or do anything unless he actually *did* something to Herb. Isn't that a laugh?" Terri said. She poured the last of the gin into her glass and wagged the bottle. Herb got up from the table and went to the cupboard. He took down another bottle of gin.

"Well, Nick and I are in love," Laura said. "Aren't we, Nick?" She bumped my knee with her knee. "You're supposed to say something now," she said and turned a large smile on me. "We get along really well, I think. We like doing things together, and neither of us has beaten up on the other yet, thank God. Knock on wood. I'd say we're pretty happy. I guess we should count our blessings."

For answer, I took her hand and raised it to my lips with a flourish. I made a production out of kissing her hand. Everyone was amused. "We're lucky," I said.

"You guys," Terri said. "Stop that now. You're making me sick! You're still on a honeymoon, that's why you can act like this. You're still gaga over each other yet. Just wait. How long have you been together now? How long has it been? A year? Longer than a year."

"Going on a year and a half," Laura said, still flushed and smiling.

"You're still on the honeymoon," Terri said again. "Wait a

while." She held her drink and gazed at Laura. "I'm only kidding," she said.

Herb had opened the gin and gone around the table with the bottle. "Terri, Jesus, you shouldn't talk like that, even if you're not serious, even if you are kidding. It's bad luck. Here, you guys. Let's have a toast. I want to propose a toast. A toast to love. True love," Herb said. We touched glasses.

"To love," we said.

Outside, in the backyard, one of the dogs began to bark. The leaves of the aspen tree that leaned past the window flickered in the breeze. The afternoon sunlight was like a presence in the room. There was suddenly a feeling of ease and generosity around the table, of friendship and comfort. We could have been anywhere. We raised our glasses again and grinned at each other like children who had agreed on something for once.

"I'll tell you what real love is," Herb said finally, breaking the spell. "I mean I'll give you a good example of it, and then you can draw your own conclusions." He poured a little more gin into his glass. He added an ice cube and a piece of lime. We waited and sipped our drinks. Laura and I touched knees again. I put a hand on her warm thigh and left it there.

"What do any of us really know about love?" Herb said. "I kind of mean what I'm saying too, if you'll pardon me for saying it. But it seems to me we're just rank beginners at love. We say we love each other and we do, I don't doubt it. We love each other and we love hard, all of us. I love Terri and Terri loves me, and you guys love each other. You know the kind of love I'm talking about now. Sexual love, that attraction to the other person, the partner, as well as just the plain everyday kind of love, love of the other person's being, the loving to be with the other, the little things that make up everyday love. Carnal love then and, well, call it sentimental love, the day-to-day caring about the other. But sometimes I have a hard time accounting for the fact that I must have loved my first wife too. But I did, I know I did. So I guess before you can say anything, I *am* like Terri in that regard. Terri and Carl." He thought about it a minute and then went on. "But at one time I thought I loved my first wife more than life itself, and we had the kids together. But now I hate her guts. I do. How do you figure that? What happened to that love? Did that love just get erased from the big board, as if it was never up there, as if it never happened? What happened to it is what I'd like to know. I wish someone could tell me. Then there's Carl. Okay, we're back to Carl. He loved Terri so much he tries to kill her and winds up killing himself." He stopped talking and shook his head. "You guys have been together eighteen months and you love each other, it shows all over you, you simply glow with it, but you've loved other people too before you met each other. You've both been married before, just like us. And you probably loved other people before that. Terri and I have been together five years, been married for four. And the terrible thing, the terrible thing is, but the good thing, too, the saving grace, you might say, is that if something happened to one of us—excuse me for saying this—but if something happened to one of us tomorrow, I think the other one, the other partner, would mourn for a while, you know, but then the surviving party would go out and love again, have someone else soon enough and all this, all of this love—Jesus, how can you figure it?—it would just be memory. Maybe not even memory. Maybe that's the way it's supposed to be. But am I wrong? Am I way off base? I know that's what would happen with us, with Terri and me, as much as we may love each other. With any one of us for that matter. I'll stick my neck out that much. We've all proved it anyhow. I just don't understand. Set me straight if you think I'm wrong. I want to know. I don't know anything, and I'm the first to admit it."

"Herb, for God's sake," Terri said. "This is depressing stuff. This could get very depressing. Even if you think it's true," she said, "it's still depressing." She reached out to him and took hold of his forearm near the wrist. "Are you getting drunk, Herb? Honey, are you drunk?"

"Honey, I'm just talking, all right," Herb said. "I don't have to be drunk to say what's on my mind, do I? I'm not drunk. We're just talking, right?" Herb said. Then his voice changed. "But if I want to get drunk I will, goddamn it. I can do anything I want today." He fixed his eyes on her.

"Honey, I'm not criticizing," she said. She picked up her glass.

"I'm not on call today," Herb said. "I can do anything I want today. I'm just tired, that's all."

"Herb, we love you," Laura said.

Herb looked at Laura. It was as if he couldn't place her for a minute. She kept looking at him, holding her smile. Her cheeks were flushed and the sun was hitting her in the eyes, so she squinted to see him. His features relaxed. "Love you too, Laura. And you, Nick. I'll tell you, you're our pals," Herb said. He picked up his glass. "Well, what was I saying? Yeah. I wanted to tell you about something that happened a while back. I think I wanted to prove a point, and I will if I can just tell this thing the way it happened. This happened a few months ago, but it's still going on right now. You might say that, yeah. But it ought to make us all feel ashamed when we talk like we know what we were talking about, when we talk about love."

"Herb, come on now," Terri said. "You are too drunk. Don't talk like this. Don't talk like you're drunk if you're not drunk."

"Just shut up for a minute, will you?" Herb said. "Let me tell this. It's been on my mind. Just shut up for a minute. I told you a little about it when it first happened. That old couple who got into an accident out on the interstate? A kid hit them and they were all battered up and not given much chance to pull through. Let me tell this, Terri. Now just shut up for a minute. Okay?"

Terri looked at us and then looked back at Herb. She seemed anxious, that's the only word for it. Herb handed the bottle around the table.

"Surprise me, Herb," Terri said. "Surprise me beyond all thought and reason."

"Maybe I will," Herb said. "Maybe so. I'm constantly surprised with things myself. Everything in my life surprises me." He stared at her for a minute. Then he began talking.

"I was on call that night. It was in May or June. Terri and I had just sat down to dinner, when the hospital called. There'd been an accident out on the interstate. A drunk kid, a teenager, had plowed his dad's pickup into a camper with this old couple in it. They were up in their mid-seventies. The kid, he was eighteen or nineteen, he was DOA when they brought him in. He'd taken the steering wheel through his sternum and must have died instantly. But the old couple, they were still alive, but just barely. They had multiple fractures and contusions, lacerations, the works, and they each had themselves a concussion. They were in a bad way, believe me. And, of course, their age was against them. She was even a little worse off than he was. She had a ruptured spleen and along with everything else, both kneecaps were broken. But they'd been wearing their seatbelts and, God knows, that's the only thing that saved them."

"Folks, this is an advertisement for the National Safety Council," Terri said. "This is your spokesman, Doctor Herb McGinnis, talking. Listen up now," Terri said and laughed, then lowered her voice. "Herb, you're just too much sometimes. I love you, honey."

We all laughed. Herb laughed too. "Honey, I love you. But you know that, don't you?" He leaned across the table, Terri met him halfway, and they kissed. "Terri's right, everybody," Herb said as he settled himself again. "Buckle up for safety. Listen to what Doctor Herb is telling you. But seriously, they were in bum shape, those old people. By the time I got down there the intern and nurses were already at work on them. The kid was dead, as I said. He was off in a corner, laid out on a gurney. Someone had already notified the next of kin, and the funeral home people were on the way. I took one look at the old couple and told the ER nurse to get me a neurologist and an orthopedic man down there right away. I'll try and make a long story short. The other fellows showed up, and we took the old couple up to the operating room and worked on them most of the night. They must have had incredible reserves, those old people, you see that once in a while. We did everything that could be done, and toward morning we were giving them a fifty-fifty chance, maybe less than that, maybe thirty-seventy for the wife. Anna Gates was her name, and she was quite a woman. But they were still alive the next morning, and we moved them into the ICU where we could monitor every breath and keep a twenty-four-hour watch on them. They were in intensive care for nearly two weeks, she a little longer, before their condition improved enough so we could transfer them out and down the hall to their own rooms."

Herb stopped talking. "Here," he said, "let's drink this gin. Let's drink it up. Then we're going to dinner, right? Terri and

I know a place. It's new place. That's where we'll go, this new place we know about. We'll go when we finish this gin."

"It's called The Library," Terri said. "You haven't eaten there yet, have you?" she said, and Laura and I shook our heads. "It's some place. They say it's part of a new chain, but it's not like a chain, if you know what I mean. They actually have bookshelves in there with real books on them. You can browse around after dinner and take a book out and bring it back the next time you come to eat. You won't believe the food. And Herb's reading *Ivanhoe*! He took it out when we were there last week. He just signed a card. Like in a real library."

"I like *Ivanhoe*," Herb said. "*Ivanhoe*'s great. If I had it to do over again, I'd study literature. Right now I'm having an identity crisis. Right, Terri?" Herb said. He laughed. He twirled the ice in his glass. "I've been having an identity crisis for years. Terri knows. Terri can tell you. But let me say this. If I could come back again in a different life, a different time and all, you know what? I'd like to come back as a knight. You were pretty safe wearing all that armor. It was all right being a knight until gunpowder and muskets and twenty-two pistols came along."

"Herb would like to ride a white horse and carry a lance," Terri said and laughed.

"Carry a woman's garter with you everywhere," Laura said.

"Or just a woman," I said.

"That's right," Herb said. "There you go. You know what's what, don't you Nick?" he said. "Also, you'd carry around their perfumed hankies with you wherever you rode. Did they have perfumed hankies in those days? It doesn't matter. Some little forget-me-not. A token, that's what I'm trying to say. You needed some token to carry around with you in those days. Anyway, whatever, it was better in those days being a knight than a serf," Herb said.

"It's always better," Laura said.

"The serfs didn't have it so good in those days," Terri said.

"The serfs have never had it good," Herb said. "But I guess even the knights were vessels to someone. Isn't that the way it worked in those days? But then everyone is always a vessel to someone else. Isn't that right? Terri? But what I liked about knights, besides their ladies, was that they had that suit of armor, you know, and they couldn't get hurt very easy. No cars in those days, man. No drunk teenagers to run over you."

"Vassals," I said.

"What?" Herb said.

"Vassals," I said. "They were called *vassals*, Doc, not *vessels*."

"Vassals," Herb said. "Vassals, vessels, ventricles, vas deferens. Well, you knew what I meant anyway. You're all better educated in these matters than I am," Herb said. "I'm not educated. I learned my stuff. I'm a heart surgeon, sure, but really I'm just a mechanic. I just go in and fix things that go wrong with the body. I'm just a mechanic."

"Modesty somehow doesn't become you, Herb," Laura said, and Herb grinned at her.

"He's just a humble doctor, folks," I said. "But sometimes they suffocated in all that armor, Herb. They'd even have heart attacks if it got too hot and they were too tired and worn out. I read somewhere that they'd fall off their horses and not be able to get up because they were too tired to stand with all that armor on them. They got trampled by their own horses sometimes."

"That's terrible," Herb said. "That's a terrible image, Nicky. I guess they'd just lay there then and wait until someone, the enemy, came along and made a shish kabob out of them."

"Some other vassal," Terri said.

"That's right, some other vassal," Herb said. "There you have it. Some other vassal would come along and spear his fellow knight in the name of love. Or whatever it was they fought over in those days. Same things we fight over these days, I guess," Herb said.

"Politics," Laura said. "Nothing's changed." The color was still in Laura's cheeks. Her eyes were bright. She brought her glass to her lips.

Herb poured himself another drink. He looked at the label closely as if studying the little figures of the beefeater guards. Then he slowly put the bottle down on the table and reached for the tonic water.

"What about this old couple, Herb?" Laura said. "You didn't finish that story you started." Laura was having a hard time lighting her cigarette. Her matches kept going out. The light inside the room was different now, changing, getting weaker. The leaves outside the window were still shimmering, and I stared at the fuzzy pattern they made on the pane and the Formica counter under it. There was no sound except for Laura striking her matches.

"What about that old couple?" I said after a minute. "The last we heard they were just getting out of intensive care."

"Older but wiser," Terri said.

Herb stared at her.

"Herb, don't give me that kind of look," Terri said. "Go on with your story. I was only kidding. Then what happened? We all want to know."

"Terri, sometimes," Herb said.

"Please, Herb," she said. "Honey, don't always be so serious. Please go on with the story. I was joking, for God's sake. Can't you take a joke?"

"This is nothing to joke about," Herb said. He held his glass and gazed steadily at her.

"What happened then, Herb?" Laura said. "We really want to know."

Herb fixed his eyes on Laura. Then he broke off and grinned. "Laura, if I didn't have Terri and love her so much, and Nick wasn't my friend, I'd fall in love with you. I'd carry you off."

"Herb, you shit," Terri said. "Tell your story. If I weren't in love with you, I damn sure well wouldn't be here in the first place, you can bet on it. Honey, what do you say? Finish your story. Then we'll go to The Library. Okay?"

"Okay," Herb said. "Where was I? Where am I? That's a better question. Maybe I should ask that." He waited a minute, and then began to talk.

"When they were finally out of the woods we were able to move them out of intensive care, after we could see they were going to make it. I dropped in to see each of them every day, sometimes twice a day if I was up doing other calls anyway. They were both in casts and bandages, head to foot. You know, you've seen it in the movies even if you haven't seen the real thing. But they were bandaged head to foot, man, and I mean head to foot. That's just the way they looked, just like those phony actors in the movies after some big disaster. But this was the real thing. Their heads were bandaged—they just had eye holes and a place for their mouths and noses. Anna Gates had to have her legs elevated too. She was worse off than he was, I told you that. Both of them were on intravenous and glucose for a time. Well, Henry Gates was very depressed for the longest while. Even after he found out that his wife was going to pull through and recover, he was still very depressed. Not just about the accident itself, though of course that had gotten to him as those things will. There you are one minute, you know, everything just dandy, then blam, you're staring into the abyss. You come back. It's like a miracle. But it's left its mark on you. It does that. One day I was sitting in a chair beside his bed and he described to me, talking slowly, talking through his mouth hole so sometimes I had to get up to his face to hear him, telling me what it looked like to him, what it felt like, when that kid's car crossed the center line onto his side of the road and kept coming. He said he knew it was all up for them, that was the last look of anything he'd have on this earth. This was it. But he said nothing flew into his mind, his life didn't pass before his eyes, nothing like that. He said he just felt sorry to not be able to see any more of his Anna, because they'd had this fine life together. That was his only regret. He looked straight ahead, just gripped the wheel and watched the kid's car coming at them. And there was nothing he could do except say, 'Anna! Hold on, Anna!'"

"It gives me the shivers," Laura said. "Brrrr," she said, shaking her head.

Herb nodded. He went on talking, caught up in it now. "I'd sit a while every day beside the bed. He'd lay there in his bandages staring out the window at the foot of his bed. The window was too high for him to see anything except the tops of trees. That's all he saw for hours at a stretch. He couldn't turn his head without assistance, and he was only allowed to do that twice a day. Each morning for a few minutes and every evening, he was allowed to turn his head. But during our visits he had to look at the window when he talked. I'd talk a little, ask a few questions, but mostly I'd listen. He was very depressed. What was most depressing to him, after he was assured his wife was going to be all right, that she was recovering to everyone's satisfaction, what was most depressing was the fact they couldn't be physically together. That he couldn't see her and be with her every day. He told me they'd married in 1927 and since that time they'd only been apart from each other for any time on two occasions. Even when their children were born, they were born there on the ranch and Henry and the missus still saw each other every day and talked and were together around the place. But he said they'd only been away from each other for any real time on two occasions—once when her mother died in 1940 and Anna had to take a train to St. Louis to settle matters there. And again in 1952 when her sister died in Los Angeles, and she had to go down there to claim the body. I should tell you they had a little ranch seventy-five miles or so outside of Bend, Oregon, and that's where they'd lived most of their lives. They'd sold the ranch and moved into the city of Bend just a few years ago. When this accident happened, they were on their way down from Denver, where they'd gone to see his sister. They were going on to visit a son and some of their grandchildren in El Paso. But in all of their married life they'd only been apart from each other for any length of time on just those two occasions. Imagine that. But, Jesus, he was lonely for her. I'm telling you he *pined* for her. I never knew what that word meant before, *pined*, until I saw it happening to this man. He missed her something fierce. He just longed for her company, that old man did. Of course he felt better, he'd brighten, when I'd give him my daily report on Anna's progress—that she was mending, that she was going to be fine, just a question of a little more time. He was out of his casts and bandages now, but he was still extremely lonely. I told him that just as soon as he was able, maybe in a week, I'd put him into a wheelchair and take him visiting, take him down the corridor to see his wife. Meanwhile, I called on him and we'd talk. He told me a little about their lives out there on the ranch in the late 1920s and during the early thirties." He looked around the table at us and shook his head at what he was going to say, or just maybe at the impossibility of all this. "He told me that in the winter it would do nothing but snow and for maybe months at a time they couldn't leave the ranch, the road would be closed. Besides, he had to feed cattle every day through those winter months. They would just be there together, the two of them, him and his wife. The kids hadn't come along yet. They'd come along later. But month in, month out, they'd be there together, the two of them, the same routine, the same everything, never anyone else to talk to or to visit with during those winter months. But they had each other. That's all and everything they had, each other. 'What would you do for entertainment?' I asked him. I was serious. I wanted to know. I didn't see how people could live like that. I don't think anyone can live like that these days. You think so? It seems impossible to me. You know what he said? Do you want to know what he answered? He lay there and considered the question. He took some time. Then he said, 'We'd go to the dances every night.' 'What?' I said. 'Pardon me, Henry,' I said and leaned closer, thinking I hadn't heard right. 'We'd go to the dances every night,' he said again. I wondered what he meant. I didn't know what he was talking about, but I waited for him to go on. He thought back to that time again, and in a little while he said, 'We had a Victrola and some records, Doctor. We'd play the Victrola every night and listen to the records and dance there in the living room. We'd do that every night. Sometimes it'd be snowing outside and the temperature down below zero. The temperature really drops on you up there in January or February. But we'd listen to the records and dance in our stocking feet in the living room until we'd gone through all the records. And then I'd build up the fire and turn out the lights, all but one, and we'd go to bed. Some nights it'd be snowing, and it'd be so still outside you could hear the snow falling. It's true, Doc,' he said, 'you can do that. Sometimes you can hear the snow falling. If you're quiet and your mind is clear and you're at peace with yourself and all things, you can lay in the dark and hear it snow. You try it sometimes,' he said. 'You get snow down here once in a while, don't you? You try it sometimes. Anyway, we'd go to the dances every night. And then we'd go to bed under a lot of quilts and sleep warm until morning. When you woke up you could see your breath,' he said.

"When he'd recovered enough to be moved in a wheelchair, his bandages were long gone by then, a nurse and I wheeled him down the corridor to where his wife was. He'd shaved that morning and put on some lotion. He was in his bathrobe and hospital gown, he was still recovering, you know, but he held himself erect in the wheelchair. Still, he was nervous as a cat, you could see that. As we came closer to her room, his color rose and he got this look of anticipation to his face, a look I can't begin to describe. I pushed his chair, and the nurse walked along beside me. She knew something about the situation, she'd picked up things. Nurses, you know, they've seen everything, and not much gets to them after a while but this one was strung a little tight herself that morning. The door was open and I wheeled Henry right into the room. Mrs. Gates, Anna, she was still immobilized, but she could move her head and her left arm. She had her eyes closed, but they snapped open when we entered the room. She was still in bandages, but only from the pelvic area down. I pushed Henry up to the left side of her bed and said, 'You have some company, Anna. Company, dear.' But I couldn't say any more than that. She gave a little smile and her face lit up. Out came her hand from under the sheet. It was bluish and bruised-looking. Henry took the hand in his hands. He held it and kissed it. Then he said, 'Hello, Anna. How's my babe? Remember me?' Tears started down her cheeks. She nodded. 'I've missed you,' he said. She kept nodding. The nurse and I got the hell out of there. She began blubbering once we were outside the room, and she's a tough lot, that nurse. It was an experience, I'm telling you. But after that, he was wheeled down there every morning and every afternoon. We arranged it so they could have lunch and dinner together in her room. In between times they'd just sit and hold hands and talk. They had no end of things to talk about."

"You didn't tell me this before, Herb," Terri said. "You just said a little about it when it first happened. You didn't tell me any of this, damn you. Now you're telling me this to make me cry. Herb, this story better not have an unhappy ending. It doesn't, does it? You're not setting us up, are you? If you are, I don't want to hear another word. You don't have to go any farther with it, you can stop right there. Herb?"

"What happened to them, Herb?" Laura said. "Finish the story, for God's sake. Is there more? But I'm like Terri, I don't want anything to happen to them. That's really something."

"Are they all right now?" I asked. I was involved in the story too, but I was getting drunk. It was hard to keep things in focus. The light seemed to be draining out of the room, going back through the window where it had come from in the first place. Yet nobody made a move to get up from the table or to turn on an electric light.

"Sure, they're all right," Herb said. "They were discharged a while later. Just a few weeks ago, in fact. After a time, Henry was able to get around on crutches and then he went to a cane and then he was just all over the place. But his spirits were up now, his spirits were fine, he just improved every day once he got to see his missus again. When she was able to be moved, their son from El Paso and his wife drove up in a station wagon and took them back down there with them. She still had some convalescing to do, but she was coming along real fine. I just had a card from Henry a few days ago. I guess that's one of the reasons they're on my mind right now. That, and what we were saying about love earlier.

"Listen," Herb went on. "Let's finish this gin. There's about enough left here for one drink all around. Then let's go eat. Let's go to The Library. What do you say? I don't know, the whole thing was really something to see. It just unfolded day after day. Some of those talks I had with him . . . I won't forget those times. But talking about it now has got me depressed. Jesus, but I feel depressed all of a sudden."

"Don't feel depressed, Herb," Terri said. "Herb, why don't you take a pill, honey?" She turned to Laura and me and said, "Herb takes these mood elevator pills sometimes. It's no secret, is it, Herb?"

Herb shook his head. "I've taken everything there is to take at one time or another. No secret."

"My first wife took them too," I said.

"Did they help her?" Laura said.

"No, she still went around depressed. She cried a lot."

"Some people are born depressed, I think," Terri said. "Some people are born unhappy. And unlucky too. I've known people who were just plain unlucky in everything. Other people—not you, honey, I'm not talking about you, of course—other people just set out to make themselves unhappy and they stay unhappy." She was rubbing at something on the table with her finger. Then she stopped rubbing.

"I think I want to call my kids before we go eat," Herb said.

"Is that all right with everybody? I won't be long. I'll take a quick shower to freshen up, then I'll call my kids. Then let's go eat."

"You might have to talk to Marjorie, Herb, if she answers the phone. That's Herb's ex-wife. You guys, you've heard us on the subject of Marjorie. You don't want to talk to her this afternoon, Herb. It'll make you feel even worse."

"No, I don't want to talk to Marjorie," Herb said. "But I want to talk to my kids. I miss them real bad, honey. I miss Steve. I was awake last night remembering things from when he was little. I want to talk to him. I want to talk to Kathy too. I miss them, so I'll have to take the chance their mother will answer the phone. That bitch of a woman."

"There isn't a day goes by that Herb doesn't say he wishes she'd get married again, or else die. For one thing," Terri said, "she's bankrupting us. Another is that she has custody of both kids. We get to have the kids down here just for a month during the summer. Herb says it's just to spite him that she won't get married again. She has a boyfriend who lives with them, too, and Herb is supporting him as well."

"She's allergic to bees," Herb said. "If I'm not praying she'll get married again, I'm praying she'll go out in the country and get herself stung to death by a swarm of bees."

"Herb, that's awful," Laura said and laughed until her eyes welled.

"Awful funny," Terri said. We all laughed. We laughed and laughed.

"Bzzzzzz," Herb said, turning his fingers into bees and buzzing them at Terri's throat and necklace. Then he let his hands drop and leaned back, suddenly serious again.

"She's a rotten bitch. It's true," Herb said. "She's vicious. Sometimes when I get drunk, like I am now, I think I'd like to go up there dressed like a beekeeper—you know, that hat that's like a helmet with the plate that comes down over your face, the big thick gloves, and the padded coat. I'd like to just knock on the door and release a hive of bees in the house. First I'd make sure the kids were out of the house, of course." With some difficulty, he crossed one leg over the other. Then he put both feet on the floor and leaned forward, elbows on the table, chin cupped in his hands. "Maybe I won't call the kids right

now after all. Maybe you're right, Terri. Maybe it isn't such
a hot idea. Maybe I'll just take a quick shower and change
my shirt, and then we'll go eat. How does that sound,
everybody?"

"Sounds fine to me," I said. "Eat or not eat. Or keep drinking. I could head right on into the sunset."

"What does that mean, honey?" Laura said, turning a look
on me.

"It just means what I said, honey, nothing else. I mean I
could just keep going and going. That's all I meant. It's that
sunset maybe." The window had a reddish tint to it now as the
sun went down.

"I could eat something myself," Laura said. "I just realized
I'm hungry. What is there to snack on?"

"I'll put out some cheese and crackers," Terri said, but she
just sat there.

Herb finished his drink. Then he got slowly up from the
table and said, "Excuse me. I'll go shower." He left the
kitchen and walked slowly down the hall to the bathroom. He
shut the door behind him.

"I'm worried about Herb," Terri said. She shook her head.
"Sometimes I worry more than other times, but lately I'm
really worried." She stared at her glass. She didn't make any
move for cheese and crackers. I decided to get up and look in
the refrigerator. When Laura says she's hungry, I know she
needs to eat. "Help yourself to whatever you can find, Nick.
Bring out anything that looks good. Cheese in there, and a
salami stick, I think. Crackers in that cupboard over the stove.
I forgot. We'll have a snack. I'm not hungry myself, but you
guys must be starving. I don't have an appetite anymore. What
was I saying?" She closed her eyes and opened them. "I don't
think we've told you this, maybe we have, I can't remember,
but Herb was very suicidal after his first marriage broke up and
his wife moved to Denver with the kids. He went to a psychia-
trist for a long while, for months. Sometimes he says he thinks
he should still be going." She picked up the empty bottle and
turned it upside down over her glass. I was cutting some
salami on the counter as carefully as I could. "Dead soldier,"
Terri said. Then she said, "Lately he's been talking about suicide again. Especially when he's been drinking. Sometimes I

think he's too vulnerable. He doesn't have any defenses. He doesn't have defenses against anything. Well," she said, "gin's gone. Time to cut and run. Time to cut our losses, as my daddy used to say. Time to eat, I guess, though I don't have any appetite. But you guys must be starving. I'm glad to see you eating something. That'll keep you until we get to the restaurant. We can get drinks at the restaurant if we want them. Wait'll you see this place, it's something else. You can take books out of there along with your doggie bag. I guess I should get ready too. I'll just wash my face and put on some lipstick. I'm going just like I am. If they don't like it, tough. I just want to say this, and that's all. But I don't want it to sound negative. I hope and pray that you guys still love each other five, even three years from now the way you do today. Even four years from now, say. That's the moment of truth, four years. That's all I have to say on the subject." She hugged her thin arms and began running her hands up and down them. She closed her eyes.

I stood up from the table and went behind Laura's chair. I leaned over her and crossed my arms under her breasts and held her. I brought my face down beside hers. Laura pressed my arms. She pressed harder and wouldn't let go.

Terri opened her eyes. She watched us. Then she picked up her glass. "Here's to you guys," she said. "Here's to all of us." She drained the glass, and the ice clicked against her teeth. "Carl too," she said and put her glass back on the table. "Poor Carl. Herb thought he was a schmuck, but Herb was genuinely afraid of him. Carl wasn't a schmuck. He loved me, and I loved him. That's all. I still think of him sometimes. It's the truth, and I'm not ashamed to say it. Sometimes I think of him, he'll just pop into my head at any old moment. I'll tell you something, and I hate how soap opera a life can get, so it's not even yours anymore, but this is how it was. I was pregnant by him. It was that first time he tried to kill himself, when he took the rat poison. He didn't know I was pregnant. It gets worse. I decided on an abortion. I didn't tell him about it either, naturally. I'm not saying anything Herb doesn't know. Herb knows all about it. Final installment. Herb gave me the abortion. Small world, isn't it? But I thought Carl was crazy at the time. I didn't want his baby. Then he goes and kills himself. But after that, after he'd been gone for a while and there was no Carl anymore to talk to and listen to his side of things and help him when he was afraid, I felt real bad about things. I was sorry about his baby, that I hadn't had it. I love Carl, and there's no question of that in my mind. I still love him. But God, I love Herb too. You can see that, can't you? I don't have to tell you that. Oh, isn't it all too much, all of it?" She put her face in her hands and began to cry. Slowly she leaned forward and put her head on the table.

Laura put her food down at once. She got up and said, "Terri. Terri, dear," and began rubbing Terri's neck and shoulders. "Terri," she murmured.

I was eating a piece of salami. The room had gotten very dark. I finished chewing what I had in my mouth, swallowed the stuff, and moved over to the window. I looked out into the backyard. I looked past the aspen tree and the two black dogs sleeping in amongst the lawn chairs. I looked past the swimming pool to the little corral with its gate open and the old empty horse barn and beyond. There was a field of wild grass, and then a fence and then another field, and then the interstate connecting Albuquerque with El Paso. Cars moved back and forth on the highway. The sun was going down behind the mountains, and the mountains had gotten dark, shadows everywhere. Yet there was light too and it seemed to be softening those things I looked at. The sky was gray near the tops of the mountains, as gray as a dark day in winter. But there was a band of blue sky just above the gray, the blue you see in tropical postcards, the blue of the Mediterranean. The water on the surface of the pool rippled and the same breeze caused the aspen leaves to tremble. One of the dogs raised its head as if on signal, listened a minute with its ears up, and then put its head back down between its paws.

I had the feeling something was going to happen, it was in the slowness of the shadows and the light, and that whatever it was might take me with it. I didn't want that to happen. I watched the wind move in waves across the grass. I could see the grass in the fields bend in the wind and then straighten again. The second field slanted up to the highway, and the wind moved uphill across it, wave after wave. I stood there and waited and watched the grass bend in the wind. I could feel my heart beating. Somewhere toward the back of the house the shower was running. Terri was still crying. Slowly and with an effort, I turned to look at her. She lay with her head on the table, her face turned toward the stove. Her eyes were open, but now and then she would blink away tears. Laura had pulled her chair over and sat with an arm around Terri's shoulders. She murmured still, her lips against Terri's hair.

"Sure, sure," Terri said. "Tell me about it."

"Terri, sweetheart," Laura said to her tenderly. "It'll be okay, you'll see. It'll be okay."

Laura raised her eyes to mine then. Her look was penetrating, and my heart slowed. She gazed into my eyes for what seemed a long time, and then she nodded. That's all she did, the only sign she gave, but it was enough. It was as if she were telling me, Don't worry, we'll get past this, everything is going to be all right with us, you'll see. Easy does it. That's the way I chose to interpret the look anyway, though I could be wrong.

The shower stopped running. In a minute, I heard whistling as Herb opened the bathroom door. I kept looking at the women at the table. Terri was still crying and Laura was stroking her hair. I turned back to the window. The blue layer of sky had given way now and was turning dark like the rest. But stars had appeared. I recognized Venus and farther off and to the side, not as bright but unmistakably there on the horizon, Mars. The wind had picked up. I looked at what it was doing to the empty fields. I thought unreasonably that it was too bad the McGinnises no longer kept horses. I wanted to imagine horses rushing through those fields in the near dark, or even just standing quietly with their heads in opposite directions near the fence. I stood at the window and waited. I knew I had to keep still a while longer, keep my eyes out there, outside the house as long as there was something left to see.

One More Thing

L.D.'s WIFE, Maxine, told him to leave one night after she came home from work and found him drunk again and being abusive with Bea, their fifteen-year-old. L.D. and his daughter were at the kitchen table, arguing. Maxine didn't have time to put her purse away or take off her coat.

Bea said, "Tell him, Mom. Tell him what we talked about. It's in his head, isn't it? If he wants to stop drinking, all he has to do is tell himself to stop. It's all in his head. Everything's in the head."

"You think it's that simple, do you?" L.D. said. He turned the glass in his hand but didn't drink from it. Maxine had him in a fierce and disquieting gaze. "That's crap," he said. "Keep your nose out of things you don't know anything about. You don't know what you're saying. It's hard to take anybody seriously who sits around all day reading astrology magazines."

"This has nothing to do with *astrology*, Dad," Bea said. "You don't have to insult me." Bea hadn't attended high school for the past six weeks. She said no one could make her go back. Maxine had said it was another tragedy in a long line of tragedies.

"Why don't you both stop?" Maxine said. "My God, I already have a headache. This is just too much. L.D.?"

"Tell him, Mom," Bea said. "Mom thinks so too. If you tell yourself to stop, you can stop. The brain can do anything. If you worry about going bald and losing your hair—I'm not talking about you, Dad—it'll fall out. It's all in your head. Anybody who knows anything about it will tell you."

"How about sugar diabetes?" he said. "What about epilepsy? Can the brain control that?" He raised the glass right under Maxine's eyes and finished his drink.

"Diabetes, too," Bea said. "Epilepsy. Anything! The brain is the most powerful organ in the body. It can do anything you ask it to do." She picked up his cigarettes from the table and lit one for herself.

"Cancer. What about cancer?" L.D. said. "Can it stop you from getting cancer? Bea?" He thought he might have her there. He looked at Maxine. "I don't know how we got started on this," he said.

"Cancer," Bea said and shook her head at his simplicity. "Cancer, too. If a person wasn't afraid of getting cancer, he wouldn't get cancer. Cancer starts in the *brain*, Dad."

"That's crazy!" he said and hit the table with the flat of his hand. The ashtray jumped. His glass fell on its side and rolled toward Bea. "You're crazy, Bea, do you know that? Where'd you pick up all this crap? That's what it is too. It's crap, Bea."

"That's enough, L.D.," Maxine said. She unbuttoned her coat and put her purse down on the counter. She looked at him and said, "L.D., I've had it. So has Bea. So has everyone who knows you. I've been thinking it over. I want you out of here. Tonight. This minute. And I'm doing you a favor, L.D. I want you out of the house now before they come and carry you out in a pine box. I want you to leave, L.D. Now," she said. "Someday you'll look back on this. Someday you'll look back and thank me."

L.D. said, "I will, will I? Someday I'll look back," he said. "You think so, do you?" L.D. had no intention of going anywhere, in a pine box or otherwise. His gaze switched from Maxine to a jar of pickles that had been on the table since lunch. He picked up the jar and hurled it past the refrigerator through the kitchen window. Glass shattered onto the floor and windowsill, and pickles flew out into the chill night. He gripped the edge of the table.

Bea had jumped away from her chair. "*God*, Dad! *You're* the crazy one," she said. She stood beside her mother and took in little breaths through her mouth.

"Call the police," Maxine said. "He's violent. Get out of the kitchen before he hurts you. Call the police," she said.

They started backing out of the kitchen. For a moment L.D. was insanely reminded of two old people retreating, the one in her nightgown and robe, the other in a black coat that reached to her knees.

"I'm going, Maxine," he said. "I'm going, right now. It suits me to a tee. You're nuts here, anyway. This is a nuthouse. There's another life out there. Believe me, this is not the only life." He could feel the draft of air from the window on his face. He closed his eyes and opened them. He still had his hands on the edge of the table and was rocking the table back and forth on its legs as he spoke.

"I hope not," Maxine said. She'd stopped in the kitchen doorway. Bea edged around her into the other room. "God knows, every day I pray there's another life."

"I'm going," he said. He kicked his chair and stood up from the table. "You won't see me again, either."

"You've left me plenty to remember you by, L.D.," Maxine said. She was in the living room now. Bea stood next to her. Bea looked disbelieving and scared. She held her mother's coat sleeve in the fingers of one hand, her cigarette in the fingers of her other hand.

"*God*, Dad, we were just talking," she said.

"Go on now, get out, L.D.," Maxine said. "I'm paying the rent here, and I'm saying go. Now."

"I'm going," he said. "Don't push me," he said. "I'm going."

"Don't do anything else violent, L.D.," Maxine said. "We know you're strong when it comes to breaking things."

"Away from here," L.D. said. "I'm leaving this nuthouse."

He made his way into the bedroom and took one of her suitcases from the closet. It was an old brown Naugahyde suitcase with a broken clasp. She used to pack it full of Jantzen sweaters and carry it with her to college. He'd gone to college too. That had been years ago and somewhere else. He threw the suitcase onto the bed and began putting in his underwear, trousers and long-sleeved shirts, sweaters, an old leather belt with a brass buckle, all of his socks and handkerchiefs. From the nightstand he took magazines for reading material. He took the ashtray. He put everything he could into the suitcase, everything it would hold. He fastened the one good side of the suitcase, secured the strap, and then remembered his bathroom things. He found the vinyl shaving bag up on the closet shelf behind Maxine's hats. The shaving bag had been a birthday gift from Bea a year or so back. Into it went his razor and shaving cream, his talcum powder and stick deodorant, his toothbrush. He took the toothpaste too. He could hear Maxine and Bea in the living room talking in low voices. After he washed his face and used the towel, he put the bar of soap into the shaving bag. Then he added the soap dish and the glass from over the sink. It occurred to him that if he had some cutlery and a tin plate, he could keep going for a long time. He couldn't close the shaving bag, but he was ready. He put on his coat and picked up the suitcase. He went into the living room. Maxine and Bea stopped talking. Maxine put her arm around Bea's shoulders.

"This is good-bye, I guess," L.D. said and waited. "I don't know what else to say except I guess I'll never see you again," he said to Maxine. "I don't plan on it, anyway. You too," he said to Bea. "You and your crackpot ideas."

"*Dad*," she said.

"Why do you go out of your way to keep picking on her?" Maxine said. She took Bea's hand. "Haven't you done enough damage in this house already? Go on, L.D. Go and leave us in peace."

"It's in your head, Dad. Just remember," Bea said. "Where are you going, anyway? Can I write to you?" she asked.

"I'm going, that's all I can say," L.D. said. "Anyplace. Away from this nuthouse," he said. "That's the main thing." He took a last look around the living room and then moved the suitcase from one hand to the other and put the shaving bag under his arm. "I'll be in touch, Bea. Honey, I'm sorry I lost my temper. Forgive me, will you? Will you forgive me?"

"You've made it into a nuthouse," Maxine said. "If it's a nuthouse, L.D., you've made it so. You did it. Remember that, L.D., as you go wherever you're going."

He put the suitcase down and the shaving bag on top of the suitcase. He drew himself up and faced them. Maxine and Bea moved back.

"Don't say anything else, Mom," Bea said. Then she saw the toothpaste sticking out of the shaving bag. She said, "Look, Dad's taking the toothpaste. Dad, come on, don't take the toothpaste."

"He can have it," Maxine said. "Let him have it and anything else he wants, just so long as he gets out of here."

L.D. put the shaving bag under his arm again and once more picked up the suitcase. "I just want to say one more thing, Maxine. Listen to me. Remember this," he said. "I love you. I love you no matter what happens. I love you too, Bea. I love you both." He stood there at the door and felt his lips begin to tingle as he looked at them for what, he believed, might be the last time. "Good-bye," he said.

"You call this love, L.D.?" Maxine said. She let go of Bea's hand. She made a fist. Then she shook her head and jammed her hands into her coat pockets. She stared at him and then dropped her eyes to something on the floor near his shoes.

It came to him with a shock that he would remember this night and her like this. He was terrified to think that in the years ahead she might come to resemble a woman he couldn't place, a mute figure in a long coat, standing in the middle of a lighted room with lowered eyes.

"Maxine!" he cried. "Maxine!"

"Is this what love is, L.D.?" she said, fixing her eyes on him. Her eyes were terrible and deep, and he held them as long as he could.

Notes

Abbreviations

Base-Text Gordon Lish Manuscripts: Raymond Carver, *What We Talk About When We Talk About Love*, Manuscript–first draft; Lilly Library, Indiana University (Bloomington, Indiana). Net editorial reduction of word count of each story is expressed as a percentage of the base-text.

C   *Cathedral*, first edition (New York: Alfred A. Knopf, 1983)

F_1 *Fires: Essays, Poems, Stories*, first edition (Santa Barbara: Capra Press, 1983)

F_2 *Fires: Essays, Poems, Stories*, second expanded edition (New York: Vintage Books, 1989)

FS   *Furious Seasons and Other Stories* (Santa Barbara: Capra Press, 1977). First and only edition limited to 100 numbered hardback copies signed by the author and 1,200 paperback copies, neither numbered nor signed. The Capra Press mss. are housed at the Lilly Library.

GL   Gordon Lish (1934–)

ms(s). Manuscript(s)

RC   Raymond Carver (1938–1988)

TG   Tess Gallagher (1943–)

ts(s). Typescript(s)

WICF   *Where I'm Calling From: New and Selected Stories,*
            first edition (New York: Atlantic Monthly Press,
            1988)

WICFv   *Where I'm Calling From: New and Selected Stories*
            (New York: Vintage Books, 1989). First paperback
            edition, published posthumously, with pagination
            different from that in *WICF.*

WWTA   *What We Talk About When We Talk About Love,*
            first edition (New York: Alfred A. Knopf, 1981)

WHY DON'T YOU DANCE?

Title in *WWTA*: "Why Don't You Dance?" *WWTA* 3-10. Base-Text in *Beginners*: RC's 8-page ts., which GL cut by 9% for publication in *WWTA*, is fully restored. Previous Publication: "Why Don't You Dance?" was published in *Quarterly West* [University of Utah, Salt Lake City, Utah] 7 (autumn 1978): 26-30. A version of the story later appeared in the *Paris Review* 23:79 (spring 1981): 177-82. The text in the *Paris Review* was the product of GL's first edit of the base-text. In 1977 RC submitted a version of "Why Don't You Dance?" to GL for possible publication in *Esquire*. GL edited the text and changed the title to "I Am Going to Sit Down," but the story was not accepted by *Esquire*. The version in *Quarterly West* included many but not all of GL's suggested revisions. The text in *Quarterly West* is virtually identical to the base-text. Note on *WWTA*: In GL's first edit he changed "Max" to "the man," "Carla" to "the girl," and "Jack" (except once) to "the boy." Subsequent Publication: "Why Don't You Dance?" was collected in *WICF* 116-21 (*WICFv* 155-61) in the version that appeared in *WWTA*.

VIEWFINDER

Title in *WWTA*: "Viewfinder" *WWTA* 11-15. Base-Text in *Beginners*: RC's 6-page ts., which GL cut by 30% for publication in *WWTA*, is fully restored. Previous Publication: The story was published as "View Finder" in the *Iowa Review* [University of Iowa, Iowa City, Iowa] 9:1 (winter 1978): 50-52. A virtually identical version was published in *Quarterly West* [University of Utah, Salt Lake City, Utah] 6 (spring/summer 1978): 69-72. The magazine version included many of GL's changes to "The Mill," an earlier, longer version that exists in unpublished ts. only. The title was based on the handless man's observation: "You're going through the mill now." GL renamed the story "View-Finder" after a word used twice in RC's original ts. Efforts to publish the story in *Esquire* came to a halt when GL departed as editor in

September 1977. The version in *Quarterly West* is identical to the base-text. Note on *WWTA*: GL corrected the title's spelling to "Viewfinder" near the end of the editing process. Subsequent Publication: None.

WHERE IS EVERYONE?

Title in *WWTA*: "Mr. Coffee and Mr. Fixit" *WWTA* 17-20. Base-Text in *Beginners*: RC's 15-page ts., which GL cut by 78% for publication in *WWTA*, is fully restored. Previous Publication: "Where Is Everyone?" was published in *TriQuarterly* [Northwestern University, Evanston, Ill.] 48 (spring 1980): 203-13. The version in *TriQuarterly* is identical to the base-text, except for slight differences in punctuation. Note on *WWTA*: The base-text contains light edits in RC's handwriting. In GL's first edit he changed the daughter's name from "Kate" to "Melody," changed the wife's name from "Cynthia" to "Myrna," and eliminated all references to the son, "Mike." GL renamed the story "Mr. Fixit" but later changed the title to "Mr. Coffee and Mr. Fixit." Subsequent Publication: RC republished "Where Is Everyone?" in F_1 155-65 (F_2 155-65). The version in *Fires* restored the text from *TriQuarterly* with light edits by RC, including his deletion of the title line "I don't know where everyone is at home." As a result, the title line appears only in *TriQuarterly* and the base-text. None of GL's alterations in *WWTA* were included in *Fires*.

GAZEBO

Title in *WWTA*: "Gazebo" *WWTA* 21-29. Base-Text in *Beginners*: RC's 13-page ts., which GL cut by 44% for publication in *WWTA*, is fully restored. Previous Publication: A version of "Gazebo" was published in the *Missouri Review* [University of Missouri, Columbia, Mo.] 4:1 (fall 1980): 33-38. The text in the *Missouri Review* was the product of GL's first edit of the base-text. Subsequent Publication: "Gazebo" was collected in *WICF* 104-109 (*WICFv* 139-46) in the version that appeared in *WWTA*.

WANT TO SEE SOMETHING?

Title in *WWTA*: "I Could See the Smallest Things" *WWTA* 31-36. Base-Text in *Beginners*: RC's 11-page ts., which GL cut by 56% for publication in *WWTA*, is fully restored. Previous Publication: "Want to See Something?" appeared in the *Missouri Review* [University of Missouri, Columbia, Mo.] 4:1 (fall 1980): 29-32. The version in the *Missouri Review* was the product of GL's first edit of the base-text. Note on *WWTA*: In GL's first edit he deleted most of the original ending. In his second edit GL changed the title to "I Could See the Smallest Things." Subsequent Publication: None.

THE FLING

Title in *WWTA*: "Sacks" *WWTA* 37-45. Base-Text in *Beginners*: RC's 21-page ts., which GL cut by 61% for publication in *WWTA*, is fully restored. Previous Publication: "The Fling" was published in *Perspective: A Quarterly of Modern Literature* [Washington University, St. Louis, Mo.] 17:3 (winter 1974): 139-52. The story was collected in *FS* 62-78. The source of the text in *FS* was a photocopy of pages from *Perspective*. The versions in *Perspective* and *FS* are virtually identical to the base-text. Note on *WWTA*: In GL's first edit he changed the title to "Sacks." Subsequent Publication: None.

A SMALL, GOOD THING

Title in *WWTA*: "The Bath" *WWTA* 47-56. Base-Text in *Beginners*: RC's 37-page ts., which GL cut by 78% for publication in *WWTA*, is fully restored. Previous Publication: A version of the story was published as "The Bath" in *Columbia: A Magazine of Poetry and Prose* [Columbia University, New York, N.Y.] 6 (spring/summer 1981): 32-41. The text in *Columbia* was the product of GL's first edit of the base-text. Note on *WWTA*: In GL's first edit he canceled the last 18 pages and changed the title to "The Bath." Subsequent Publication: RC restored the story to nearly its original length and published it as "A Small, Good Thing" in *Ploughshares* [Cambridge, Mass.] 8:2/3 (1982): 213-40. The version in *Ploughshares* follows the base-text, except for minor changes in words and phrasing, as well as the deletion of a 4-page flashback section found only in the base-text. None of GL's changes in "The Bath" were incorporated into the *Ploughshares* version, except for slight rephrasings in the first few paragraphs. RC republished "A Small, Good Thing" in *C* 59-89. The version in *C* included RC's light edits of the *Ploughshares* text and several suggestions by TG. At RC's insistence, GL's editing of *C* was kept to a minimum, largely restricted to matters of spelling and punctuation. "A Small, Good Thing" was collected in *WICF* 280-301 (*WICFv* 377-405) in the version that appeared in *C*.

TELL THE WOMEN WE'RE GOING

Title in *WWTA*: "Tell the Women We're Going" *WWTA* 57-66. Base-Text in *Beginners*: RC's 19-page ts., which GL cut by 55% for publication in *WWTA*, is fully restored. Previous Publication: The story was published as "Friendship" in *Sou'wester Literary Quarterly* [Southern Illinois University, Edwardsville, Ill.] (summer 1971): 61-74. RC wrote GL in 1969 to thank him for giving "Friendship" a careful review. RC hoped to publish the story in *Esquire*, where GL had been named fiction editor, but the story never appeared. RC later proposed to collect "Friendship" in *FS*, but the publisher Noel Young deemed the story "too gruesome for my quavering senses" (Capra Press mss., letter of 24 April 1977). The version in *Sou'wester Literary Quarterly* is nearly identical to the base-text, except for the title, incidental word changes, and an expanded ending in the base-text. Subsequent Publication: None.

IF IT PLEASE YOU

Title in *WWTA*: "After the Denim" *WWTA* 67-78. Base-Text in *Beginners*: RC's 26-page ts., which GL cut by 63% for publication in *WWTA*, is fully restored. Previous Publication: "If It Please You" was published in *New England Review* [Kenyon Hill Publications: Hanover, N.H.] 3:3 (spring 1981): 314-32. The version in *New England Review* is virtually identical to the base-text. Note on *WWTA*: The base-text includes several handwritten corrections by RC. In GL's first edit he changed the title to "Community Center" and canceled the last 6 pages. GL later retitled the story "After the Denim." Subsequent Publication: RC republished "If It Please You" in a limited edition of 226 copies, *If It Please You* (Lord John Press: Northridge, Calif., 1984). The text in the limited edition followed the version in *New England Review* except for minor editing. RC repeatedly revised the final sentence of the story:

> "If it please you," he said in the new prayers for all of them, the living and the dead. ~~Then he slept.~~ (Base-text, final sentence hand-canceled by RC)

> "If it please you," he said in the new prayers for all of them, the living and the dead. (*New England Review*)

> "If it please you," he said in the new prayers for all of them. (Lord John Press limited edition)

SO MUCH WATER SO CLOSE TO HOME

Title in *WWTA*: "So Much Water So Close to Home" *WWTA* 79-88. Base-Text in *Beginners*: RC's 27-page ts., which GL cut by 70% for publication in *WWTA*, is fully restored. Previous Publication: "So Much Water So Close to Home" was published in *Spectrum* [University of California, Santa Barbara, Calif.] 17:1 (1975): 21-38. The story was collected in *FS* 41-61. The source of the text in *FS* was a set of tear sheets from *Spectrum*. An editorially abridged version of the story appeared in *Playgirl* [Santa Monica, Calif.] 3:9 (February 1976): 54-55, 80-81, 110-11. The *Playgirl* editor made substantial cuts but also added two final sentences that are unique to this version: "I begin to scream. It doesn't matter any longer" (111). The text in *FS* is identical to the base-text, except for slight differences in punctuation. Subsequent Publication: RC republished "So Much Water So Close to Home" in *F₁* 167-86 (*F₂* 167-86). The version in *Fires* restored the text from *FS* and also included several changes suggested by TG. "So Much Water So Close to Home" was collected in *WICF* 160-77 (*WICFv* 213-37) in the version that appeared in *Fires*. None of GL's alterations in *WWTA* were incorporated into *Fires*.

DUMMY

Title in *WWTA*: "The Third Thing That Killed My Father Off" *WWTA* 89-103. Base-Text in *Beginners*: RC's 24-page ts., which GL cut by 40% for publication in *WWTA*, is fully restored. Previous Publication: "Dummy" was published in *Discourse: A Review of the Liberal Arts* [Concordia College,

Moorhead, Minn.] 10:3 (summer 1967): 241-56. The story was collected in *FS* 9-26. The source of the text in *FS* was an offprint of pages from *Discourse* on which RC made incidental corrections. The version in *FS* is virtually identical to the base-text. Note on *WWTA*: In GL's second edit he changed the title to "The First Thing That Killed My Father Off" after adding then canceling the title "Friendship." He later revised the title to "The Third Thing That Killed My Father Off." Subsequent Publication: "The Third Thing That Killed My Father Off" was collected in *WICF* 149-59 (*WICFv* 198-212). Except for a few changes in word choice, the version in *WICF* is identical to that in *WWTA*.

PIE

Title in *WWTA*: "A Serious Talk" *WWTA* 105-13. Base-Text in *Beginners*: RC's 11-page ts., which GL cut by 29% for publication in *WWTA*, is fully restored. Previous Publication: A version of the story was published as "A Serious Talk" in the *Missouri Review* [University of Missouri, Columbia, Mo.] 4:1 (fall 1980): 23-28. The text in the *Missouri Review* was the product of GL's first edit and partial second edit of the base-text. Several months later "Pie" appeared in *Playgirl* [Santa Monica, Calif.] 8:7 (December 1980): 72-73, 83, 92, 94-95. "Pie" was an earlier version of the story than "A Serious Talk," but the *Playgirl* editor delayed publication until the Christmas holidays. The version in *Playgirl* is nearly identical to the base-text. Note on *WWTA*: In GL's second edit he changed the title to "A Serious Talk." Subsequent Publication: "A Serious Talk" was collected in *WICF* 122-27 (*WICFv* 162-69) in the version that appeared in *WWTA*.

THE CALM

Title in *WWTA*: "The Calm" *WWTA* 115-21. Base-Text in *Beginners*: RC's 9-page ts., which GL cut by 25% for publication in *WWTA*, is fully restored. Previous Publication: "The Calm" was published in the *Iowa Review* [University of Iowa, Iowa City, Iowa] 10:3 (summer 1979): 33-37. The text in the *Iowa Review* is identical to the base-text. Note on *WWTA*: In editing the final sentence of the story GL initially changed RC's description of the barber's touch from "sadness" to "tenderness" and subsequently to "sweetness." Subsequent Publication: "The Calm" was collected in *WICF* 178-82 (*WICFv* 238-44) in the version that appeared in *WWTA*.

MINE

Title in *WWTA*: "Popular Mechanics" *WWTA* 123-25. Base-Text in *Beginners*: This is the only story for which no ts. exists in the first draft ms. of *WWTA*. The base-text is found in the second revised ms. of *WWTA*, which corresponds to GL's second edit. RC's 3-page ts., which GL cut by 1% for publication in *WWTA*, is fully restored. Previous Publication: "Mine" was published in *FS* 92-93. An identical version appeared under the title "Little

Things" in *Fiction* [City College of New York] 5, nos. 2 & 3 (1978): 241-42. "Mine" was reprinted in *Playgirl* [Santa Monica, Calif.] 6:1 (June 1978): 100, in the same version as that in *FS*. In April 1977 RC sent "a three-page mini-story" entitled "A Separate Debate" to Noel Young of Capra Press, together with a signed contract for *FS*. RC simultaneously submitted the story to GL, who edited it for possible publication in *Esquire*. GL cut "A Separate Debate" by 7% and asked RC to propose a different title. RC changed the title to "Little Things" and subsequently to "Mine," but the story never appeared in *Esquire*. The version published as "Mine" in *FS* incorporated many but not all of GL's editorial suggestions and is virtually identical to the base-text. Note on *WWTA*: In GL's second edit he changed the title to "Popular Mechanics." Subsequent Publication: The story was collected as "Little Things" in *WICF* 114-15 (*WICFv* 152-54). Except for RC's restoration of the earlier title, the version in *WICF* is identical to that in *WWTA*.

DISTANCE

Title in *WWTA*: "Everything Stuck to Him" *WWTA* 127-35. Base-Text in *Beginners*: RC's 13-page ts., which GL cut by 45% for publication in *WWTA*, is fully restored. Previous Publication: "Distance" was published in *Chariton Review* [Northeast Missouri State University, Kirksville, Mo.] 1:2 (fall 1975): 14-23. The story was collected in *FS* 27-36. The source of the text in *FS* was a photocopy of pages from *Chariton Review* on which incidental corrections were made. "Distance" was reprinted in *Playgirl* [Santa Monica, Calif.] 5:10 (March 1978): 101-04, in virtually the same version as that in *FS*. The version in *FS* is identical to the base-text. Note on *WWTA*: In GL's second edit he changed the title to "Everything Stuck to Him." Subsequent Publication: RC republished "Distance" in F_1 113-21 (F_2 113-21). The *Fires* version largely restored the *FS* text but also incorporated a few of GL's alterations from *WWTA*, as well as several changes suggested by TG. "Distance" was collected in *WICF* 140-48 (*WICFv* 186-97). Except for minor changes in word choice, the version in *WICF* is identical to that in *Fires*.

BEGINNERS

Title in *WWTA*: "What We Talk About When We Talk About Love" *WWTA* 137-54. Base-Text in *Beginners*: RC's 33-page ts., which GL cut by 50% for publication in *WWTA*, is fully restored. Previous Publication: A version of the story was published as "What We Talk About When We Talk About Love" in *Antaeus* [Ecco Press, New York, N.Y.] 40/41 (winter/spring 1981): 57-68. The text in *Antaeus* was the product of GL's second edit of the base-text and his subsequent corrections to the printer's ms. Note on *WWTA*: The base-text contains light edits in RC's hand, including his cancellation of the final 2 sentences: ~~Then it would get better. I knew if I closed my eyes, I could get lost.~~ In GL's first edit of the base-text he deleted the last 5 pages. In his second edit he changed the title to "What We Talk About When We Talk About Love" and eliminated the names of the old couple

"Anna" and "Henry [Gates]." Subsequent Publication: "What We Talk About When We Talk About Love" was collected in *WICF* 128-39 (*WICFv* 170-85) in the version that appeared in *WWTA*. "Beginners" was published in the *New Yorker*, 24-31 December 2007, 100-09, in a version identical to the base-text.

ONE MORE THING

Title in *WWTA*: "One More Thing" *WWTA* 155-59. Base-Text in *Beginners*: RC's 7-page ts., which GL cut by 37% for publication in *WWTA*, is fully restored. Previous Publication: "One More Thing" was published in the *North American Review* [University of Northern Iowa, Cedar Falls, Iowa] 266:1 (March 1981): 28-29. The text in the *North American Review* is nearly identical to the base-text. Note on *WWTA*: In GL's first edit he deleted the original ending of the story. GL later changed the fictional daughter's name from "Bea" to "Rayette" and finally, at RC's suggestion, to "Rae." Subsequent Publication: "One More Thing" was collected in *WICF* 110-13 (*WICFv* 147-51) in the version that appeared in *WWTA*.

www.vintage-books.co.uk